THE
BLACK
ACE

ALSO BY G.B. JOYCE

The Code
Every Spring a Parade Down Bay Street

THE BLACK ACE

G.B. JOYCE

PENGUIN
an imprint of Penguin Canada

Published by the Penguin Group
Penguin Group (Canada), 90 Eglinton Avenue East, Suite 700, Toronto, Ontario, Canada M4P 2Y3

Penguin Group (USA) Inc., 375 Hudson Street, New York, New York 10014, U.S.A.
Penguin Books Ltd, 80 Strand, London WC2R 0RL, England
Penguin Ireland, 25 St Stephen's Green, Dublin 2, Ireland (a division of Penguin Books Ltd)
Penguin Group (Australia), 707 Collins Street, Melbourne, Victoria 3008, Australia
(a division of Pearson Australia Group Pty Ltd)
Penguin Books India Pvt Ltd, 11 Community Centre, Panchsheel Park, New Delhi – 110 017, India
Penguin Group (NZ), 67 Apollo Drive, Rosedale, Auckland 0632, New Zealand
(a division of Pearson New Zealand Ltd)
Penguin Books (South Africa) (Pty) Ltd, 24 Sturdee Avenue, Rosebank,
Johannesburg 2196, South Africa

Penguin Books Ltd, Registered Offices: 80 Strand, London WC2R 0RL, England

First published 2013

1 2 3 4 5 6 7 8 9 10 (WEB)

Copyright © Penguin Group (Canada), 2013

*Publisher's note: This book is a work of fiction. Names, characters, places and incidents either are the product of the author's
imagination or are used fictitiously, and any resemblance to actual persons living or dead, events, or locales is entirely coincidental.*

Manufactured in Canada

LIBRARY AND ARCHIVES CANADA CATALOGUING IN PUBLICATION

Joyce, Gare, 1956–
The black ace / G.B. Joyce.

"A Brad Shade thriller".
ISBN 978-0-14-318760-8

I. Title.

PS8619.O957B53 2013   C813'.6   C2012-905938-2

Visit the Penguin Canada website at **www.penguin.ca**

Special and corporate bulk purchase rates available; please see
www.penguin.ca/corporatesales or call 1-800-810-3104, ext. 2477.

For Trent Kresse,
Scott Kruger, Chris Mantyka and
Brent Ruff and their families

SUNDAY

A hangover laced with dread had Derek Jones in a crushing headlock and drenched in a cold sweat as he crawled and lurched across the empty streets of Swift Current in an F-150 that had rolled off the dealer's lot sometime late in the previous century. It was minus twelve outside and the truck's heater sighed uselessly. Jones's blood had thinned over four years of waiting tables and banging waitresses on a Caribbean cruise ship and it hadn't thickened since coming home six weeks before. His breath, redolent of mouthwash, frosted the windshield and his lone working headlight left the world ahead a black void. At every stoplight and stop sign he worried that his truck would conk out and strand him. He needed this job like he needed the other two just to get by, and if he was fired for showing up late and half in the bag, his old man would kick him to the curb.

Jones wiped a tiny porthole on the windshield to peer out. It was about the size of a bar coaster, and when he wiped his dripping nose afterward on the sleeve of his lumberjack jacket he thought he could smell Jack Daniel's and his last pack of duty-free Marlboros. His head and eyelids dipped and he drifted into the wrong lane, a couple of raced heartbeats away from a head-on with an oncoming car. He swerved hard and took a deep breath. Ice pellets bounced off the windshield like a thousand rounds of frozen machine-gun fire and reassured him that he was, in fact, still alive, even if under siege. It could have ended right there, he thought, and he let himself be buoyed by the notion, previously unimaginable, that things could be worse.

Jones was the morning man at the full-service gas station at the town's easternmost exit on Highway 1, and he was twenty minutes late to open up. Six A.M. Sunday wasn't a quiet shift like it would be in other jurisdictions. He could count on the Sabbath rush, locals who had morning appointments with redemption at one of the thirty-two churches in Swift Current, locals who were going to be awaiting his arrival with their pickups idling and righteous indignation revving. He meditated as his one-eyed rustbucket fishtailed around the last corner: If the parishioners were as righteous as they played it, they wouldn't complain to the proprietor. They'd just say a prayer for him that might land him once again and forever after in tanning butter.

When Jones finally pulled into the station, he didn't have to touch the key in the ignition, the motor intuitively stalling just as he skidded into his parking spot out front. Three pickups were sitting by the pumps, engines running and windows fogging up. Three farm families in their Sunday best watched Jones jog across the lot with his collar up against the wind and unlock the front door. The wind howled, but he wasn't worrying about what was blowing so much as the blowback. If he had been on time, 5:50, he'd have done a quick check of the premises, just to make sure that the night man had left the washrooms in acceptable shape and the back doors were shut. And he would have counted out his till in the station's main building. In that time inside the station, the little space heater in the booth out by the pumps would have kicked in and made it almost fit for human habitation. This was a routine that had been instituted with good cause, and the boss insisted on compliance to the letter and minute. But Jones was only getting used to it. He skipped the warm-up. His customers' reserve of patience was about to hit E.

It was 6:40 before a window opened for Jones to make his rounds. The first thing he did was hit the lights for the sign out front. It glowed red. Six storeys tall, it was Swift Current's highest free-standing structure. The second thing he did was turn on the radio in the station. The singer sounded familiar but before his time, he figured. He didn't know it was another Jones, George, and didn't recognize "Still Doin' Time." He was thankful that the gospel stuff wasn't going to crank up until the top of the hour. He listened to a couple of verses and started to go about his rounds. Only then did it occur to him that the guy who closed the night before had failed to set the alarm. Jones was going to have to call it in to the security company and his manager. Someone else was going to land in the shit, he thought, and for that he felt a sense of undeserved relief.

Flush with this wishful *schadenfreude*, he worked through the checklist. The washrooms were acceptable. Everything seemed to be in its place up at the front desk. There were a couple of coffee cups in the sink in the closet that passed for the lunchroom. A Taurus had been a guest for the night on one hoist in the two-car repair bay. The other hoist was down and unoccupied. That figured. Saturday was overtime for the guys wielding the wrenches and grease guns. Overtime was done in half days. The mechanics had checked out and there'd been no one in the bay since noon Saturday. Jones checked the back door. It was secure. He unlocked it and peered out into the snow drifting around the dumpster and old wrecks left to rust out back.

There were three other cars parked close to the door, out of sight from the road. The nearest was a snow-covered Volkswagen microbus of a Summer of Love vintage. It needed some TLC and STP and maybe even an EKG. Farthest from the door was an old Impala that was acned with rust. The microbus and the Chevy had been there since Jones worked his Friday night shift, left in auto-repair limbo while their owners mulled over the costs versus benefits of throwing more money into their geriatric rides. Between them was a car that had only a thin sheet of ice over the trunk. First impression, it had been on the empty hoist, had been serviced, and had been left in the back for the owner to pick up after hours, the keys under the visor or floor mat.

The keys weren't in either place, though. They were in the ignition and the engine was running, eight cylinders on a low rumble. Jones didn't realize that right away. He couldn't see the exhaust. The wind would have been blowing it down the Trans-Canada and across the prairies at the speed limit. Even if his toque hadn't been pulled down over his ears, the wind drowned out the low, finely tuned hum. Jones recognized the car. It was his boss's ride. Jones dry-heaved. Busted for showing up late, for sure.

On closer inspection, though, looking through the thoroughly defrosted and even sweating window, he took faint hope. His boss's head was tilted back, like he was asleep. Jones walked over to the driver-side door and tapped on the window. His boss didn't respond. He tapped a little harder. Still nothing. Not even when Jones opened the door. And only when Jones opened the door did he notice the hose running into the passenger-side window. And only when Jones walked around the back of the car did he see that the hose was hooked up to the exhaust.

Fifteen minutes later the snow was speckling a corpse as the pair of medics lifted it into the back of the ambulance and Jones was telling a couple of veteran Mounties exactly what happened, right down to the song on the radio, even though he couldn't name the singer and didn't recognize the song. He tried humming a couple of bars. He was a good-looking kid, too good-looking to be smart. Looks didn't deceive. He had smoked enough dope to leave behind a dozen IQ points at various Caribbean ports of call.

But he was telling them what they already knew. They would have recognized that old Mercedes 280SE anywhere.

So would I.

2

It was five hundred bucks I would have earned the hard way: buck-naked in the back seat of that Mercedes, steaming up the windows. It was broad daylight and we were pulled over on the not-so-soft shoulder of a freeway in plain view of passing cars and risking charges of gross public indecency, a hard thing to do in Orange County.

It was September '91. Martin Mars was behind the steering wheel. The Benz was his single indulgence. It was all he could manage on a one-year deal paying him the league minimum, a two-way contract that kept the threat of a return to the minors hanging over his helmet like the sword of Damocles. He never said anything to me about his plight, even though I was his roommate on the road. Then again, he never said much about anything. He had suffered a crushed larynx years back. His nickname was Whisper. It seemed like it physically hurt him to talk, and days would go by without much more than a shrug or a wink or a wave out of him. I never saw his eyes redden when he'd walk into the dressing room before a game and see his name

6

among the night's healthy scratches. It was hard to make out his eyes behind his thick horn-rims.

Ivan Borzov was sitting beside Mars. He was twenty-six but this was his first trip to North America so he was still just a rookie. He had a haircut from a Red Army stylist and a head so big that the trainers didn't have a helmet to fit him. He had the grill of a Moscow watchdog that had kissed the bumper of a speeding Volga. He would have beaten out Dolph Lundgren for the part of Ivan Drago in *Rocky IV*. Normally I would have had my choice of seat as the veteran in our little group, but Borzov was about six foot six and as stiff as Dr. Frankenstein's monster. I volunteered to sit in the back.

Beside me was Van Stone. He was called Stoner, of course, and the epithet fit, on looks anyway. He was just eighteen, but with his stringy mullet he looked like a greasy fifteen-year-old skipping class to hang out in the poolroom. On the ice he had the hockey sense of a ten-year veteran. This was his first pro camp. We all knew that he was going to be sent back to junior in a couple of weeks but the team had signed the Next Big Thing to a deal over the summer. He had his bonus, endorsement deals for sticks and skates. If his agent had been sharp he would have had his picture on tubes of Clearasil or packs of Zig-Zag rolling papers. Didn't matter. Stoner was already worth seven figures and didn't even have his driver's licence. He was a good kid. Didn't mean we didn't envy him.

It was a ritual every September, first week of training camp. On the first really hot day I'd set up a bet. Everyone throws in fifteen hundred dollars. Driver turns off the air conditioning and cranks the heat with the windows up. First one to open a window loses his stake, five hundred to each of the survivors. I always made sure that I brought along a six-pack, well chilled.

I figured Boris Badenov would be easy to beat. He took every shortcut on the ice and I predicted this was going to be the same.

Not even close.

We had been in the car for almost an hour and Borzov hadn't even blinked, staring straight forward, not making a sound. Stoner and I had split the six-pack but it didn't help. The kid and I were pressing our faces to the windows, the only relief from the heat in this German-crafted rolling steam bath. Mars had to be even warmer under a beard that was as dense as an SOS pad and ran uninterrupted from his chin to his shag bath mat of chest hair. We had sweated right through our clothes. We had taken them off. We were going to leave butt prints on the black leather upholstery. No one had ever gone this long on the bet.

Stoner looked woozy. His eyes rolled back in his head.

"I think we're going to lose this kid," said Mars, whose glasses were densely fogged.

"He'll be okay," I said. I figured his contract was insured against cataclysmic injury or illness. The risk was even greater than we knew. I had, in fact, served Evan Stone the first and last beers of his life. I didn't read *The Hockey News*. How was I supposed to have known he was an evangelical Christian? Or that he had ulcerative colitis?

It was at that point that Boris lit a cigarette, a Russian dart with the aroma of raw sewage. He looked into the back seat with menace and blew smoke in my face. I coughed. And then he held the smouldering butt like he was going to grind it out on his seat.

"Is burn?" he said.

"You win," Martin Mars rasped, powering his window down. "Throw it out."

The next day, the Russian bragged to our teammates. "Is easy," he said. Martin Mars was a laughingstock at practice. He had to fork out five hundred to Boris. I told Martin Mars that I didn't want his five hundred dollars. Stoner did the same thing. I told the kid it would help us if he didn't say anything about the bet to the coaches or reporters. If it ever got out that Mars and I were corrupting a near minor who happened to be the Future of the Franchise, we'd be in deep shit with management. Management would try to trade me and Mars would be exiled to the minors without the faintest hope of ever being called up again.

Mars was our Black Ace. He wore the black sweater in practices on game days and had to stay on the ice after we came off. While we were hitting the showers, our Black Ace was out on the ice, doing hard time, pushed through drills and miles of hard slogging by a coach who had no use for him, who actually had it in for him. Martin Mars did his best to conceal what had to be existential despair, but for all he knew back in training camp in '91 he might have already played his last game in the league. Whenever I looked at Mars in his black sweater I thought of my classics class at Boston College and reading *The Iliad*: "The goal of all men is to be the first and superior to others." The Black Ace, he was the guy in sandals chasing after the chariot, left behind as the heroes headed off to war. I couldn't have taken his money in good conscience.

Stoner said he trembled all night long, drank gallons of water, and hadn't pissed in thirty-six hours.

Mars thanked us and told us he'd pay us back someday.

Funny thing, Borzov was back in Moscow a week later. Boris didn't want anything bad enough on the ice. He just went through the motions in camp and he definitely wasn't sticking around to get sent to the minors. He went back home with five hundred bucks, a third-degree sunburn, and a thousand Aeroflot points to show for his cameo in Hollywood.

It was Martin Mars who spent the season in the game's gulag.

3

Derek Jones was still taking the Mounties' questions when I stepped off the plane in Regina.

Scouts enter a few assignments with guarded enthusiasm, like a mid-winter date in Vancouver, my previous stop on a ten-day swing through the West. Occasionally an excursion dovetails with real life. For me that was two weeks away, when I'd head off to Minnesota for a few days of college and high school games. That would be my chance to reconnect with a goaltender at a boarding school in a town near the Twin Cities, the goaltender being my daughter. But this was going to be two nights in Regina. In February. While I waited to get my keys at the car rental desk I checked my BlackBerry for my departing flight Tuesday. Out at 11 A.M. Forty-seven and a half hours couldn't pass fast enough.

I checked into the Hotel Saskatchewan. I've stayed there on each of my trips to Regina.

My first time I was in grade seven and was with my family. My mother, the Queen, liked nothing better than entering contests and finally landed the grand prize: an all-expenses-paid trip by

train across Canada. We stayed in the old railroad hotels at each
stop, even at the Banff Springs. We had to pose for some publi-
city pictures and, as patriarch, Sarge did some interviews with
newspapers as we went down the line. At the Hotel Saskatchewan
I dropped a postcard down the slots that were beside the elevator
on each floor. I remember it was an old-fashioned glass shaft
and the lettering in brass said CULVER MAIL DELIVERY SYSTEM.
I waited by it until I saw other people's cards and letters drop
down, like it was raining Wish-You-Were-Heres.

Regina Trip number two was even more memorable. I was on
the Ontario team that went to the national Junior A champion-
ships in Regina. We beat a team from Vancouver in the final
and I started to get calls and letters from U.S. colleges the week
after. I didn't get a goal in that game, but I did manage to score
that night with a tall blond cowgirl who was in town on her high
school's tour of the university. I told her I was two years older
than I really was. That's what I told the bartender too, and I had
the fake ID to prove it. She flashed her card and she ordered a
tequila sunrise, something she picked up from a movie. She had
freckles and I asked her if she'd show me all of them. She said she
didn't do that sort of thing, but she did that sort of thing with
me all night long.

And so I always check into the Hotel Saskatchewan when
duty puts me out there. Call me a stealthy sentimentalist.

It was 11 A.M. when I dropped my bags in my room and the
game wasn't until two. The one surviving ligament in my knee
was on fire. Arthur had taken up residence in the small apartment where my cartilage used to call home. This souvenir from
my playing days had fetched the dirty bastard Lavery a two-game
suspension for a cheap hit and was going to keep the needle in
the red on the meter that clocked my pain threshold. Yeah, his
knee-on-knee hit left me with a Neon Knee, one made of thin

glass, filled with compressed gas that pulsed and glowed in the dark. I downed a Celebrex and counted six left in the vial. I was going to have to manage my dosage to make it until Tuesday. I got a load off my feet, jumped up on the bed in my street clothes. Normally I can't nap, but I hadn't slept at all the night before and I can never sleep on planes, especially sitting next to some fat slob in economy, as I had been. I couldn't have been more lights out if I'd been up onstage with a hypnotist.

I was dreaming about running but before I could get where I wanted to go I woke up. It was twelve thirty and I didn't have time to sit around tearing the dream apart. I had to go to the rink.

I collected my car off Victoria Avenue. For a second I forgot what make and model it was. I booted it over to the arena, giving myself enough time to catch up with Chief, our regional scout. Enter his name on YouTube and you'll get forty-five hits with some of his classic fights from the '80s and '90s. Chief played with five teams in the league and a dozen more in the minors. Wherever he strapped them on he was the most popular guy with fans. And with his teammates. From what he tells me he had a rough time in junior. "Never had been off the reserve farther than Yorkton down the road before I went to tryouts in Moose Jaw," he told me once. "That's the one time I can remember that I was ever scared of anything."

One look at him and you'd think that he got his nickname because he's a ringer for Nicholson's sidekick in *Cuckoo's Nest*. Not so. Sure, there is a resemblance: six foot four, straggly hair down to his shoulders that look like a football player's in pads. Fact is, though, every native guy in the game gets saddled with the handle.

Chief wasn't an affirmative-action hiring. Not by a long shot. Teams might do that sort of thing in the front office or the

arena, but out in the field there's no sense dressing a window
that no one sees. Chief was on the staff on merit and because
of a track record. His nickname would be in bad taste in other
realms, but we attached a healthy helping of respect to it. He
had great gut instincts about players, uncanny, even unnerving.
Some guys can tell you that you're holding an apple. Some guys
can tell you that you're holding an apple seed. Chief can tell if
you have an apple seed in your pocket. I've pushed other scouts
to explain why they liked a kid or why they crossed him off the
file. I only pushed Chief once. "No need to ask me why," he said.
"*Why* doesn't matter. *Why* is wasting your time. Ask me how
much I like a kid or not. That's what counts." Which had never
occurred to me and was absolutely true. Chief was intuitive, so
I never asked him why. I wasn't going to waste his time either.

Chief was in the scouts' room at the arena when I limped in.
He had a coffee going and had one bite left of a maple glazed.

It was Chief who told me Martin Mars had died.

"Was he sick?" I asked.

"Suicide is what I heard," Chief said.

Other scouts started to file in. It was all over the grapevine.
Why was a question that hung out there and no one had an
answer.

4

I wouldn't have pegged Martin Mars as the Happily-Ever-After Guy.

I was his roomie for most of that season, his only stretch in the league and my last go-round in L.A. I couldn't have claimed to know him that well. There was nobody I could pump for his story. Most players have family and friends visit them in L.A. No one ever showed up to catch up with Whisper. I tried to read between the lines. They say all happy families are alike, but each unhappy family is unhappy in its own way. Almost every player tells the story of his parents, the father who made him. That's how every player frames it, all alike and some of it is even true. Maybe five guys in the whole league volunteer hardship when it's undeniable, usually because it's already a matter of public record. An abusive father, a guy with a restraining order, a celebrity father with a drug problem, whatever. I figured that the vacuum of Whisper's history was the by-product of a unique dysfunction.

On the hockey end he was a decently talented guy, a bit over six feet, a bit under two hundred pounds, a good skater whose hands were better with a wrench than a stick, true of a lot of career minor-leaguers. He had spent five full seasons in the bus leagues with only a couple of call-ups that lasted no more than two weeks. It was easy to see why. Sometimes when he mishandled the puck, I wondered if maybe he needed a different prescription for his contacts. If you get down to it, a player without vision isn't a player. With one fairly famous exception, Whisper never seemed to be angry about being the Black Ace in L.A. Everybody else in the game would have been burning up. I saw guys trash rooms over smaller indignities. Whisper took it all with beatific calm, like he had skipped all the stages of denial and grief and gone directly to acceptance. I remember hearing Grant Tomlin on a broadcast talking about the difference between those who play and those who don't. "Gord, it comes down to need," he said. "The best don't want. They need." Bullshit. It isn't *need*. It's *greed*. A player not only wants it but he wants it for himself. Whisper didn't have the greed to play his way in from the margins.

Whisper's bio in the team's program listed "cars" as his hobby but it wasn't that he collected big-ticket rides. No, he liked fixing them. Nothing made him happier than getting under the hood of 99's Jaguar. Whisper's '69 Benz was his first love, though. He changed its oil like a first-time mother changed a diaper and spoiled it with high-test. The owner of our team back then, long ago RIP, missed the occasional dialysis appointment if he was getting rogered by his secretary. Martin Mars would never miss his biweekly appointment to have his ride detailed.

Mars's second-biggest night with L.A. had nothing to do with a goal or anything else on the ice. That year we had some guys who would rather gamble than fuck and we had a bullshit game of poker going on road trips. I hosted one in our hotel room and dealt a reluctant Whisper in. He anted and folded every hand. The last deal of the cards was Match-the-Pot Guts. Everybody anted five hundred bucks each, cheques would do. Each player was dealt two cards and made the best poker hand he could with those two cards. Ace high is pretty good. Ace-king close to a lock, and any pair you can start counting your money. The tough part: You have to drop a coin on a count of three to declare you're in. If you drop the coin and lose to a guy you have to match the pot, which, with seven players, was thirty-five hundred. I kept my straightest face when I looked at my cards: a pair of eights. We put our cards down and our hands behind our backs so no one would know who was loading or off-loading a coin for the drop. Blakey, our trainer, acted as emcee, calling for the drop and then counting it down. A quarter fell out of my hand, a penny out of Whisper's. Anyone else I would have been licking my chops but I felt sorry for him. I wasn't even sure he understood the rules. He flipped over the ace of clubs.

"No good," I said. "Eights."

I started to sweep in the pot.

Whisper put his hand on my sleeve and gave me the universal sign of Not-So-Fast. He flipped over the other card: ace of spades.

"Shadow, you got done in by the Black Ace," Hunts crowed.

Hunts was and is my best friend so I pretended that I had a stick with too much flex in it at the next practice when I drifted a head-high slapshot that had him ducking for cover under the crossbar.

5

Regina versus Red Deer was game 120 for me that season. Hogan, the kid who interested me on Red Deer, had two goals and an assist, and if he'd been six foot two he would have been looking at first-round money. But you can say that about a hundred kids in any season. He was listed at five foot eleven in the program but stretched to only five nine and a quarter when the Central Scouting Registry dropped in to inspect the meat. He had great hockey sense and all kinds of try in him, but scouts are whores for size. If he had showed another gear I could have liked him more, and I already liked him more than the rest of the L.A. staff. Hogan was Mr. Close but Not Enough.

Chief did the drive out to Moose Jaw. He wanted the lowdown on the doings at our offices. All the regional scouts wanted that. The farther they were from L.A., the more they wanted to know.

"I'm just asking you," Chief said. "Should I take out a long-term loan?"

Chief could see through the standard answer. I gave it to him anyway. It's my job, even with a good worker like him, even with a friend. "I can't tell you anything beyond July 1. It was a two-year deal you had, right?"

"Yeah," he said.

"Well, Hunts is all twisted. I know he'd want to give you another two years, but a lockout in the fall is a done deal from what I hear. Hunts told the owner that we have to keep our staff together, but he's tuning Hunts out a lot lately."

Chief sighed but said nothing as we sped along Highway 1. I filled in the unnecessary detail.

"I'm lucky I'm still around. We had a good draft and we have some good kids in our system. I don't think the owner can have any complaints. But when Tomlin came in, everything changed."

Grant Tomlin had never been a player above the college ranks, had been an assistant coach in the league for about fifteen minutes, and had weaseled his way into a broadcast gig. He developed this Smartest Man in Hockey role so convincingly that Joe Public thought he was that. Real hockey men just figured he had done a theatre degree and laughed at him, at least until they found out that he was making seven figures to wear makeup and talk out of his ass. Then Tomlin wormed his way into the president's job in L.A. He had campaigned for it on the air and practically speed-dated our owner, Galvin, the Society Page's Favourite Tech Baron, Founder of Fideligence Smartware. Tomlin was as subtle as a slapshot off your cup. At the draft he had gone up to Galvin's box with a copy of *Fast Company* that featured its Man of the Year on the cover, the man who just happened to be signing our cheques.

"You know Tomlin threw Hunts under the bus," I said. "The rest of us too, I guess. If I hadn't re-signed with the team before Tomlin came aboard he was going to replace me. I still don't figure I'll be around the team in two years' time."

Chief was phlegmatic about our office intrigue. Then again,

he was phlegmatic about almost everything. "Nothing guaranteed on the ice, nothing guaranteed off," Chief said.

"I'm thinking of getting out anyway," I said.

Chief took his eyes off the road for a second to see my expression. It was dead serious.

"This isn't for public consumption and deny it if you hear it," I told him. "I got a call a while back from the investigations outfit I used to work for before Hunts brought me in. They've moved up into corporate stuff. It's good money. Since I left the company really took off. They might even give me a piece of it."

That was the upside. I left out my past history in investigations, an awful stew of bogus insurance claims and cratering marriages seasoned with missing persons, the majority of them missing by their own volition. I left out the awful fact that a couple of hours into my working day I hit the daily recommended requirement for other people's heartache.

Chief didn't bother with the particulars. "That's good ... for you," Chief said, leaving out that the fact that it might be bad for him.

The prospect of a minty life after scouting was hanging there like an air freshener from the rear-view mirror when Moose Jaw was finally in sight. We were greeted by Mac the Moose, the twenty-foot statue of Bullwinkle's brother that stands at the first exit westbound.

We grabbed burgers at Harvey's. Chief didn't go for fine dining. He had four patties and squeezed them into one bun. Chief didn't go for vegetables, either. He'd be more likely to offer you a slice of bacon than a stick of Juicy Fruit. I didn't want to disrupt his digestion so I kept work talk to a minimum.

"You played with Martin Mars back then," he said.

"Couple of years, as much as he played," I said. "And that last game too."

6

I try to avoid getting asked about the game, but I can't always duck out of it. People ask me over and over again about the same themes. *What was it like shutting down 99 in the Cup final?* Nerve-racking, I tell them, feigning modesty. *Where's your ring?* In storage, I tell them, leaving out the part about it being stored by the guy who bought it at an auction after I had to declare bankruptcy. *What was it like being married to a starlet and going to Hollywood parties?* Overrated, I tell them, absolutely straight up and praying that they don't want any gory tabloid-worthy details of how it all came apart. I regularly get asked about Whisper. *What happened with that Martin Mars thing in L.A.?* They don't need to get specific about it. I know exactly what they're talking about: his last game. All anybody remembers about him is his last game, and all they really remember is his last shift and the aftermath. I've always used the standard answer: I don't know and I was there.

I played in the league with guys with less talent, but I never played with anyone whose makeup was like Whisper's. Fear is the worst thing you can accuse a player of, but I always thought that Whisper might have been afraid of success. He wouldn't skate that last half inch that separates players from pretenders. In most other walks of life there are a lot of people like that. In the league all the guys like that could have fit in Mars's Benz with room left over for two tubas. It's hard to get to the league. It's almost impossible if that's your attitude.

In the spring of '92 we snuck into the playoffs and faced Edmonton in the first round. Edmonton had racked up thirty more points than we had during the regular season. People figured we were going to lose four straight. And none of us figured that Martin Mars was going to be a factor at all. He had played only a dozen games since Christmas. That's when the front office fired Al Hampton, an easygoing lout, and replaced him with John B. Harris, a.k.a. Iron John. I played for a few coaches like Iron: Surrounded by players in the prime of their lives, these guys worry that in the autumn of their years they might seem unmanly. To compensate they become inhuman. The hiring of this scowling despot had no obvious effect on our performance during the regular season, just soaring numbers on our misery index. His too. Blakey had to get Iron out of the hotel bar and back to his room six times in three months using the fireman's carry. Iron managed to miss a couple of practices with recurring cases of "the flu" and spent shivering hours with room-service coffee and aspirin while we skated on game days.

The game is sometimes beyond explaining, one notable occasion being our series against Edmonton. Somehow we won games one and two in Alberta. Hunts was in the zone. "I played pro sixteen years and earned my millions over the course of a week," he always says and it's absolutely true.

By the time we came to L.A. for game six we had a chance to close out the series, but that afternoon Hines, the left winger on our second line, a dependable but not flashy guy, came down

with food poisoning. It didn't come out until later that he had
been done in by a bad fish taco served up at a beachside joint
near Malibu way, an establishment with a history of health-code
violations. Iron John couldn't have felt worse if he'd had a couple
of those spoiled tacos washed down by a forty-ouncer of JD. We
were banged up. Three guys had broken bones in five games. I
was playing through a fractured wrist. We had one open spot in
the lineup and no one except Whisper to fill it.

Iron John's modus operandi was known to all of us. He ignored
the top half of the roster and treated the rest with withering
contempt. He had mixed results with six franchises over twenty
years, teams that made it to the finals, teams that finished in the
cellar. The bigger the stakes, the worse his mood. By game six,
with the opportunity that we faced and the physical state we
were in, Iron showed up in satellite photos as a giant black cloud
hovering over SoCal.

"You guys gotta get it done tonight," he said, shaking,
reddening. "We got three lines, 'cause Edwards is all shot up and
can't hold a stick and this guy, the Black Ace, can't play at all,
healthy or not. He can't play so he won't play. We don't want to
go back to Edmonton. We win this, we can send this clown back
to the press box and we can get healthy. We can have a real shot
at the Cup, but it's gonna take a big effort from our best. If you
don't do it, no one else can do it for us. You can't go looking for
the Fuckin' Black Fuckin' Ace to get us there. Hey Ace, do you
hear me?"

Bud Sutherin tried to peel Iron Manic off Whisper, going so
far as to tug him by the sleeve. But an assistant coach, even if
he's the general manager's brother, can *only* tug on the sleeve of a
tyrant like Iron the Terrible.

My stall was next to Whisper's. His head was hanging down
as he listened to Iron's rip job. His face was in there, somewhere

folded up under his beard. I was the only one who could see his grill. He took it hard, really hard, harder than I ever saw anyone take it in the league.

Iron was good to his word through sixty minutes. Edmonton came at us in waves. We hung on by our fingernails and Hunts was playing out of his mind again. It was 1–1 at the end of regulation. At the end of the first overtime. And at the end of the second OT. Martin Mars's ass was nailed to the bench throughout. In the third OT the trainer pulled off Malloy because he seemed delirious. I thought he might have had his bell rung, but it was dehydration and our team doctor had to hook him up to an IV. That left Iron with no choice but to throw Whisper out there. Iron did his best to raise Mars's spirits. "Don't fuckin' lose it," he said. Whisper, as usual, said nothing.

Whisper played four short shifts on my left wing in the third OT. He hadn't even worked up a sweat and I felt like I was skating in sand. In the last minute of the third OT Edmonton got the puck by Hunts twice, but both times it rang off the post. The game was going to a fourth OT. I felt better than most and still felt like the game had taken years off my life.

It was a hot day and night in L.A., and by overtime number four fog was hanging over the ice surface. We had been outshot 63 to 34. In the 138th minute we had a little pressure in Edmonton's end, but it looked to have abated when Robertson, the league's most fearsome punisher on the blueline, smoked Whisper, running him face-first into the boards. Robertson then skated to the front of the net and had his back turned to Whisper, who was slow getting to his knees and then his skates. He had blood pouring from his broken nose and the hit had probably knocked all the sound and light out of his world, but he still went to the front of the net. I drifted a shot from the top of the circle and it caromed off two sticks and a leg or two legs and a stick. Darryl

Brown stopped that shot, kicking out a pad, but the rebound went right to Whisper, who had about four feet of net to bury it. Robertson turned too late. I saw the big thug looking skyward in despair as the bloodied Whisper skated by him toward me and jumped into my arms. The next day, sports sections across the continent ran an award-winning image of a crushed loser, Robertson, and his misshapen nemesis, Whisper, and a found-in, me.

The rest of the team poured over the bench and piled on Whisper. We were a little more delicate with Hunts, whose twelve pounds of sweat had been soaked up by his pads over the course of the night. After he straightened his comb-over, Iron threw his hands up in the air, all but waving over the television cameras so he could stake his claim as author of the upset of upsets. But with cameras trained on the unbeloved scene-stealer and fans cheering, Martin Mars skated up to the bench, pointed to Iron threateningly, and broke his stick in half over the boards. Whisper picked up the pieces and headed straight for the dressing room.

Mars was the first one off the ice and he changed without a word. He didn't even bother with showering. He rushed like he had left his Benz running. He walked out of the dressing room with his skates and the remnants of his stick. That's the last I ever saw of him. He walked out on the team. He gave no explanation. Maybe it would have turned out differently if I had said something when Iron was carving him. But nobody spoke up and Whisper wouldn't or couldn't defend himself.

We went out in four straight against St. Louis in the next round. I watched our season end with my arm in a sling. It turned out that Martin Mars had scored the winning goal in Iron John's final victory. That summer Iron had his cigarette boat out on Lake Rosseau, suffered a massive heart attack, and collapsed over the steering wheel. He was probably already dead when the boat, wide open, hit a well-buoyed slab of granite that jutted out of the water. The boat went airborne, did a lateral one-eighty, and landed top down on the water.

I figured it would take all that and a stake through his heart to keep Iron down.

7 ————————————

Chief drove up to the arena. The Crushed Can. I had heard about it for years but had never seen it until Hunts bumped me up into the amateur-scouting director's job. I don't know whose idea it was to put a concave aluminum roof on a half million cinderblocks but it wasn't a professional architect's. Once you got by that, though, it was a pretty cool barn. The scouts' room down at ice level between the dressing rooms was the size of a broom closet and had just a couple of benches, uncomfortable but all occupied. Chief and I were standing outside it with our coffees, waiting for the teams to go out for their warm-ups, when my BlackBerry vibrated in my hand. It was Hunts on the line.

"How may I direct your call?"

Hunts took a deep breath. "Is there anything left in your mini-bar?" he asked.

"I'm as sober as you are," I said. Hunts was okay with talk about his sobriety.

"Did you watch the Hogan kid?" he asked.

26

"I've talked myself out of him and there's nobody who's going to talk me back into him," I said. Letting go of a player you like is harder than letting go of a lot of things.

"Where are you tonight?"

"In Moose Jaw with Chief," I said. "Just heard today that Whisper died."

"Martin Mars?"

"Yeah, Chief told me. It was on the news."

"I figured he would be one of those guys who lived forever," Hunts said. "Didn't drink or smoke. No bad habits. Lived pretty clean. The only risk he took was dying of boredom."

Part of me wanted to say that the onset of chronic boredom saved Hunts's life and career, but I decided against cracking wise for once. It was me who'd played the lead role in getting Hunts off the bottle, and it was Hunts who'd called me up cold when he had an open spot on his scouting staff.

"Boredom might have been what did it," I said. "He committed suicide. They found him in his Mercedes ..."

"Shit, the sauna."

"Yeah, the sauna. Except it wasn't the heat that killed him. It was the hose he rigged up running from his exhaust into the window."

"Jesus."

"Yeah, we were talking to Gravy in Regina this afternoon," I said. Gravy scouted the West for Jersey before retiring two summers ago. He still came out to every game in Regina to see old friends. "He said that Whisper moved back to Swift Current after he played in Germany for years. He had a number for him. I was gonna give Mitzi a call."

"Mitzi? He was still with her?" Hunts was amazed. Both he and I had been through marital meltdowns, him thrice, me just the painful and very public once.

"Yeah, that's what Gravy said. He said that Mars came back from Germany and made some big money with a chain of gas stations and truck stops on the Trans-Canada."

Hunts hated to seem out of the loop. "I think I heard something about that," he offered unconvincingly.

"I'm gonna give the Widow Mars a call tomorrow," I said. "There'd be so much going on right now. They only found him this morning, I guess. But I figure if I don't call, no one else from the team will. Maybe no one in the league. Gravy said he had some sort of connection to minor hockey in Swift Current. Had something to do with the junior team. Not coaching or anything, but it would probably look bad if no one from L.A. offered condolences."

"Yeah," Hunts said, not particularly moved. I'd taken any pressure off him to make a call. There wasn't much, anyway. "We'll have to do a moment of silence at our next home game and show the goal on the big screen ..."

"But not when he threatened the late, great Iron and he broke his stick."

"We'll leave that out. I don't think we'll do anything else. He's not quite up there enough that we'd wear black armbands or a patch with his number or name on it. Besides, it's a suicide."

"Yeah, it's a bit awkward, for sure." I didn't think that should have been a factor but I wasn't about to contradict my boss.

8

In the first intermission I called Sandy. Like almost all of my teammates over the years, I had tried the Trophy-Wife Gambit and I had met with uniquely disastrous results. Only when we were surrounded by divorce lawyers and social workers did I realize that my ex was fine when she had a script to read but otherwise had nothing to say. Only then did I realize I had to be with a woman who could at least keep up with me in conversation about things that matter, affairs of state, the stuff of life, culture high and low. In Sandy I had found a woman who could run laps around me but kindly let me stay close enough to think I was almost her intellectual equal. She had launched her practice, child psychology, fifteen years before and, yes, I had met her when my daughter was struggling, normal teenage stuff compounded by tabloid stories of my ex, her mother, landing in and then busting out of rehab. Sandy had helped my daughter through it. I'll always owe her for that. She said that she didn't like to get involved with her patients' fathers, and why she made an exception for me is one thing I never asked her and never will. Probably couldn't resist the challenge.

Sandy had just wrapped up with patients, three kids whose parents were divorcing and going to separate penalty boxes while the offspring prepared to play short-handed the rest of their lives.

I reminded her that I was going to be home Tuesday. She did her best to be enthused about my return. Our summer had been great, back when we rented a place in the Finger Lakes, when we went to Watkins Glen to catch a race, which was her idea, not mine. Those were good times, but we hadn't seen much of each other since the season started. She knew that went with my job but she still resented the game. She didn't have to be a clinical psychologist to recognize that hockey turns some people's values inside out, upside down, and through the looking glass. But she was, and that just made her resent it even more.

"I found out today a teammate died, guy named Martin Mars," I said.

"I never heard you talk about him," she said.

I hadn't. It was of a piece with the ongoing *negotiations* since the season had started, Sandy's unsolicited analysis of someone who didn't think of himself as a patient, the guy holding my BlackBerry to my ear. She thought I was something less than a good boyfriend to her because I was a lot less than a good friend to one and all in my life. "Mr. Independent," she called me. That was Her Term of Endearment. It was downhill from there. She said I had romanticized my Outsider Status so much that I couldn't let anyone in. She said that she didn't say any of this clinically and it wasn't a complaint, but almost everything she said had a clinical ring and this thumbnail reading of me would have had to improve a lot just to become a complaint. She made jokes about it too often for them to be jokes and just often enough to be a warning.

"Truth is stranger than fiction," I said, trying not to seem too cold. "He was my roomie for a while. Not much of a player. If he'd scored as much as he snored he would have made five mil a season. He sounded like a car with a bad muffler and his jaw made this cracking sound like bones breaking."

"You should talk about noisy sleepers. How did he die?"

"Suicide."

"Oh, how terrible for his family."

"Yeah, I'm gonna put in a call tomorrow. I'd go out there ..."

"You should. It's what a friend would do."

The dreaded F-bomb again. She said *friend* like I was a kid in the spelling bee and had just asked the moderator to use the word in a sentence. She phoned in the prescription. I treated it like our connection had cut out at the most opportune moment.

"I'd go but I've got to catch a game tomorrow," I said. "Just my job. Nothing I can do about that."

Maybe she'd judge me harshly, again, but no one in the game would. We all know the etiquette, know what should be done, what has to be done. In this case, a call would have to suffice.

"It's a shame, especially how it happened. If only he could have had help. Suicide is an avoidable death."

Sandy was jumping way ahead. Then again, she was staking her professional claim. Suicide and lesser heartbreaks were either mostly mitigated or entirely avoidable with the help of a psychologist, and that was the bottom line on her shingle. "Well, I don't know that he didn't try to get help," I said. "I hadn't been in touch with him for a long time. No one had as far as I can tell."

"Maybe you should have been."

Again with the should-haves. "Maybe other guys were trying to connect with him," I said. "I don't know. People drift off by choice sometimes."

9

Chief and I left the game with three minutes to go. Moose Jaw's team wasn't much—the best prospect was a sixteen-year-old, a six-foot-three defenceman as skinny as an exclamation mark. He wasn't eligible until next year's draft, but it was good to keep tabs on the prospects that far ahead. Even if Chief and I couldn't count on having a job in L.A. after July 1 we had to be ready in case a job came up with another organization. Medicine Hat was not even as interesting. The Hat's best prospect was shut down for the season with his second concussion. Chief cornered the Hat's coach before the game. They were ex-teammates in junior. His buddy told him that the kid's symptoms were still pretty bad. "Solitary confinement," he told Chief. "The kid is locked in a dark room all day." God bless him. I hoped he'd get better but I still wouldn't want to invest seven figures in a Potential Casualty. My advice would be to get out of the game and get on with your life. Of course he wouldn't take it.

Bad news must have been metastasizing when Chief and I hit the highway back to Regina. It was a starless night, the roads were nasty, and the winds could blow your ride sideways. While Chief was weaving through a fleet of eighteen-wheelers, we formalized our plans to head out to Wilcox Monday, a late-afternoon game against the team from Yorkton. Wilcox is a hamlet of a hundred hardy souls about an hour due south of Regina. We'd give ourselves just over the minimum time. If we were in Wilcox early, there was just no place other than the rink to kill time and get out of the cold.

I hit Seek on the radio. Against all odds I found a station, a five-thousand-watt outfit, that had Steve Earle on the playlist. If it had been his later, long-haired, subversive stuff, that would have been begging for a boycott by local businesses and listeners. But this was his early stuff, when he was still singing about Nashville staples: a kid left behind in a small town while his friends went off to school, a pump jockey counting out-of-state plates.

Just when the chorus of "Someday" started, Chief's BlackBerry vibrated. Chief grabbed it off the dashboard, checked the number of the incoming call and took no time to decide to answer it. The conversation was brief and to the point.

"Shit," he said. "Okay, thanks. Bye."

"What's up? Family?"

"No, it's from Wilcox. The Notre Dame kid. He was scratched in Kindersley this afternoon."

"The shoulder?"

"No, flu. Won't be back 'til Friday night."

"Shit," I reaffirmed. "He didn't get a flu shot?"

"His folks are Christian Scientists, that's why he's not playing major junior and wanting to go to college in the States. They figure he'll be allowed ..."

Chief searched for words. I jumped in.

"... the religious freedom to piss away his career."

I was less interested in the kid now than ever. I'm not looking for a player with issues or questions or problems, because they will end up being my issues or questions or problems. I've never had an interest in becoming a social worker.

We had no reason to go to Wilcox Monday, the odds were against my being able to book an earlier flight back to Toronto, and Sandy's should-haves were eating at me. I had no excuses. I'd fill her prescription. I'd swallow the bitter medicine.

"You got anything going on tomorrow?" I asked Chief. "We should go out to Swift Current in the morning."

Chief didn't have a problem with my shoulds. I was his friend but I was also his boss. There wasn't much call for him to be there for Whisper and the widow. It wasn't a consideration for them. It was a consideration for me. It's a long drive out to Swift Current. It would feel a lot longer if I was going on my own.

"It's four hours each way," he said, thinking I might be a weak-willed and soft-assed Easterner not up for what folks in Saskatchewan think of as a short commute.

"Still," I said. I figured that he needed a reminder and an incentive. "You can expense the mileage. We'll split the drive."

He had already assumed that would be the case. "Your car?"

"If I get a big rental bill plus a bunch of mileage claimed for the same dates here it's going to look bad," I said. "Let me drop this off at the airport. I'll make it back to you some way."

IO

The usual: I couldn't sleep. It happens on the road every night and at home most nights. Could a half-hour nap at lunchtime mess me up that much?

I was staring up at the ceiling like it was the Jumbotron. I was projecting the scene after Whisper scored that goal of all goals. He had his back to me and had just taken off his sweater. I put my hands on his shoulders and gave him a shake. "You fuckin' showed him, Whisper," I said.

He didn't turn around. He said nothing. He stripped off his pads.

"We're going to get rehydrated," I said. "Come on out for once. It's the night of your life."

No reaction. He put on his cheap suit and his one pair of dress shoes and then started to walk out of the dressing room with his skates and the shards of his stick. His MARS 8 sweater was at the bottom of the pile of equipment that he didn't bother to hang up to dry.

A reporter tried to ask him a question. "Get out of my way,"

Whisper said, head down. He looked as mad as a guy sent down to the minors. The video clip showed up on sportscasts that night. So did Iron John, in full preen, announcing that he knew what this team had and had seen the epic victory coming.

I thought of the newspaper the next day, the one column in the *Times* that started: *After banging in a timely rebound and ending the longest game in franchise history, Martin Mars beat a hasty retreat like Cinderella grabbing the homebound train after midnight. The only difference was that Mars didn't leave behind a glass slipper.*

The scene on the ceiling of my room flashed ahead. It was a couple of days after the marathon game. Reporters were asking me about Martin Mars. I told them I didn't know anything, which was true. They said that the GM was giving them the No Comment Treatment. Three days later he could keep up the embargo no longer. He was in front of the cameras and lights and microphones, saying that Martin Mars had left the team without notice and was under suspension. It was a distraction that our exhausted and beat-up team didn't need.

We had a team meeting before the start of the St. Louis series. "He didn't figure in our plans, anyway," Iron John said. I looked at my watch. It was ten forty-five. That was the minute when Iron lost the last team he'd ever coach.

Reporters came to me every day, fishing for the scoop. They knew I was his roommate and should have known him better than anyone else on the team. They thought that I was giving them the slip. They figured I had talked to him. I hadn't.

I was excited, or at least fairly excited, by the win over Edmonton. Still, I had been in a bad mood that season. My contract negotiations had stalled the summer before and I had ended up in salary arbitration, where my agent screwed the pooch. He prepped a bad case, the team won the arb, and I was out a good 150 K. That's peanuts by today's standards but it was a good chunk twenty years back. I felt sick to my stomach coming out of the hearing. People said I shouldn't have taken it so hard. After all, my wife at the time had just landed her first big television series and she was the bigger breadwinner. No matter, my pride took a shit-kicking. Gatorade tasted like Schweppes Bitter Lemon all season. I tried not to let on in the room, and I wasn't anxious to get traded out of L.A. because of my other half's ties to Hollywood.

I took one reporter aside and told him to meet me in the parking lot. I told him what had happened in the dressing room before game six, Iron John carving Whisper like a Thanksgiving turkey. I told the reporter to do with it what he wanted so long as he didn't out me as the source.

The final scene that played out on the ceiling was a video clip that was on the sportscasts the next day.

The media covering the team was all over Iron John's ripping Martin Mars. Every question made Iron's eyes bulge out. "Lies," he said. "All lies."

That came from one of the best, gone but not mourned.

MONDAY

I was back in California. And, yeah, I was with her. We were in the studio and she was on a set that didn't change over her five seasons on the show. She was twenty-one years old and had been cast as a high school freshman when the series and our marriage debuted. Her role wound up outlasting her status as network TV's It Girl and Whatever It Was We Had Vowed. In the dream it must have been around the third season. It was between takes and I had a front-row seat in the studio audience while she teased her hair and had her eyes lined with surgical precision by the makeup girl. She looked at me and said, *You're mine when school's out.* And, and, and, and a couple more ands, and it was all lost.

I reached and fumbled and could hear it at a pillow-width distance.

"This is your wake-up call."

I fought off the urge to fall back asleep and back in time. I don't mind dreams but can do without hauntings. I reached for my laptop on the side table and went online before I rubbed my eyes clear. Google and four clicks found the name and phone number of the funeral home where my ex-teammate was in a deep sleep. I told the funeral director my story. I didn't ask him to give me the number Chez Mars. He wouldn't have given it up, anyway. I just asked him to pass on the message that I was going to come out to the visitation.

I splashed some cold water on my face, force of habit, and went downstairs to breakfast only half-exhausted. I didn't exactly blend in with the businessmen who were heading into meetings and conferences, but I didn't care. I put in my order: eggs over, bacon and sausage, hash browns, brown toast, grapefruit juice, and a coffee. I needed a comprehensive meal in advance of the drive out.

Chief called me when the plates landed in front of me. He was on his way.

An hour after that we turned onto the Trans-Canada. "You're sure you still want to go out there?" Chief asked. He was sure he didn't want to and just as sure he had to.

Time dragged on. I did a double take and then another. I was sure that those eighteen-wheelers were the same ones we had seen the night before, and I took some satisfaction in the thought that whatever hardships I might encounter in my workaday life it beat hauling loads up and down Highway 1. Most of the time, anyway.

Chief had rustled up his best threads. He was sitting bolt upright behind the wheel, making the noble effort not to crease his suit. I looked casual by comparison. I was travelling light. The two ties I own were hanging in the closet of my apartment. My suits were too—hadn't worn one since the draft last June.

We rolled past the hard stare of Mac the Moose and I struggled to stay awake. Nodding off would have been bad form as a passenger. And I didn't want to drift off and land back in the studio.

2

Cruise control set at the speed limit plus ten. The heat on high.

"No, you can ask why. Lots of people wanted to know back then. 'Chief, you're thirty, you can still play, you can still fight, so why'd you quit?' I told my wife. I'll tell you 'cause you're good with this stuff. Thing is, day before I played, maybe two days before sometimes, I'd see the fight I was going to be in. The guy I was gonna fight. Sometimes waking up, sometimes going to bed, maybe even driving my car. Could be doing anything and all of a sudden I'd get this feeling down deep in my gut and I'd see the fight clear as spring water. Every punch he'd throw and I'd throw. And the fight would go down just like that. Mess used to say that my eyes spun like someone had pulled the handle of a slot machine, but I was just seeing something that I'd seen before. Anyway, at the end of that last season, one game to go, we're out of the playoffs, and I saw the fight, right before the game. And I saw that I got hurt real bad. Stretchered and everything. So I went out there and I didn't drop him when Wilson wanted to go. I just told him I can't. Maybe he understood. I had a year left on my contract but I knew I was going to keep having that same thing happen over and over. It was good for me all those years, you know. And it probably saved me that last game. No going back after that."

A school bus slowing at an exit ramp. A kid in the back of the bus turning around to wave at strangers.

"I don't like Swift much. I have no idea why they call it Swift Current. It's neither swift nor current."

A tractor-trailer spraying slush against the windshield. A tractor-trailer left behind.

"You heard about the bus crash in Swift Current all those years back? Were you still in college when it happened?"

An email soliciting Boston College alumni donations unopened on the screen of a BlackBerry. Another inviting players from the 1987 hockey team to a reunion also unopened.

"Four died. Everyone out here knows the story. I played against that team. The one guy I had a fight with. A big tough kid. When he died he was caught underneath the bus. Another one of the kids was going to be a first-round pick, just sixteen but he had it all. Two of them were the leading scorers. One grew up right around the corner from the team. I guess they were playing cards in the back. A bunch of them were hurt bad too. Bus went off the road barely two minutes out of town, rickety old school bus that the town had paid for. Team was in its first year in the league. Right around New Year's."

A gas station left behind. A half-full tank that could wait.

"Our coach had us all go to the funeral. They had the ceremony in the arena. I didn't have a suit but the good thing was they had us all wear our sweaters, same with the teams in the rest of the league who showed up. We were in seats down on the floor of the arena. I was sitting behind a guy from Saskatoon whose nose I'd broken a couple of weeks before. He gave me a dirty look but it wasn't the time to do anything."

Eyes on the road. A glance at the rear-view mirror with nothing in it except a dead-straight road disappearing into the horizon.

"So many guys on that team ended up all messed up. Drinking, a lot of them. Drugs. They won a national championship a couple of years later with guys who'd been on the bus and everyone thought it was a great story, but they had a diddler as a coach. You know the guy. Went to jail years later. Messed with one kid on the team who made the league and he nearly went completely off the rails. There was just too much shit. People in Swift had to know *something* was going on. Half the league knew things weren't right there. Someone should have stepped up."

On the north side of the shoulder, snow that had fallen since October perfectly preserved. A million sections of farmland promising an infinite white harvest.

"You talk to people out there about it and all you get back is this blank look. It was awful stuff but people just don't want to know. Sort of like you can put the secrets back in the bottle if you try hard enough."

Old wooden hydro poles looking like crucifixes on the north side of Highway 1. A westbound train pulling a hundred boxcars like so much inescapable and freighted history on the south side.

"You weren't working for us yet, but a few years back there was one kid I really liked out with Swift, kid from a small town, not far from Hunts's hometown. Word was he was drinking a lot. Hunts had me look into it. It was bad. Team was bad. Into all the bad places downtown by the railway tracks. The kid missed practices hungover. You can't fix problems like that."

Wind blowing Chief's Jeep around the road. The Jeep coughing indignantly when asked to pass a couple of senior citizens in a beat-up station wagon.

"I meant to take it in for a tune-up the other day."

A sign warning for a bridge that ices. A cigar-sized index finger pointing to a rise in the road.

"That's the overpass that the team bus came off of going east. If there wasn't any snow you'd be able to see right where the bus rolled over. I heard a scout say one time it looked like God was golfing and he left a divot. I think it's more like a scar."

A train snaking its way east under traffic heading west. Snow evenly covering the town's best-kept lawn, a cemetery, on the south side at the first exit.

3

I had only heard about that bus crash in passing. Back when it happened I was at BC and I read the *Globe* and the *Times*, but they had almost no hockey in them so I didn't bother with the sports sections at all. When we pulled up to the funeral home's parking lot it occurred to me that the victims of that crash would have been brought to this same place.

Chief parked his Jeep in an empty lot framed by piles of plowed snow seven feet high. I had thought we were travelling to the edge of the world but now wondered if we were standing in the shallow end of the abyss beneath it. Snow and ice were hard-packed under our boots. It was a solemn occasion but still too cold for dress shoes.

We were met at the front door by the only funeral-home staffer in the house. I told him that we were there for Martin Mars before I noticed that Whisper's visitation was the only event on the board in the lobby. The guy's grief was genuine. Whisper's death had separated him from a day off.

Mitzi Mars sat there alone with her husband, my ex-teammate

lying in the casket, eyes closed, hands crossed, expression blank. Whisper was in a suit that looked never worn. He had stayed in pretty good shape. He probably wasn't even ten pounds over his playing weight. Fat lot of good it did him.

Mitzi had aged well. Yeah, the hair was still a sculptural and chemical miracle, but the face under it didn't look like it belonged to a woman in her late forties. Maybe they had been drilling outside Swift Current and struck Oil of Olay.

A funeral home in Swift Current is one place I have to admit I never expected to see Mitzi Mars, a girl Whisper had met one night in Vegas over the all-star break and married the next. He'd been on the wrong end of so many pranks that we thought he was trying to pull one on us when she came to practice with him after they got back. When it finally sank in that this was no joke, that the buxom broad with three storeys of bottle-blond hair was in fact Mrs. Mars, we tried to piece together her story. She went for skimpy outfits that Saran Wrapped her prodigious curves. Her skin was as pale as pancake mix, obviously the type of girl who was up at night and slept all day.

Mars told us that she was a dancer. "In a show," he whispered.

"Peeler, call girl, and/or grifter," read the collective thought bubble in the dressing room.

"Jesus, Whisper, we should have had a bachelor party," I said. "It's just that we would have needed more than an hour's notice."

We were sure that she was out to fleece him for all he was worth. She wouldn't have been the first out to sucker a player, though if she had known the league and its salary structure, she would have aimed her sights higher than the Black Ace. We figured she'd stick around until the first or, if she was in for the long haul, the fifteenth. Just long enough for the gold digger to realize she'd struck a vein of pyrite. Instead, she stuck with him to what turned out to be the bitter end for him in L.A. She'd

show up in the wives' lounge and none of the other brides would
even look at her. "She comes to the arena to watch games that
her husband doesn't play in?" my then-wife asked me. I told her
it didn't make sense to me either.

I looked over at the casket and hated myself for thinking that
he was scratched one last time.

"Mitzi, I'm Brad Shade," I said. "I'm so sorry for your loss. I
don't know if you remember me but ..."

"Brad, of course," Mitzi said, dabbing tears with each word.
"Thanks so much for coming. It would have meant a lot to
Martin. He always talked about you. I know he was so happy for
you when you won the Cup in Montreal. He always said that he
wished he'd stayed in touch with you."

That rattled me. Maybe it was just because I was his roomie.
Maybe it was because I was on the ice for his final shift in the
league. Maybe it was because I had reached out to him after the
game. Maybe he knew it had to be me who ratted out Iron John
for being so brutal toward him. Maybe he resented me less than
others. All those maybes and I didn't have a good reason why he
would have always talked about me.

Mitzi's voice had been sandpapered by hours of bawling. Her
accent was fainter than I remembered. It was south, although
of no specific place as far as I could tell. She had no particular
pedigree to brag about. She never had a chance to be a deb or go
to a good school, that was for sure.

"This is Warren Bear," I said and pointed back to Chief. "He
played in the league back when Martin played. He came down
with me from Regina."

"I'm sorry," Chief said. "I didn't know Martin 'cept to play
against him."

Mitzi tried to recover her composure and catch her breath.
"As you can see, Martin and I don't have any family here," she

said. "We don't have any family at all. And really we kept to ourselves. We used to joke that no couple had ever spent more time together. We were together just about every day and the odd night he was away on business he'd call, call once during the day and then again at night, and I could tell he wasn't happy away from home. We had just celebrated our twentieth anniversary."

She collapsed into tears again. She bowed her head and raised her left hand to her brow. Her hands gave away her age more than anything else. The rock in her wedding ring was a healthy size, upgraded from what he had purchased on a Black Ace's pay.

A couple of painfully quiet minutes passed and a search party wouldn't have come back with something to say. I felt a little guilty leaving it up to Mitzi to try to restart the conversation.

"What have you done all these years, Brad? Martin always wondered."

Shit, what a perfect time and place to discuss what might have been and what was lost. I skipped by the worst of it: my failed marriage to a very modestly talented actress, my knee surgeries and the arthritis that came out of them, my agent's acquittal for bilking my career earnings and those of others. I wasn't about to do the Old Woe-Is-Me, though so many things still kept me up at night.

"After my career was over I worked for an investigations agency in Toronto," I said.

She jumped in before I could flesh out the thumbnail profile.

"Martin said that you had studied criminology in school and that your father was a police officer," she said. "He played hockey too, right?"

I knew that Whisper had answered the phone and taken messages when Sarge called my room a couple of times. How Whisper knew that I had majored in criminology at Boston College I did not know.

"Yeah, I did that for four years and then Hunts ... I don't know if you remember him ..."

"The little goalie," she said.

"Yeah, he ended up with the general manager's job in L.A. and hired me as a scout ..."

I had to change the subject. I couldn't count on Chief to jump in. He's a good man but not a smooth operator.

"You stayed in Swift Current all these years?"

"After we came back from Germany," Mitzi said. She was going back to the good times. "When I met Martin, he said that he didn't want to play in the league anymore. I didn't even understand what that meant. He told me that he wanted to play in Europe. I liked that idea. It sounded like an adventure."

An adventure. Everyone on the team had her all wrong back when she met Whisper on a Friday night and married him on the Saturday. Leave it to him to find a babe in the woods in Las Vegas.

"He made me a promise that we'd go. I think he regretted going to Germany at first, but we had five great years there. Martin's parents ran the family business here. We never visited. They were very old and he had no brothers or sisters or relatives, but they had a good business adviser and their business really took off. Martin always said he wanted to play until his fortieth birthday, but we came back after his father died and his mother developed dementia. Martin knew the business really well. Worked in it since he was a kid."

That explained the love of cars.

4

The lone funeral-home scrub working that day had driven Mitzi to the funeral home. I was sure she was going to be billed and gouged for that. Chief drove us back to the Mars home. It was a big spread, on the east side of town, a few blocks from the arena and a few blocks from the ramp to the highway that the team bus had rolled up that day all those years ago.

Mitzi invited us in. I have been in a few multi-millionaires' homes, those of star players, those of big hitters in Hollywood, and Château Whisper was undoubtedly the least pretentious I had ever seen. It was a three-bedroom split-level and it looked well preserved but unrenovated. It wasn't even the nicest-looking house on the block. A couple of teachers lived in the home on one side and the realtor who'd sold them the house lived on the other. It was a Just-Folks Street. The decor was consistent with the packaging. No pool, understandable given the climate, I guess, but no great creature comforts either. No big entertainment centre, no crystal chandeliers, no sauna. Most of the furniture was bought off the floor of the big-box store down at the mall, the same place where his employees bought their stuff. There were a few antiques, not the fancy European kind, just a handcrafted cabinet and dining table and other wood pieces that would have fit in a Prairie heritage theme park. There was a blanket of homesteader vintage hanging on the largest of the living-room walls. Mitzi would show us around later and talk about each piece. When she got to the blanket all she could muster was: "Well, Martin didn't really have any time for art."

It didn't look like Whisper had any time for hockey, either. There wasn't a sign that Whisper had ever played a game, not a single photo in a game or anything lifted from a program, no mounted puck or framed sweater. Not a thing. At the centre of the mantel over the fireplace was an eleven-by-fourteen photo of bride and groom at the wedding chapel in Vegas. The flash from the camera reflected off Whisper's horn-rims. On the left side of the mantel were smaller pics of the couple from back in the '90s, his playing days in Germany, the pair of them in front of European landmarks: the Eiffel Tower, the Leaning Tower of Pisa, and the Matterhorn. On the right side were photos of more recent vintage, the pair of them fishing and tanning at their place up on the lake. The beard was gone in all of them, and in none of them was he wearing glasses.

I was in the kitchen with Mitzi when she checked her messages on speakerphone.

You have two new messages.

Message One, received today at 12:37 P.M. "Mrs. Mars, this is Ron Beckwith. I'm sorry for your loss. We on the board are going to have to go ahead with our meeting as scheduled at four o'clock, however. Unfortunately, the board members have set aside this time. Given what we're up against and time constraints, we will have to move ahead with our planning. If you're not up to attending in your husband's stead, I completely understand."

Mitzi deleted it.

Message Two, received today at 1:14 P.M. *Click.*

A hang-up. Mitzi checked to see if there was a return number. NUMBER UNKNOWN. Probably an auto-call, a consumer poll, a giveaway, one of those You've-Been-Selected cons.

Message One was strange enough that it begged an explanation, and Mitzi gave it without my asking. "Martin sits, *sat*, on the board of the juniors. The team is community-owned. About a hundred and fifty people have shares. Martin has more than most." Still, Beckwith's call seemed ghoulish. A pharmacist invests more emotion in a recommendation to take a pill on an empty stomach.

"Can you go to the meeting, Brad?"

"Did Wh— *Martin* have anyone on the board he'd have trusted for a proxy on his vote?"

"No."

The worst grifters are the vultures who smell death and opportunity. The criminals who are at least artful are no worse than the Chamber of Commerce types who make their pillages while proclaiming their good intentions. Chief and I had come all the way to Swift Current to help out, though we figured we'd take a largely ceremonial role. I didn't need to stick around the scene any longer than a cup of coffee, but I allowed myself to get sucked into a small vortex.

"I'll go and let you know what happens," I told Mitzi.

She was deeply appreciative. She gave me the details. The board met at a conference room at the arena.

I kept waiting for a knock at the door, a friend to prepare dishes that will go uneaten, deliver flowers that will go unnoticed, and let us make a graceful exit for the meeting. The knock never came. I thought it might have been the way Whisper died. A small-town scandal. This was sort of a nineteenth-century attitude, but from what I could tell and all Chief had told me,

Swift Current hadn't moved very much beyond it. The good citizens didn't want to be stained by associating with the widow.

Mitzi's hands were folded in her lap and she had her head down. The only sounds were the furnace churning up and Chief clattering in the kitchen as he got the coffee percolating.

"I have to know how he died," she said.

I wanted to say that only the mentally ill commit suicide and mental illness isn't something that's there for explaining. Not by family and friends. Not by scientists who can confidently explain most things. Not by men of the cloth who can doubtlessly explain everything. Not by a mope like me who struggles to explain anything. If I had known her better or if she had been a total stranger, I would have managed to spit that out.

I couldn't say a thing, couldn't do a thing. We just sat there like a fruit-in-the-bowl still life until Chief brought us our coffees.

"I don't know how these things go, Brad," she said. "I don't know what to do."

I had a sinking feeling that I was going to be roped into something that I didn't want to do by someone I was in no position to say no to.

"Can you go talk to them about it? They called me and brought me in to identify him, but I couldn't ask them about anything that ..."

Mitzi couldn't finish the sentence.

I heard a car rattle up in the drive and a car door open and slam, then the side door of the house do the same.

"That's Walt," Mitzi said. "He lives in our basement apartment. He's been working at the station for a year now. A few months after Martin hired him we brought him in. Martin said he was struggling with things but he was a good kid. We've had a bunch of Martin's workers, old and young, stay here. We never charged them rent, they just help us out with things, cutting the lawn, watching the house when we'd go on holidays. Walt's a good boy. He was with me at the funeral home before you got there. He was embarrassed because he didn't have any good clothes to wear. Martin was closer to him than other boys we've had. We never had kids. Couldn't. They're the closest thing we've had to sons."

Mitzi was still stuck in the present tense.

"Mrs. Mars?" came the voice from the basement.

"We're here," she said. "It's all right, Walt."

Chief came out of the kitchen. "Cream?" he asked.

Mitzi brought her voice down to a hush. "Poor Walt," she said. "He works at the other station across town and last week he was mugged and robbed and beaten up on the night shift. He thought he was going to lose his job over the two hundred dollars they took from him at gunpoint. He's been shaken up ever since."

Walt came upstairs. He was a kid, if a kid could be about twenty. He was too big to be a jockey, too little to be much else. He had hair messed by a toque and a chalky complexion messed by persistent adolescence, like a pool of Polyfilla flecked with pomegranate seeds. He had good manners, a gash on his forehead, and a look of worry that Mr. Mars's death might end his employment, his rent-free address, and the insulin on his health plan. He froze when Mitzi introduced him. He wasn't comfortable in his own skin, even less so around those in other people's skin. He added nothing to the conversation except silent witness. Ten minutes later Walt said, "Yes, Mrs. Mars." Five minutes after that he was sizzling some pork chops.

"They're off local farms," Mitzi pointed out, mustering Swift Current Tourist Board Pride. "I go out to a farm just outside of town and pick them up once or twice a week." The pork chops were the best I had ever sampled, as if grief were a rare and special seasoning. Chief had seconds. I couldn't remember ever having a home-cooked meal on the road as a player or scout. I couldn't even remember making myself a sandwich. They were only pork chops but they tasted as good as any filet mignon I had dropped a C-note on.

5

Dinner hadn't hit bottom when Chief and I headed over to the arena. It was adjacent to a working-class neighbourhood on the east side of town and south of Highway 1, not even two minutes from the station where they found Whisper. The arena was the utilitarian centrepiece of the town's parks and rec department, but from the looks of it there wasn't a lot of recreating going on. On the playground beside the arena, monkey bars climbed out of a couple of feet of snow and the foot of the slide was a pile of hard brown slush. The outdoor rink for shinny was likewise snowed under. The park was a plain unbroken by a single boot print and there wasn't a kid in sight.

Chief and I walked into the conference room at the arena. Seven men and one woman, septuagenarians, lined a long table. Their clothes were made for business if the business had been conducted in 1964, which was around the time they had made their respective wads. The man I took for Beckwith had taken centre stage. He was all of seventy and had been a member of the original board that had landed Swift Current the junior team.

His construction company had missed out on the contract to build the arena back in the '80s, but Beck-Bilt's drab piles of cinderblocks were all around the town. He wore a grey suit a half shade darker than his skin, a timeless outfit in that it never has nor ever will be in style. He had a white-knuckled grip on his coffee mug, and I imagined that his hold on the proceedings was just as viselike. He offered me what passed in Swift Current for a warm welcome.

"Who are you?"

I tried to tidy it up in proper business fashion. "I'm Brad Shade. I'm serving as proxy for the late Martin Mars. This is my friend Warren Bear."

Chief nodded. A couple of members of the board rewarded him with a look of toxic distrust.

"So you say you're acting as a proxy for Mars," said the master of ceremonies, whose voice I now recognized as that in the voice-mail. His impulse to close ranks was deep-seated and indigenous to the town. Given tragic precedent in the team's history, you'd think that a correction would have been made, that complete transparency would have become standard procedure. Instead, Beckwith and company liked to keep things opaque. "I suppose you have documents to indicate that. Dated. Witnessed."

He supposed right. Mitzi had signed and Chief and Walt had put their scrawl as witnesses beneath it.

"It seems to be valid," the lone woman conceded with undisguised regret. She was, I'd learn later, a long-standing member of the town council and a vice-principal at the local high school. From the looks of the bespectacled harridan, she was a scold of the first order. If I spoke out of order she'd probably hand me a detention. The vice-principal slapped a copy of the minutes from the last meeting down in front of me like she was trying to squash a beetle crossing the table.

A couple of points of order, a couple of motions, a couple of secondeds-and-all-in-favour-say-ayes later we got down to business. I wasn't surprised to learn that the team as a going concern was not going so well at .500 on its ledgers. The arena was the smallest in the league. So was the market. In fact, other Prairie towns had bigger population bases and bigger arenas yet were content to have teams in lower and less-expensive leagues. The cost of travel was eating into the bottom line. The shortfall on a yearly basis steamrolled into mid-range six figures. It had been booster hubris to take on a major–junior franchise back in the day. The market had been too small to break even twenty-five years ago. Twenty-five years of cost escalation and the town's almost completely stagnant economy made it an even bleaker picture. The only reason the team was still in Swift Current was its tragic arc. The board saw it as a point of honour; taking the franchise out of Swift Current would have been giving the brush to the four teenagers who'd died in the crash on the outskirts of town. But the realities were plain as the numbers in the ledgers: It could no longer be sustained with this ownership set-up.

"We have no choice," Beckwith said. "We can only go to the community so often to cover these losses. We can't pay for the best European players. We can't convince the best players from other provinces to come here. Any coach worth anything won't work for what we pay him, and if we do get someone who's any good at all he'll jump at the first decent job offer. Let's face it, there's no future here, the way things are. I've taken the liberty of talking to some people who would be in the market to buy the franchise for relocation. Victoria is strongly interested. There's a group in Winnipeg and businessmen in the States who are also prepared to make offers. I can't see the league's board of governors standing in our way. Bidding will go up to four or five million to the right buyer. We can pay dividends to our shareholders and ice a team in the Saskatchewan league."

I didn't trust Beckwith after listening to him on the voice-mail. I trusted him even less now. I would have liked to play poker against him. His words came faster and his voice rose when he got around to the prospect of a sale. With that much at stake, Beckwith could have cooked a deal, an inside job that, if he swayed the board, might get him a nice reward from an appreciative new owner above and beyond what he was fairly due.

6

I called Mitzi and said I'd write up the details for her to pass on to her lawyer. She asked us to stay the night. I told her that I had to get back to Regina, that I had a flight out in the morning. I told her I'd go by the RCMP office and ask them what they could tell me about Whisper's death. It seemed the least I could do short of staying over. Chief and I climbed into his Jeep, he put RCMP into his GPS, and we followed the arrow downtown to the Mounties' offices.

The good news was that it had heated up a bit in Swift Current. The bad news was a forecast of freezing rain.

We stopped to fill up the Jeep. Chief looked at the sky, down to its last few minutes of daylight, washed-out grey directly above us, heavy weather on the horizon directly into the wind.

"Maybe we should try and beat that back to Regina," Chief said. "It looks like it's going to be bad."

"We'll be all right, so long as you're driving," I said. I gave Chief my corporate card and went inside to the counter of the convenience store. I grabbed a couple of Red Bulls and the local paper, *The Southwest Booster*. Whisper's death got five paragraphs on page 4.

> *Martin Mars, a former pro hockey player and the owner of a province-wide chain of service stations and truck stops, died Sunday morning. He was 48.*
>
> *Mars, who grew up in Herbert, Sask., played briefly for the Swift Current juniors before he was traded to Prince George and drafted by Los Angeles.*
>
> *He kept roots in Southwest Saskatchewan, returning to oversee his family's business, one that started with a small two-pump gas station in Herbert and later branched out with more than a dozen service centres along the Trans-Canada.*
>
> *In recent years Mars branched out into retailing, including Mars Farm Equipment and Repair on Main Street in Swift Current.*
>
> *Mars also served on the board of the junior hockey team and the Swift Current Arena, and in an advisory role with the city's triple-A teams.*

There was no mention of suicide. Then again, in Swift Current, word would get around fast. It probably had made it around already.

I got out my BlackBerry while Chief waited for the pump to spit out the receipt. I Googled Martin Mars. I thought his death might fly under the national media's radar. It didn't. *The Globe and Mail* picked up on it. I guess no political heavyweights, artistes, or socialites bit the dust that day.

> *Martin Mars, a journeyman hockey pro who scored a goal that ended one of the longest overtime games in modern history, died in Swift Current, Sask., Sunday morning. He was 48 years old. A*

cause of death has not been announced but authorities are treating Mr. Mars's death as a suicide.

We pulled up beside the yellow brick RCMP offices. From his south-facing window an officer would have a view of a line of the town's thirty-two registered churches. Each of them promised some sort of deliverance, the assurance that Mountie and citizen alike are in Swift Current as part of God's plan. From his north-facing window an officer would have a pictur-esque view of Highway 1 and a line of old rundown motels and new big-box stores that run alongside the Trans-Canada artery. No doubt each and every one of the boys in uniform envisioned one day getting in a car and going down that road in one direc-tion or the other with his worldly possessions packed up in the delivery truck behind him.

The crusty bastard at the front desk had no window. He stood six-four and would have been a handful in his day, but that day was long gone. He had gone soft across the middle and added a chin, but his deskside manner was the residue of his once legit tough-guy attitude. Chaining him to the front desk was best for all involved. Let him out of the office and someone could get hurt, including him. He was suspicious of us at first, hostile a minute later.

"I'm wondering if I could speak to the officer or officers who went to the scene of Martin Mars's death," I said.

"And you are ...?"

I told him. My name didn't register with him. He was no hockey fan.

He gave Chief the hairy eyeball. "And he is ...?"

I told him Chief was with me. A curl of his lip betrayed deep-seated intolerance.

"And you want to know about this fellow because ...?"

And I told him that we were there because Mars's widow asked us to be.

"And why isn't she here asking herself?"

I said that she had spent the day at the funeral home looking after the inevitable particulars and was in no shape to come out that night. And that maybe she'd find it all too painful.

"And no family, I suppose?"

I let that go with a nod.

"Well, sir, you can 'wonder' all you like," he said, shutting a notebook. "My job isn't to help you get past your wondering. It is ..."

And he went on. I gave up with the eye contact. As if the day hadn't been long enough. I should have known that the guy who was working the desk on the night shift, especially an older guy, was going to be sour.

Finally I'd had enough. I took out my BlackBerry, wrote a note to myself with his name and number, and saved it. "That's fine, officer," I said. "I appreciate your limited help. If you want you can let whoever comes in here on the day shift tomorrow know that I'll be phoning in. If that doesn't work out, I'll call the regional headquarters."

I knew I had overstepped even before Chief put his big glove on my shoulder.

"I don't need to see you out," the old hump said before adjusting his glasses and burying his head in some paperwork.

7

God in his Providence must have decided that Swift Current needed a good wash or a cold shower. When we got back to the Jeep freezing rain was pelting down. Chief and I took it to a run. Arthur checked in and as soon as I shut the passenger-side door I popped a Celebrex. I had five left in my vial. I thought I was going to need one before the flight Tuesday morning and another after. I didn't bother trying to hide the pain around Chief. Practically every guy in the league returned from the war with a Purple Heart. I had my knee. Chief had a right shoulder that kept popping out, a career-ending liability for a tough guy who made his living with his right fist.

The radio brought bad tidings. A young thing did her weather update in a sunny voice at odds with her script.

It's six thirty. From Weather One the forecast for southwestern Saskatchewan, Monday night through Tuesday morning: Freezing rain and winds out of the west at fifty kilometres an hour with gusts up to eighty kilometres an hour and temperatures of minus five.

We have a high-winds and traffic advisory for the area. Tuesday afternoon: Cloudy with freezing rain giving way to snow ...

"What next? Hail, frogs, and smiting of the first-born?" I said. It turned out to be worse than frogs. Little Miss Sunshine gave us the traffic update.

We remind those of you heading to the east, the Trans-Canada is closed. Two separate accidents involving multiple vehicles and tractor-trailers jackknifing. The local authorities are strongly advising against drivers getting out on the road tonight.

I thought of my luggage sitting there at the Hotel Saskatchewan. I didn't have even a toothbrush with me. Then I thought of dying in an icy ditch beside the highway. "Forget it. Let's get rooms before they're all booked. I don't know if I'm up for imposing on Mitzi. I haven't seen the guy in twenty years and then I'm sleeping in his house while he's sleeping in a casket. No thanks."

We must have been the last ones on the road to get the news. After five Sorry We're Full for the Nights, we secured the last remaining room at some dump. One queen-size bed at that. Spread out, Chief could have spilled out over all four sides of it, I thought, while I filled out the standard personal-information file and declined to have my email registered. And while I waited for my credit card to be processed, I thought of the one trip out to Brandon last winter when I had the room next to Chief and I realized that it was him snoring and not a muscle car revving at 3 A.M.

We had nothing to take to our room. We went there out of habit and surveyed the crib. Bed, end table, and desk wouldn't have moved for a dollar at a lawn sale. I sent texts to my daughter at the prep school in Minnesota,

> *how it go vs St Paul Kennedy ... looks like I won't make it 4 coupla weeks stuff came up*

to Sandy, who was expecting to go out to dinner with me Tuesday night,

> *went out to swift current to pay respects to my good friend martin storms stuck here now bunking with good friend Chief*

and to Hunts to tell him that my road trip wasn't ending when or how I had hoped.

Chicago was in L.A. that night and the game was televised. The set in the room was older than we were and the motel owner must have forgotten to pay the cable bill. And I didn't have my laptop, not that there was wireless. "Let's grab a bite and then we'll find somewhere to watch the game," I said. "I need a drink. Let's call a cab."

8

.The Imperial Tavern in downtown Swift Current adjoined
a by-the-night-week-month flophouse and one of western
Canada's greasiest spoons. I felt like we were being watched even
before we ducked into the Big I's lounge. An eye, two storeys
high, was painted on the facade of the building. I'm sure a critic
somewhere would consider it a fine example of primitivism,
but I imagined that the artist had painted a ceiling and didn't
want to waste any leftover paint before cleaning his brushes with
vodka. If his inspiration was an eye he had seen in the bar, it
would have been VLT-glazed and bloodshot.

The Imperial's fixtures and decor were as old as I was. The
room smelled of fermented urine and mildew. At the side of
the bar closest to the front door sat the joint's only two women.
Flora and Fauna were skanks in bad repair. Their matching
lipstick was a shade of pickled beet and looked like it had been
applied with a three-inch brush. Their complexions matched
the filters of the Marlboros they had stubbed out in the smokers'
room. Their expressions said No Good Men. Their expressions

were commentary on market supply and personal history. They gave Chief and me the Once Over Twice, felt some old embers almost glow, and then worked up the strength to drain their glasses down to the ice cubes.

"I got a bad feeling, Shadow," Chief said. He did a three-sixty scan of the room. "Let's get out of here. Let's go someplace else."

"C'mon."

"No, seriously. This is gonna be ugly, I know it."

"C'mon Chief, when in Rome, you know," I said. "Let's just have a couple. Watch the game."

Any analogy to Rome proved non-operative. On a much later, fully sober second thought, Chief had got it right.

I spied two huge bikers in your standard-issue 4XL leather vests sitting at the far end of the bar. Maybe they were an inch shorter than Chief, but the smaller of the two had forty pounds on him. Guessing their age, I would have put them at forty or so, using the fading of their tattoos to carbon date them. Though beer and years had softened them around the middle, their biceps would have spanned twenty inches, the product of thousands of hours of gym work when they had thousands of days to serve as guests of the Correctional Service of Canada. Typical thing: These boys didn't lift for chiselled bodybuilder looks or anything remotely athletic. They wanted size to intimidate and strength to do damage and the tag team had both. It turned out that Butch had spent a few years as a jobber on *Stampede Wrestling*, donning a mask for an easy gig that enabled him to deal steroids and pharmaceuticals to the other members of the circus. Sundance's backstory was a little less colourful. He had been tried and dubiously acquitted in a double murder of a lawyer who had represented members of his former club and her husband. When I would pass Butch and Sundance on my way to the head I couldn't tell if they were a source of the reek of the joint or if they just wore it as a result of their residence in this shithole. Either way, it was as anti-social as hell, which I suppose was the desired effect. When I would pass on the way back I didn't bother checking out their advertised allegiances. I pitied them. They had made some questionable career choices. All of us in the room had. All of us didn't have a Something More than Recreational Bag of Weed out in plain sight. They did. All of us weren't running a Cash and Carry Recreational Pharmacy with a stream of losers coming into the I as a customer base. They were and were blatant about it. Turned out meth was the Special of the Day.

They didn't seem to mind our presence. Maybe I'd look like a cop somewhere, but they probably knew them all in Swift Current by sight. And Chief didn't look like a cop at all.

Chief and I were damp and weary but Mitzi's pork chops had provided us the necessary stomach liner for a few beers. Draught was out of the question. The last time the lines were cleaned was the Year of the Great Flood. I stuck to a Canadian. Chief nursed a Blue. He wasn't a drinker and that was probably a good thing for his health and the physical well-being of those around him.

Last week's *Southwest Booster* was on an empty seat at our table. There, on the front page, was a photo of Martin Mars. He was sitting at his desk, as it turned out, at the gas station where he heaved his last sigh. He had both hands clasped around a souvenir coffee mug with a raven on its side. I recognized it from my days in the German league when my career was winding down, the Berlin Ravens. Whisper managed a slight smile for the photographer.

Mars Petroleum Co., the Swift Current—based gasoline distributor, could have another significant link in its thriving chain.

Reports out of Regina suggest that MPC will be entering into an agreement with Garageland Canada, which has 50 big-box auto-parts and hardware stores across Canada.

"It's not done by any stretch," said MPC president Martin Mars yesterday. "There are some details to iron out. It was a bidding process to have exclusive ties to Garageland and we feel that we came up with a successful bid. Exactly how it's going to play out, I can't really say right now, but it's a great growth opportunity for our company."

Hopeful, forward-looking, happy: It fit with Mitzi's theory. Swift Current probably had its fair share of despair, and a few of its citizens would like to choose their own time to exit. A guy looking to close deals like that didn't seem to be a prime candidate.

We parked ourselves at a table in line of sight of an old TV hung precariously on chains strung from the ceiling. The game was in L.A. and they showed the brief tribute and pre-game moment of silence at the top of the broadcast. No surprise, Grant Tomlin butted his way in front of a camera and started flashing his cosmetic dental work and his even less-genuine insight into the game. "Isn't that the way it goes, Gord," Tomlin said, looking squarely at the camera, as if Gord were a thousand miles away and not holding the microphone. "Every once in a while a player is never noticed until the moment of greatest need presents itself. And that's the Martin Mars story, Gord. God rest his soul."

"He never even met Whisper," I said. My indignation amped the volume of the fact-checking and the bartender gave me a nonchalant inspection lest I had been over-served. He skipped over to Chief and shot him a hateful glance, obviously holding back the urge to say, "We don't get your kind in here," or to goad him by asking if he was with the native outreach down the road.

My stomach knotted when Chicago scored on the second shift. Our goaltender, Fournier, shit the bed, *again*. His wife had given birth to twins in August and, doubly sleep-deprived, he was having a small disaster of a season. Hunts said we should have traded him when the rabbit died.

By the third period I had a serious steam on. Bad news for my company: Fournier was pulled after giving up four goals on nine shots. Our backup was a backup for a good reason. He stopped a few shots but gave up three more, even though it looked like Chicago was easing up with a 7–2 lead in the last minutes.

I didn't take my eyes off the dirty screen, mostly because I found the setting so depressing, but Chief did a scan of the room and the alarm light started to flash.

"I don't like it," he said.

I had no idea what he was talking about. I was lost in the game. "Don't like what?" I asked.

"The way those kids are looking at us."

I still didn't clue in, but when I turned my head to look at him I saw two eyes burning a hole in me, eyes belonging to a thick-chested kid in his not-so-old high school football sweater. He was standing over by the pool table and it was his shot, but he dropped his cue on the vomit-stained felt. He then walked away from the table and over toward us, stopping at spitting distance. And then he spat on the floor, close enough to my pant leg to make me look down.

The bartender looked on wearily. There was no need to bring in entertainment on a Monday night. This stuff always sufficed.

No. 51. I made him to be a linebacker. Maybe six-one, maybe 210, jacked, 'roided, maybe a year or two out of high school. The number suited him, one short of a full deck.

"Where'd you say you were from?" No. 51 said. It wasn't a question that gave me hope of having a civil drink in an uncivil place. His three other playmates fell in behind him and worked up their toughest looks. For reasons that escaped me at that moment but not for long they seemed awfully brave.

"Just passing through," I said and forced a smile. It was a Pick 6 Lottery Longshot that it would defuse a confrontation. "We're in town for a funeral."

"Whose?"

"Martin Mars. We were friends of his a long time ago," I said.

There was no chance he'd let us grieve peacefully. "He doesn't have any friends," the linebacker said. "Not in this town."

He turned to smile at his friends. I could see the name on his back. HANLEY. He was too young and too unthinking to come to any conclusions beyond his basic wants, occasional needs, and animal instincts. He voiced received opinion, I figured, probably from an authority figure he never bothered to question.

Chief had his thousand-yard stare on. He didn't see me at all. The handle had been pulled and his eyes were all Cherries, Lemons, Bars, Bells, and Sevens.

I saw everything. Out of one eye I could see that Chicago had scored again. Out of the other I saw the kid take one step inside spitting distance. With the room temperature rising I grew a third eye, and it saw three of his buddies walking over from the pool table with cues in hand. With my fourth eye I saw the bartender back away to the farthest neutral corner and turn his back on the proceedings. And they were proceeding to go ugly.

"Why don't you go back to where you come from, city boy, take your girlfriend with you?" No. 51 said. It was four-beer courage and home-field advantage that made him and his buddies so bold, though why Martin Mars would get their backs up I didn't know.

I looked over at Chief. He was lost somewhere, like a veteran haunted by what he'd seen at war. For Chief it wasn't grenades lobbed up to the trench or a hill that had to be won, but it was something close. It was Mangler in Fort Wayne or Dog in Muskegon or Kayo in Worcester. Or maybe it was in the league, Joey K in Detroit or the Reaper wherever he was playing.

No. 51 pushed the table in and it bumped Chief just below the rib cage. My winger shot to his feet and that launched the table into the linebacker, though it wasn't heavy enough to knock him back more than a couple of steps. Fight or flight kicked in for me and I was strongly leaning to the latter.

The adrenalin was flowing but my toggle switch was flipped from flight to fight when one of No. 51's buddies swung a cue at me. No. 54. He swung from the left side of the plate. I jumped back and he fouled one off my chest. While this went on, No. 51 flung the table back at Chief. All four rushed us. Chief had a handful of the linebacker's sweater and one-punched him with a right hand. I heard a nose crunch like a wafer. The poor kid, he found out the hard way that life's different without a face mask.

No. 54 must have read the scouting report. He broke a cue over Chief's bum shoulder. I had never seen the Big Man wince before. His lips went thin as a dime. It lasted a tenth of a second.

They were just boys in their twenties and they outnumbered us, but we would have been more than all right all things being no more unequal. However, my fifth and sixth eyes and all other sensory tools at my disposal failed to pick up a meteorological shift: Six hundred pounds of biker in two pairs of boots with steel shanks and steel toes were blowing in at the backs of the hometown heroes. I was in against two high school punks and Sundance, who had a full eighty pounds on me. I took my best shot at him and landed it but he kept coming, wrapping me in a bear hug, lifting me off the floor, and then driving me into the wall, my head cracking the already cracked plaster. While he was crushing my ribs and blood ran down the back of my neck, Nos. 51 and 58 took potshots at me from the side. Sundance dropped me in a heap on the floor and it was only then that I realized Chief's fight with Butch had rolled into the back of the room by the door to the parking lot. Like me, Chief was dealing with a three-on-one. Unlike me, he had a chair cracked over his back. Unlike me, the next time he'd look in the mirror he'd see the imprint of Butch's skull ring.

And then, suddenly, the shit-kicking subsided and the room went quiet.

Someone once said that in a game success rides on having a sense of Where You Are. For bikers, it must be about having a sense of Where Not to Be, and for these two at that moment Where Not to Be was the I. Butch and Sundance left Chief and me in messy piles on the messy floor, then picked up their weed and wares and blew out the back door with less than a minute to spare. They were on their home turf and had the benefit of local knowledge. They were down the evolutionary chain but up the grid in some sort of network. They must have been tipped off, had to have been the bartender who didn't make a peep when they set up shop. I didn't hear him say anything. Then again, there was a lot going on and I had an earful of blood.

I had dropped a couple of bucks in the jukebox a half hour before but my songs came up when I was too busy and bruised to enjoy them. I had told Chief that I wanted to play "something for Whisper." One was playing when a pair of Mounties walked through the front door and our party. They were big boys and had big guns. Something for Whisper was playing as they strongly recommended that we cease and desist. It was Moe

Bandy singing about watching his children grow and the Lord letting the cold wind blow. We were out the door before the last verse of "Till I'm Too Old to Die Young."

9

"Welcome back," the bastard at the front desk at headquarters said. "You've been out seeing the sights."

Chief shot me the Another Fine Mess You Got Us Into look. Provoking a bitter guy exiled to the desk on the night shift moved to the top of my List of Lifetime Do-Overs.

We were uncuffed. My BlackBerry and Chief's cell were tossed in a drawer. We were ushered back to a holding area that was marginally less comfortable than the motel room we'd booked. It had been an eventful day and at its close I had two hotel rooms booked in two cities and was staying in neither.

"You might as well get comfortable," the desker said. "This is going to be handled by the day shift and they don't start coming in until five thirty. I hope the weather doesn't hold them up."

We waited for this fat prick to go back to his station and finish his crossword.

"I know we should spend more time with a better class of people," I said, wiping the blood and shaking the plaster out of

78   G.B. JOYCE

my hair. "What the hell do they have against Whisper that these
punks would come after us?"

Radio silence.

There was no figuring it out. We had no call to make. There
was no calling Mitzi to bail us out. She had her own grief, way
worse than ours, and, besides, we didn't have her number. I'd
find out later that it was unlisted.

We saw the four kids talking to the Mounties who'd been
on the scene at the Imperial. The old hump at the front desk
fetched No. 51 a bag of ice to bring down his swollen beak. It was
pretty genial. It was pretty familiar. There was no third degree,
no reading of the riot act. I suspected the boys had a bit of a rep
around town and didn't go much beyond busting each other up.
That's par for the course when a joint like the Imperial passes
for the local cultural centre.

Chief had started to nod off when I saw a tomato-faced guy
of about sixty with a bushy hyphen for a moustache go back to
the room where the four kids were being held. He had folds in
his forehead deep enough to swipe a credit card through. The
broken blood vessels in his nose and cheeks formed a minute red
paisley. He gave off the look of a guy who was unhealthy but also
unhealthy for you. I thought he might have been a lawyer, but
then a lawyer wouldn't have walked out with the four of them
while messing No. 51's hair like he had made the game-saving
tackle on a goal-line stand. I had seen it all before, after games,
proud as punch, wishing it had been him and not his son. To
Old Man Hanley's mind, a broken nose was a character builder
if it had been earned for the right reason, and from the look on
his face it had been. And I figured that No. 51's enmity toward
Martin Mars issued from pronouncements from an authority
figure who had bailed his son out of scrapes because of his affec-
tion in part and influence in practice.

The old hump at the front desk shook No. 51's father's hand and was given reassurances that the boys would get home safely. "It's an awful night out there," the old hump said, though he was relying on hearsay because he didn't have a window. It was an awful night where we sat too, and as the gash on the back of my head congealed, night bled into morning.

I

TUESDAY

Morning came but not dawn. I didn't need a window to see that the sun was reluctant to shine on Swift Current and wouldn't rise until a couple of hours after the first day shift began to file in. I saw it in the faces of the long-time vets and in the citizenry at large. The collective environmental despair tracked back not just to the harshness of the weather but to sunlight deprivation. It was a place where days of work were infinitely long and light shining on lives was unmercifully short.

In the morning Chief and I sat at a featureless table across from an old Mountie and a young one, clearly mentor and protegé. They struck me as being as ineffectual as Inspector Fenwick and Dudley Do-Right, and they only bothered with the latter half of the Good Cop, Bad Cop routine. They alternately debriefed and mocked us. The young stiff's name was Constable Prentice and he took the lead under the old master's watchful eye, the questions cascading out of him without a change in speed, volume, or expression.

"Tell me again, exactly what were you doing in town?"

I told him that we were in town paying our respects to a friend of mine from years back.

"Martin Mars, yes, I know of him, very sad," said the less-than-sage old vet, Staff Sergeant Albert D. Daulton. "There have been a few issues in town regarding Mr. Mars, the holdup at that station the other week being the latest. Well acquainted with it, nature of his business, I suppose, but no matter. His death explains how you came to Swift Current but not exactly how you ended up in ... well, in all of this."

The questions poured forth, mentor and protegé taking turns like an investigative tag team.

"And then where did you go?"

"And then what did you do?"

"And then what happened?"

We piled up the mundane details. Prentice took the notes the first time we walked through one of the longer days of our lives. The second lap he just listened to see if our accounts were in sync. The third and fourth, it was the same drill.

"Unfortunately, your version of events doesn't wash with the statement that we have from the bartender, and the Imperial doesn't have a security camera," Constable Prentice said. "From what I've been told you picked a fight with the boys. And no one has mentioned anything about these supposed gang members. Interesting story, though."

There was no use pointing out the obvious, that being the bartender taking the side of his regulars. The jocks fearing the bikers or gladly covering for them or both. All of them in it together. It would later occur to me that no mention had been made of any account from Flora and Fauna. Perhaps the RCMP kept copies of the ladies' standard witness statement and had them sign and date them.

It wasn't until we were a good hour in that I picked up on the fact that Daulton was giving us a hard study. He put his hand on Prentice's right arm to interrupt a fifth pass of the same questions.

"What do you gentlemen do for a living?"

We filled in the blanks. I had given up any hope that it was going to impress him.

"Did you play?"

I gave him the details.

"Never heard of you," he said.

I wasn't shattered.

"And you?"

Chief gave him the same sort of rundown. He started off by mentioning that he had played in Moose Jaw and Other Garden Spots of the West.

"Warren Bear," Daulton said.

"Yeah," Chief said, like it was an admission under accusation.

"Was your father in the service?" the staff sergeant asked. It was the first time I had been surprised since I'd seen the two drawn nine-millimetre service revolvers at the Imperial.

"He's dead but, yeah, he was in the service." Things you don't know.

"I'm not sure what he'd think if he could see you now," Prentice editorialized.

Again Prentice felt a pat on his right arm.

"What was your father's name?" Daulton asked.

"John Bear."

"There are lots of them. I could put together a hockey team of John Bears. Where was your father from? What did he do during the war, son?"

Where the hell did "son" come from? Maybe the sun was starting to slice through the opaque horizon.

Chief mentioned the Second Infantry. Chief mentioned the South Saskatchewan Regiment. Chief mentioned Dieppe. I hadn't picked up any credits in World War II history while finishing my degree by correspondence, but I knew surviving Dieppe was just about the worst ride.

"Roger," Daulton said again, putting his hand on his apprentice's arm, this time with the firmness of finality. "Warren's father was a war hero. Order of Canada. Prominent in his community." The staff sergeant went on with a thumbnail life story and stopped occasionally for Chief to fill in the blanks or confirm a detail where necessary. I could feel the air being let out of Prentice.

Daulton shuffled the papers in front of him and with them, his thoughts. "You two seem like nice enough fellows," he concluded. "I'd hate to see anything bad happen to you. You might think there's not much worse that can happen to you around here, but I haven't even been trying to make your life miserable. Yet. I can and will if you plan on staying around Swift Current. Others might beat me to it, from the looks of you. So I suggest the pair of you get out of town. Now is only soon enough for my liking. And pass along our condolences to Mrs. Mars."

I took everything seriously except the sympathetic afterword.

We were walked to the front desk. I was limping badly. I usually iced my aching hinge at night.

It was just after a shift change. The sour old hump had checked out. In his place was a great improvement, a bright young blonde. Her uniform accentuated her broad shoulders and hid her assets. When we had checked in for the night the Mounties had taken our various personal effects. She returned our cellphones and gave us a smile that wasn't in the RCMP handbook. Mitzi had already called a couple of times, Sandy hadn't. I told the blonde that I had a vial of pills that were held when we were taken into the back. She said she hadn't seen them. Prentice must have overheard because he came up to the front desk.

"We're going to hold on to the pills for now, just to check them out," he said.

"They're a prescription," I said.

"Well, it looks that way but they might be street drugs in a prescription vial, that's all. So we're going to check them out. Who knows, maybe they're sex pills."

"Oh yeah, they're sex pills all right. I have to take one or else I'm in too much arthritic pain to ..."

I felt Chief's hand on my shoulder. He squeezed hard enough to deflate a football.

2 _____

The cab ride was time for silent gathering of thought. Chief
and I had just about exhausted conversation. We had just
about exhausted everything. He was asleep thirty seconds after
I slammed the door and told the driver where we were going.
En route I saw a Dollarama store that was just opening and had
the driver pull over. I limped into the store and bought a plain
black toque that would keep the cut on the back of my head
covered. I put it on in front of a mirror to check out other subtle
scrapes and welts and wondered if I should go all in for a ski
mask. I decided against it.

Sixty seconds after I got back in the taxi I had to nudge Chief
awake. We were going back to check out of a room that we had
spent all of a minute in.

At first I had thought it was strange that Mitzi should be so
alone in her mourning. Eighteen hours later I had my own theory.
She had the virtual monopoly on honesty and decency in town,
at least among those I had encountered on my misbegotten
odyssey. Okay, Walt seemed like a good kid, not quick on the

uptake, maybe a bit damaged, but he seemed to genuinely care about Mitzi and mourn Whisper. Daulton's late-coming leniency gave me faint hope that, whatever his failures, he might be on the up and up. But the junior team's board members, the crowd at the Imperial, and most of the boys on the force were bastards all. I'll admit that, with 80 percent of the precincts reporting, I had a hate-on for Swift Current.

And I also thought that Mitzi might be right. Whisper had been doing well. He seemed to have had the love of a good woman and definitely a well-preserved beauty. He was in a position to sell off his thriving business so he could retire to watch sunsets at the beach. Suicide didn't fit.

I had missed my flight back to Toronto. I was going to have to use my air miles to get a flight when I got back to Regina. I'd have to use another point plan to cover another night at the hotel. There was no way I was going to be able to bill the team, not with Tomlin's hot breath on Hunts's neck. There was no way I was dipping into my own limited reserves. I called the Hotel Saskatchewan to book a room for my luggage and hopefully for me.

I roused Chief when we were back at the motel. I could see overnight losers exiting the casino on the north side of Highway 1. They were hoping that the wind would blow the stench of cigarette smoke and failure off them.

"I'm washing up and then we'll go back to say goodbye to Mitzi," I said.

The ice was slippery under my boots. I skidded. I caught my balance. Arthur shouted: "Boss, get us back to terra firma."

3 _____

Chief turned the key for the fifth or sixth time. A tenth time and more until the key clicked and the engine didn't sputter.

"Battery is as flat as the world before Columbus," I said.

Chief told me with just a look that I could have chosen my words more carefully.

I didn't bother to ask him how he was enjoying the trip so far. I had caused him too much grief already, and now the players in this grand conspiracy against us had enlisted the internal combustion engine.

"Whatever fixing it costs I'll hide it on the expenses," I said. "Just over-claim on the mileage and I'll sign off on it."

I knew he over-claimed anyway, but our owner had frozen salaries two years ago and giving the boys a break on mileage was my way of throwing them a bone.

No response. His hard stare was defrosting the window.

I Googled *auto repair* and *Swift Current*. I punched the Mars listing that came up. I recognized the voice that answered. Walt. I spelled out the situation.

"Mr. Shade, yeah, I know the hotel," he said. "I'll be right over with the tow."

"I'm surprised you're in," I said.

"I'm shaky, I'll tell you, Mr. Shade. But I had to be in here first thing. There were a bunch of cars and trucks in for repair. I gotta look after them but I wasn't going to take any more on until ..."

His voice and thoughts trailed off. I didn't wait for him to finish.

"I appreciate your doing this," I said.

He said he had a loaner he could give us if it came to that. He promised he was going to make Chief's sled Job One.

Fifteen minutes later I climbed into the cab of the tow truck with Chief after me while Walt put the hook and chain on. He clearly did this daily. He said that he would drop us off Chez Mars while he got under the hood of the Jeep back at the garage.

The cut on his forehead hadn't healed much overnight.

"Was that from the other day when the gas station got knocked over?" I asked.

"Yeah," he said. His face reddened. "It was worse before. They must have been waiting for me. I spend most of the shift in the booth at the self-serve. It's locked in and safe. But they waited until I had to use the washroom. I had the 'back in five minutes' sign up and they got me from behind. Tackled me and whaled on me. They gave me a couple more shots after I cleaned out the till. I had the minimum float in there. I told Mr. Mars he could dock it out of my pay but he said it was all right. 'The price of doing business,' he said. He was real kind to me."

Walt looked ready to cry. I tried to get him to buck up.

"I'm sure Mitzi won't have a problem with you staying on for as long as it takes to sort all this out."

Walt looked unconvinced. He had the look of a guy who had been beaten down so many times that he had just about given up caring. He had the look of a guy whose every life appointment had turned into disappointment.

4

"Thanks, Mitzi," I said. Chief and I were sitting on the well-worn leather couch in the living room and she set down desperately needed coffees in front of us. The coffee was scalding hot but Chief swallowed his in two gulps.

I told her that I appreciated Walt coming out. And I told her that we were haggard looking simply because we hadn't brought a change of clothes.

"Were you able to find anything out with the Mounties?"

I didn't bother to tell her that we were their overnight guests.

"The guy I talked to last night wasn't helpful at all. It might be different if you come with us. I can't guarantee that they're going to tell us anything more than they did last night ... which was nothing at all. But I think by rights they'll let us see the photos of the scene. They told you there was no note?"

"That's what they said," she replied.

I didn't want to dive too deep in that reflecting pool of sorrow. Only one in five or six leave notes. It figured that Kurt Cobain would. Words and sounds and gut wrench: He died as he lived.

It would have fit if Whisper had walked away from life like he walked away in L.A.: without a word or backward look.

I needed to change the subject. "We went to the board meeting," I told her. She didn't ask me about it but I followed up anyway. "The guy who left the message was saying that he's lined up buyers for the team. It looks like the team is losing money hand over fist and I suppose ... Martin ..."

I almost said Whisper.

"... and a few others had been going into their own pockets to make up the shortfall. The guy ..."

"Ron Beckwith?"

"Yeah, Beckwith says he has buyers but it doesn't look like a transparent piece of business."

"Martin was involved with it, I know."

"Well, I didn't like his act in the meeting. And it looks like he's quite happy to look after the sale of the team unilaterally."

The phone rang. Mitzi got up and went to the kitchen to get it. She still had it on speaker. Another hang-up.

I looked at Chief. He didn't have an exit strategy either. Mitzi came back into the living room and broke up our attempt at telepathy.

"What do you think, Brad? What should I do?"

I didn't even know where to begin. The requisite stuff that goes with any death, the reports put together by the Mounties, the financial considerations, especially those with the team: She wasn't up to any of it by herself, probably at the best of times, definitely at this point in extremis.

I know what I'd have *liked* to have done. I'd have liked to have gone down to the Imperial to settle my tab, get one for the road, give a piece of my mind to the chickenshit bartender, throw a scare into No. 51, wipe the smile off his old man's face, and let the air out of the bikers' tires. I doubted Chief was down with C, D, E, or F. He would probably have been okay with A and B.

Yeah, I was fading, sitting shiva, sleepily daydreaming about a getaway. Then Mitzi splashed my face with cold water.

"Please," she said. "Would you two take me over to Martin's lawyer's office at ten thirty? I mean, I don't think I can drive my car. I'm just too upset. The reading of the will should be pretty straightforward. So he told me, anyway. Martin's accountant is going to be there as well. I just have to sign some things there. Then over to the RCMP headquarters? I'm just not up to it myself."

This was the price of being a good teammate. Chief looked at me as if to say, "I want to be traded."

I told Mitzi that I had one stop to make before we made the rounds with her.

5 _____

Chief and I piled into Mitzi's Escalade and drove five minutes
to a Shoppers Drug Mart overlooking the Trans-Canada at its
downtown exit. As we pulled into the parking lot we saw an
RCMP cruiser making a slow pass-by, the two Mounties giving
me a hard stare while they sipped their coffee. Not a local,
they figured, and how is it that a guy in a hat like that drives an
Escalade?

My head began to ache. I never had a concussion that I knew
of when I was playing, and it would be my dumb luck to suffer
my first while I was drawing a cheque as a scout. Hunts would
have a field day with that one.

I went to the pharmacy at the back of the store to throw
myself on the mercy of the staff there. I thought I might have
a shot at talking a friendly pharmacist into calling the Shoppers
Drug Mart where I fill my prescription in Toronto and coming
away assured that I had refills of Celebrex on their records. No
dice. Knew it from the look of the old guy who asked if he could
help me. He made it sound like he wouldn't be too shook up if he

couldn't. He stood about five-two, light bouncing off his shiny bald dome, and he was as white as an aspirin. It was hard to tell where his lab jacket ended and skin started. He wore his reading glasses down his hypodermic-needle nose and peered over the top of them.

"I have to fax your doctor and when he confirms your prescription I can fill it for you," he said.

"Shit, that's not going to work," I said. "He's going to Myrtle Beach to golf with his buddies."

"You take this for ..."

"For my knee. For the one ligament I have left. For the sharp bits of gravel where my cartilage used to be."

"You can go over-the-counter for some relief."

"It would be no relief. Tried it. Doesn't help."

"Then you will have to get a doctor here to prescribe something. You could go to emergency ..."

I imagined sitting there for two or three hours. No thanks.

"... or maybe you can try the sports injury and physio clinic down the street. Dr. Humphreys. He's the doctor for the local hockey team."

That sounded like the better option. A team doctor would have more empathy with an ex-player on the limp.

The clinic was only two hundred yards across the sprawling parking lot but I drove it in the Escalade. I limped into the waiting room and explained my situation to the receptionist. She said she could squeeze me in before lunch if I had my health-plan info with me, which I did. I told Chief that there was no point waiting around with me and that he could go chow down in the meantime.

The only reading material in the office was a pile of year-old *Sports Illustrated*s. I was staring out the window at passing traffic when I felt my BlackBerry vibrate in my coat pocket. It was an email from Intel-Sec Canada, the investigations and security firm that I had worked for unhappily in my first years out of the game.

> Brad,
>
> We hope you're doing well. We have a lot of hockey fans in our office, and though Toronto probably gets the majority of support we followed your L.A. team with interest.
>
> We have just entered into an agreement to provide the security detail for the league, including details for the commissioner, owners, and star players at games and major events. We are also organizing a unit charged with investigating players of interest to the league office, i.e., any players who might have links to organized crime or issues with substance abuse. It is a long-term contract and a very lucrative one and we believe your background in the game would prove invaluable. We envision it being a springboard to contracts with professional leagues in other sports.
>
> It would be great to meet up with you when you're in the city to discuss a role for you on our team.
>
> Regards,
> Jay Christie
> President
> Intel-Sec Canada Inc.

I had seen the sides of beef that were the commissioner's bodyguards at the draft. They went three bills apiece and looked like the two anchors at the end of the rope for the Toronto police department's tug-of-war team. They were, in fact, ex-NYPD, former beat cops, probably run off the force before they were fully pensioned because of serial internal investigations. They should have been able to do their jobs for the Commish working in the background, but they couldn't have been more conspicuous if they had worn DayGlo vests and flashing lights atop straw hats. I hated that type of work but I couldn't rule out having to do it to put food on the table if my contract wasn't going to be renewed in L.A.

I was imagining a very different line of work than my present one when the patient with the next appointment came through the door. The kid from the night before, I thought. I could see his football sweater under his unbuttoned down jacket. The nose that Chief had pounded into bone meal was neither bandaged nor the worse for wear. No black eye, just a limp, one that looked as bad and painful as mine, nothing I had seen a trace of the night before. He was on crutches and his left leg was heavily braced. He hadn't even been limping at the end of hostilities. Must have fallen on the ice or maybe someone had lived my dream and pushed him down a flight of stairs.

"Fancy meeting you here," I said by way of an icebreaker.

"Excuse me?"

"You come here often after getting busted up in bar fights? They keep your file out just in case?"

"You've got the wrong guy," he said. And I had. He hung up his down jacket. He was wearing No. 59 but the name on the back read HANLEY. He took a seat on one of the chairs lined against the far wall, as if he couldn't stay far enough away from me. He put it together. "You must be thinking about my brother. We're twins. We get mixed up all the time. Even by people who know us."

I could see that. I could guess it probably caused this kid no small amount of grief too. Chief had done his part in giving him some relief for a while. You weren't going to need a program to tell them apart. His brother would be the one walking around with a nose encased in plaster and eyes lined in black and red and yellow rings like a psychedelic raccoon.

No. 59 checked in and the receptionist asked how he was doing. He winced and gave a look of What Can You Do Anyway. He didn't say he was doing okay. He wasn't going to lie.

"I'm sorry," I said, when he sat back down. "My buddy and I got into some sort of thing with your brother at the Imperial."

"Yeah, that makes sense," No. 59 said. "He was out late and my father was up in the middle of the night. It happens."

"I'm sure it does," I said. "Your dad got him out of the lock-up, looked like he had done it before."

The kid barely pent up the resentment. "He's been in a fight a night since he got back," No. 59 said. "He made the football team at the university as a freshman, played some special teams but got a concussion, a bad one. He got medical leave from school. His year's wiped off the books but it didn't bother him so long as he'd be eligible to play again next year. The one doctor he saw said he should never play again. Our father found him another doctor who'd clear him. When he drinks he gets wild."

"I'd bet it's more than beer," I said.

"That'd be a safe bet."

"What happened to you?"

"I tore my knee up in the first game in my last year of high school," he said. "Nerve damage. I thought they were going to have to amputate it. My father says I'm lucky but it's hard to see it that way."

I told the kid that I knew a few specialists connected with our team. I had come on to the kid and he didn't deserve it. This was a make-good. I told him that I could give him contact information for the orthopedic surgeons who are the team's first choice for major work. "Maybe there's something they can do for you," I said. I remembered exactly what it was like to spend months on crutches. Looking at him, I knew that he'd be filling a prescription for Celebrex or another anti-arthritic when he sprouted his first grey hair, just like I did.

"That would be great," he said. I gave him my card. While I typed his email into my BlackBerry I pumped him for Swift Current 411. I told him that I was in town for Martin Mars's funeral and that I had fallen out of touch with him after he left L.A. He seemed to have no working theory for why the mention of Whisper's name would have ignited the fires at the Imperial the night before.

"Mars has always been the chief competition for my father, I guess," No. 59 said. "My father didn't have a lot of time for him. He said that he made his money the easy way. 'He was the only son of a couple who built their fortune the way I built mine, through blood, tears, and sweat. I've made my own good fortune.' My father is the majority owner of a bunch of gas stations and auto-repair places and some other retail outfits. He's involved in some oil drilling south and west of here."

If the old man was also drilling his hatred of his rival into his sons, I could see why No. 51 might have seen red when I mentioned Whisper's square name, especially if No. 51 was drunk, high, or chemically wired. With shorted-out synapses as a chaser, he'd probably have taken a swing at Mike Tyson.

I tried to change the subject. "Do you have to go to Moose Jaw or Regina for rehab?" I asked him. "That's a hell of a drive."

"They actually have a good rehab facility at the hospital here, as good as the one in Moose Jaw and pretty close to Regina's," he said. "The Mars Rehab Centre."

I was leafing distractedly through an old *SI* and stopped, turning my head.

"Yeah, it was his donation," No. 59 said. "He'd come by to check in and talk to the therapist I see there."

"And people don't like him even if he's doing stuff like this?" I asked. I couldn't make any sense of it.

"Thing is, Mars is really picky ... *was* ... with what he'd give money to. He wouldn't give anything to church charities. Something like the hospital, the public school, sure. He gave money to our football program at the comprehensive school, but when our basketball team at the Catholic church wanted to go play in a tournament against teams from the States, he wouldn't even buy us water bottles."

The game of hockey and Whisper's career path would make an atheist of just about anybody, I guess.

A fourteen-year-old clad in a hockey jacket and perched on crutches exited a room in the back of the office and the receptionist told the better of the Hanley twins that he was good to go. He hobbled off. "C'mon in," Dr. Humphreys said. While I sat and waited I Googled *Hanley* and *gas* and *auto*. I landed on a couple of news stories about the Garageland Canada bidding from early January.

Mars, Hanley, BPS, and two internationals in running for Garageland.

It looked like Hanley had been cut out of the deal that had gone to his chief competitor just before that competitor decided to pack it all in. That's the type of lucky bounce that a self-made man wouldn't leave to good fortune.

6

Dr. Humphreys recognized my name. He dropped the names of a few junior players he had worked with. He was in his thirties, a no-neck lifter and recreational jock, and he told me that he had played for a bantam team with a guy who made it into the league for about a week. I suffered His Unremarkable Career Retrospective because I'd suffer more without my Celebrex. He asked to have a look at my knee, maybe just to make sure that I wasn't an imposter. He asked me the particulars and I told him when and how it had happened, Lavery and the knee-on-knee.

"You tore it up a few years too soon," he said. "They made big strides in that work by the late '90s. You might have lasted a few more seasons. You might have played until you were forty."

I'd always thought that but had never said it. I suspected only the first half was true. I might have lasted a few more seasons and ground a few more bucks out of the game. I was never going to be a forty-year-old playing in the league. I had already fallen out of love with the game when I shredded two ligaments. In fact, I could barely remember ever being in love with it. The nearest thing to a warm and fuzzy feeling I ever had about hockey these days was when I had to pop my anti-inflammatory of choice and it burned another dimple in my stomach lining.

He handed me a prescription and wished me well.

I asked him about the Hanley twin who had been in to see him.

"Very nice kid," he said. "An awful injury. Maybe it has turned out for the best. He says that all this time he has spent in doctors' offices and in surgery has made him want to go to med school. He's a very bright kid."

That was my read of him too.

I told him that I was in town to pay my respects to my former roomie and Swift Current's former chief philanthropist. And I told him that I had a sense that two more wings for the hospital and the successful drilling for the Fountain of Youth still wouldn't have earned Whisper the respect he deserved from the locals.

"It's a funny town," he said, in case that had escaped my notice. "Almost any town is at least a little envious of someone who made a fortune."

It was a token defence of a town that was, from what I had seen, not very funny at all. "Usually, it's envy of someone who throws his money around on something other than charity," I said. "Most places are pretty deferential to those with money. I would have thought most would be proud that someone with the money to live anywhere chose to stay here."

I had written him a Prescription for Truth Serum: Take One Massive Dose Immediately and Save the Shit for a Stool Sample. "Yeah, his stand with the church charities hurt him," he said in a voice low enough that it might not be picked up if I were wired. "People here put a lot of value in their churches and it doesn't seem like Mr. Mars had an affiliation. Some said Mr. Mars's charity work was all a tax dodge."

Yeah, this would have been the righteousless indignation of the appointed and self-appointed arbiters of morality. Having a good heart, a generous spirit, and unimpeachable character wasn't as important as standing in the church. A small town populated by smaller people. Yeah, I'm cynical enough to have bought that right out of the showroom without a test drive.

7 _____

The session at Robert Roth's humble offices was again proof
that Whisper had a lot to live for, not just the love of a good
woman but a net worth well into the eight figures. With just
a few small exceptions, recognition for past favours, the estate
went to Mitzi in its entirety. To Mitzi and his Mercedes, as it
turned out. Whisper's will provided for storage and care of the
car. Many dutiful children haven't made out as well as his ride.
A few other forthwiths and wherefores followed. There was a
general instruction for Mitzi to help out Walt with any expense
for schooling as she saw fit, a couple of lines that Mars had added
to his will when he updated before Christmas. Roth laid the
document on a green felt pad atop his old oak desk and didn't
look up as he gave it an abridged reading. The provisions in the
event of her predeceasing him went unread. She whimpered
when Roth came to the instructions for the burial. Roth sensed
my basic mistrust of everybody and slid the will across the desk
for my inspection and I read every last line. It was all on the up
and up.

The accountant, an obese and constantly sweaty man named Harry Friesen, opened the Excel numbers, even though it was hard for him not to hit two keys with fingers as fat as German sausages. The ledgers on the screen made his green visor glow. Mitzi Mars was set for life. There were a few charities that my old winger had named. A few last requests to look after, stuff for Roth to discharge. I had steeled myself for a longer session, Roth and Friesen sucking all the hours out of a complicated tangle. That wasn't the case. It was straightforward and they said that they were doing this pro bono.

"He was a loyal client and good friend for years, a pillar in the community," the lawyer said.

In this community I didn't imagine that there were other pillars. Whisper's virtue probably stood out like the thick metal shaft of a car hoist in an auto-repair shop. I liked Roth and was inclined to trust him. He stood no more than five foot four and was reedy enough to trespass undetected in a dressing room full of jockeys. Roth might have been as upstanding as Whisper but could aspire to be no more than a pylon in the community.

"Martin stayed with me for years when it might have been attractive for him to go to one of the big outfits," said Friesen, dabbing the southern borders of his brushcut with a damp handkerchief. "He told me that he wanted to keep his money in town and with people he knew."

I had judged Swift Current harshly. It seemed there were a few good men in town, but with Whisper's death not enough to make up a golf foursome.

I thanked Roth and Friesen for their time and good work and Mitzi followed suit, muffled by a wet handkerchief. Roth had done this before and I expected him to be all business, but he seemed legitimately concerned about Mitzi's welfare. I assured him that we'd keep an eye on her for as long as we were in Swift

Current. I didn't tell him that we were looking to get out of Swift Current post-haste.

Chief took the wheel of Mitzi's Escalade and drove us six blocks to RCMP headquarters.

I asked to see Staff Sergeant Daulton. He was fetched by Prentice, who looked reluctant but lacked the confidence to stall or put us off. Daulton looked neither happy nor irate to see our sorry asses once more, though from the twinkle I detected through his beady little spectacles I suspected Mitzi's well-preserved curves mitigated the matter. She was just out of his age bracket but a guy can dream, even an old one. Our previous meeting went unmentioned. In her presence Discretion was Albert Daulton's middle name.

He went through the particulars with a veteran's remove and efficiency. "A phone call from one Derek Jones, a station employee, age twenty-four. Time: 6:45. Our officers on the scene, Layden and Pierce, brought the boy in to take his full statement." He paused for a few seconds and scanned the transcript of the statement. In that time he would have edited out anything he considered indelicate.

"The discovery of the body appears to have been in the normal course of Jones's working day, albeit a bit later than his schedule calls for. The Mercedes was parked behind the station where it could not be seen from the road or from the pumps and the office. A hose ran from the exhaust to an opening in the passenger-side front window. It was the hose that was attached to the tailpipes of cars in the service bay and run outside. It had been pulled out of the wall. Jones said the car was running when he got there. He turned the car off and ..."

Daulton looked up from the paperwork.

"... that would seem to be a proper and consistent reaction under the circumstances."

"There was no hearing the car from out front or seeing the exhaust when he got to work?" I asked. Mitzi looked at the office wall as if she were trying to find Whisper's face in the chipped dull grey-green paint.

"It was a pretty breezy morning even by Swift Current standards, sir," he said. *Sir*, already. "It's a very quiet car. It really gets down to where the car was parked, though. It was thoroughly obscured."

He showed us a diagram in the report.

"And there are images?" I asked. Mitzi raised her right hand, placed it over her mouth, and then turned away.

"On the computer," he said.

He walked the three of us over to Prentice, who was working across the large room. A few words, a few clicks, a few misses, and he finally got his man digitally.

Image 1: "Here's the view of the car from the passenger side," Daulton said. His narration didn't spare us the obvious. "Clearly, the hose running from the exhaust."

Image 2: "Here's the view of the layout from the rear of the car," he continued on the unscenic tour. Mitzi wasn't looking. "You get an idea of how young Jones could miss it. That's a solid, reinforced back door there, no windows."

Image 3: "Here's the deceased in the front seat."

Clearly, the obvious suicide was a hell of a lot less obvious. "Can you zoom in?" I asked.

Prentice did.

"He's buckled into his seat," I said. "He has his seat belt on."

"It may have been that he was driving around prior to coming to a stop behind the gas station," the Boy Mountie offered in nonsensical colour commentary. I would have bet against him ever getting bumped up to detective.

"He was a safety-first suicide then?"

"Maybe he was afraid he'd be pulled over," Prentice tried.

It could hardly be more ludicrous. "Maybe so close to death he couldn't bear the sound of the seat belt alarm anymore," I said. Chief's deadpan was freeze-framed. "Even if he was wearing his seat belt, wouldn't you have pulled over a car that had a hose running from the exhaust to the window? It's pretty plain in the other shots. Zoom in on the shot from the front."

Prentice looked at Daulton and was given the Go Ahead and Humour Him Nod. Whisper's left arm was under the strap coming across his body.

"How the hell does he get in that position?" I said. There was no good answer so Prentice floated a couple of bad ones.

"He didn't need his left hand to strap himself in. He could have just used his right hand."

"So he would have buckled himself up, planning to commit suicide, and pretzelled himself like he was bound."

"Maybe he was in pain and reaching for his stomach."

"It's carbon monoxide. He would have gone to sleep. Painless."

In this Ping-Pong game between the obvious fact and the absurd conjecture, I had forgotten about Mitzi for a second. She was sobbing. She only caught a glimpse of the third image but it was enough to leave her in tiny little pieces.

"You're completely satisfied that this was a suicide?" I asked.

"That is what we're going with."

"Have you dusted the car?"

"No. Didn't see a point, frankly."

I didn't bother to try to reason with him. The car's interior was immaculately kept. A fingerprint would have stood out like a molten ingot in a bowl of gazpacho.

"Are you doing a tox on the body? As part of the autopsy?"

"Body" broke every tiny little piece of Mitzi into shards and splinters.

"We didn't think all of that was necessary."

It was hard to imagine how you could get months short of retirement in uniform and not know the basics from Crime Scene Investigation 101: "Autopsies are required standard practice in all cases of carbon monoxide poisoning." In a box somewhere in one of my closets I had an old textbook from back in my college days and that line was highlighted in fluorescent yellow. I suppose that when you've spent so much time in Swift Current you're more likely to become one of the locals and subscribe to their peculiar values than remember and respect your professional obligations. In Swift Current, just as it was with the bus crash and with the molester, people wouldn't want to know the details of something like a suicide. People there would think that you can know too much. Daulton seemed to have more in common with those people than law-enforcement officers. He had acclimatized himself to a place where denial and avoidance blew around in huge drifts like the snow. Local mores had become his and they had overridden good judgment.

The devil on my left shoulder wanted me to give him shit. The angel hovering on my right begged me to stay in control and I took the little winged cherub's advice. "We can ask for an autopsy and toxicology, right?"

"You can do whatever you like. What we can do we'll do if we see fit."

"Maybe I'm just used to procedures being followed. Spoiled, y'know, growing up around Metro's finest, son of a decorated officer and all that."

Our conversation, such that it was, ground to a halt. It seemed pointless to ask him if his crack crew had checked for any boot prints or tire tracks around Whisper's Benz. If they had he would have been waving them at us as fine examples of his detachment's professionalism. Any of that evidence at the scene was lost two days after the fact, washed away by the freezing rain.

I suspected it was equal parts incompetence and intransigence. The Mounties on the scene had botched their report and the official line went sideways as a result. Daulton had to have seen that, but a tow truck couldn't have budged him.

"We'll have to talk to the coroner to see if he can look at this," I said.

"Suit yourselves on that count," he said and smiled.

"We can take the car away?" I asked.

"As far as I'm concerned it would be a happy sight to see you going down the road with it," he said. Any sense of decency was the first casualty of his hostility toward me.

"Let's go," I said. Daulton was racking his brain to try to come up with another passive-aggressive form of harassment dressed up in a cloak of justice. We were out the door before he could figure out another way to make our lives miserable.

8

The blonde at the front desk had Mitzi sign a form before she handed over the keys. Her hands shaking, Mitzi passed them to me. I told her that I'd see her back at the house. I didn't need to follow Chief. We had covered this route enough.

The Mercedes was parked at the back of the lot. The windshield was frosted inside and out. Maybe more inside than out. Cold, wet air had blown inside while the window was lowered for the hose running from the tailpipe, so from the driver's seat the windshield looked like a frosted beer glass. I turned the key and the motor kicked in on cue. The sound of perfection, a collector's car as finely tuned as a Stradivarius. But it wasn't violin music I heard. It was the sound of a crowd laughing. A comedy album was in the cassette player. I waited for it. Steve Martin.

I like to get small.

The tape was muddy, practically demagnetized by the passage

of three decades, thirty winters of long refrigeration, and thousands of plays, rewinds, and fast-forwards.

> *I know I shouldn't get small when I'm drivin', but, uh, I was drivin' around the other day, you know, and a cop pulls me over. And he goes, "Hey, are you small?" I said, "No, I'm tall, I'm tall."*

I don't know how I had forgotten this. Whisper had been playing it in the Benz when we had the sweatbox challenge. I told him it was almost as bad as the heat and to put something else on. He said he had only one tape. Even back in the early '90s it seemed hopelessly dated.

I left the cassette in the deck and left the play button down. I looked under the seat and found the empty case, cracked, with the album cover in miniature, Martin with a fake nose and glasses and a hat of balloons.

I didn't feel safe hazarding a guess about the suicidal mind. If I did, though, I'd have bet against someone determined to turn out his own lights wanting to exit laughing.

While I waited for the car to warm up I looked in the glove compartment for any other cassettes, anything else to listen to. There was nothing in there except the original owner's manual in a beat-up plastic case. I supposed that original touches like that are points of pride among vintage car buffs. I took out the manual and fanned through it. A piece of yellowed paper fell out. It was beat-up, folded and unfolded a hundred times by the look of it. It had a note, printed not written, and back-leaning in a leftie's hand: ACHTEN SIE AUF DAS AUTO. I went to Google Translate and punched it in.

TAKE CARE OF THE CAR.

9

Chief and Mitzi had beaten me back to the Mars home. I had just stepped in the door when she handed her cell to me.

"Mr. Shade, it's the fuel pump," Walt said. "I don't have a part in stock. I'm not going to be able to get it until tomorrow. As soon as I do I'm on it."

The nightmare was now heading into second overtime.

Walt said he'd come back to pick me up and ferry me back to the station to get the loaner.

When he did come, I tried again to put his fears to rest about where he might find room and board for the next stretch.

"Mitzi is going to let you stay on," I said. I stopped short of saying that she was worried about him, even though, at the worst time of her life, she was.

Walt stared at the road ahead. He looked unconvinced.

"You'd probably help Mitzi just by being around. She could use the company."

Still nothing.

I did what I could to make small talk.

"From Swift Current originally?"

"No, from a ways away, grew up on a farm. Family farm."

"Did you think about staying on there?" I wasn't really hinting that he should look at that as a fallback. He could have and probably should have taken it that way, even though that wasn't what I had intended.

"No, when I came into the city to go to school, I decided I was gonna stay here."

He didn't strike me as the college man. Not with his black toque with the Mack Truck patch centred perfectly, pulled down over his eyebrows. He looked like he had reached the perfect station in his life, working the pumps, making change, checking oil, giving directions, asking if there'd be a car wash with that fill-up.

"... I was the youngest of six kids and my brothers and sisters are all farming. I had no place to go, so I just stayed here. At first I worked at the arena. Just did odd jobs there and helped out at the other things at the rec centre. Maintenance. Sweeping and mopping. Painting during the summer. That's where I met Mr. Mars."

Living large in Swift Current would be pretty unappealing. I drew a mental picture of the subsistence lifestyle you could afford at minimum wage and with insulin to buy. At least there was no nightlife to miss.

"Did you play hockey?"

"Not really. I had skates and a stick growing up but my parents wouldn't let me play in a league. I liked watching the team and all at the rink when I came to town. I never got to go see hockey like that growing up."

"Seriously? No Saturday nights sitting around the TV?"

"Not really. Our family wasn't like that."

He struck me as an earnest, luckless kid.

"Mitzi says they liked you best of all the boys who came in. She's going to pay for you to go back to school. It's what Martin wanted."

He wasn't family. The Marses didn't have any. He was the nearest thing. He grieved in his own way. He had a lot of practice, I suspected. He wouldn't know what to do with a good break.

We pulled into the station and it was hard to miss the loaner, one selected to humble customers for the convenience and discourage them from all but wholly necessary driving: a canary-yellow '99 Volkswagen New Beetle, the first year that they rolled it off the production line in Mexico. The little plastic flower in the holder on the dash, a standard feature, served as some sort of cosmic joke. As if the locals couldn't already see us coming, now Chief and I were touring Swift Current in a clown car. If it had had satellite radio I would have found the calliope channel.

IO

When Walt and I made it back to the Mars home at twelve thirty, Derek Jones and his father, Ed, were just leaving and Mitzi was giving them thank-yous for respects paid. The kid was still shaky and his father, one of Whisper's longest serving mechanics, a giant who looked like he could hoist a car all by himself, was likewise. I walked them out to their car and stood with them while the wind howled. I asked the kid the particulars of his discovery of Whisper's body and he gave me the blow-by-blow, right down to the song playing on the radio. By the end of it he was choked up.

"If I had been on time, I might have been able to save him," he said.

I assured him that was unlikely. The Mercedes was down a quarter-tank of gas when I picked it up, so it could have been idling for more than an hour, maybe more than two if the tank had been filled, long enough to do the job. Ed gave Derek a stern look, one that said that he regretted his son being pulled home from what the family had always regarded as an extended vacation.

Ed was struggling to come to grips with his boss's death. "Martin had plans to take the Mercedes to a rally of vintage cars in Vegas in the spring," he said to me as he climbed in the passenger door of his son's beat-up pickup. "I told him that it was gonna be tough riding around in the heat with the car's crappy air conditioning. He said he was going to get Freon for the air and fix 'er up when he had a chance. He'd go in at all hours to work on it ... didn't want to get in anyone's way."

I asked the kid if he had a key to the station.

Jones the son dug through several strata of crumpled bills, loose change, his driver's licence, bank and credit cars, and girls' phone numbers before hearing the familiar jangle. He excavated a key chain that probably weighed three pounds and would have put him at risk of a lightning strike. I must have given him a look that begged explanation because he gave me background I hardly needed. "I do maintenance, y'know, janitor work at nights for a bunch of stores and offices 'round here," he said.

The kid sorted through three dozen keys before finding the one to the gas station. He uncoupled it and gave it to me and I promised I'd return it. Maybe there was something in the office that Mitzi might want, a photo or something sentimental, I said.

Ed Jones seemed satisfied with that and told his son that they were going to have to go over to the station later and get the vehicles on-site over to the main garage downtown. And not a minute later the old Ford's one headlight lit up like a Cyclops waking up and the Joneses were rolling down the road, trying to warm up the cab with their body heat and no other help.

II _____

I went back inside and took a seat beside Chief on the living-room couch. Chief was big enough to make it look like he was wedged in a high chair. Mitzi sat at ninety degrees from us. In the brief time that I had been out with the Joneses, Walt had retired and gone to bed. We could hear Walt snore every now and then and acknowledged it with glances. Mitzi told us that the kid's hours at work were so irregular that it always seemed he was trying to catch up on his sleep.

Small talk could only last so long, though. After a wordless few seconds, her head dropped and she whimpered.

"He couldn't have done it," she said.

I wasn't completely convinced, but what we had heard from the lawyer and the accountant reinforced the notion. What we'd seen in the RCMP headquarters suggested that the circumstances might not have been so cut and dried.

She asked me what I thought. I unrolled the ball of string.

"I don't get the seat belt," I said. "I don't get the position of his arm. And I don't get the reason. Everything you've told me and I've heard ..."

I was going to mention Steve Martin in the cassette deck but I held back. Somehow it felt less than respectful.

"How can I find out what happened? Can you help me?"

I don't go looking for trouble but I don't mind it in reasonable amounts.

I looked at Chief. I had put him through the wringer already. I'd be hanging him out to dry if we were going to get involved any deeper.

"Can we take another hour?" I asked him. "I know your missus was expecting you last night."

The Big Man's body was exhausted but not his patience. "I'll call the bride."

Chief went into the kitchen to dial up the wife. He always sounded different with her, like he wasn't in a dark place, like he was just about to laugh. I heard him ask about their boys and she put them on. He told them not to wait up and said he'd make them breakfast and take them to school the next morning. He was the Guaranteed Nullifier of My-Dad-Can-Beat-Your-Dad. The Little Chiefs could just refer their playmates to a couple dozen blood-soaked videos on YouTube.

While Chief was doing his Dagwood Bumstead, I laid it out for Mitzi. The first promise was No Promises.

"I don't know that I can help you at all," I started.

She knew I had worked in investigations. She asked if I knew someone who could help.

It was an out that I could have taken. The snags: (1) There wouldn't be a dick for hire in Swift Current who could bring the advantage of local knowledge and contacts, (2) someone coming to the town out of the cold would take weeks to get a handle on the principals, (3) it would be impossible to gauge a hire's enthusiasm for the task and I suspect it would wane pretty quickly, and finally (4) a dick from outside might eyeball Whisper's books and think Mitzi was suitable for perpetual fleecing.

On the first count, I was no worse than anybody I'd have been able to find. On the second, I knew the principals better than any investigator because I had played with and even roomed with Whisper. On count three, I would be motivated at least by a sense of sympathy for Mitzi. And finally, there was the matter of money. When I told Mitzi I'd have a look, she said that she would pay me for my time. "You don't have to do that," I told her. "I owe it to him. You can pay me in pork chops for now."

I laid out the ground rules. I warned her about the painful exercise of plumbing the truth. Whisper had kept everything on the down low from his teammates, and if he had confided anything in Mitzi she had to open up before the window closed. All of us have secrets, but when they're bound by shame we're forced to live behind thin plaster masks that we fear will crumble when we try to take them off. Better to live locked in the darkness of regrets than to have our fictional selves reduced to so much dust in our hands and expose the unrecognizable faces behind them.

"If I'm going to help you, you're going to have to be an open book to me and I'm going to ask you some questions that you might find uncomfortable ... no, that you *will* find uncomfortable."

She said she understood.

"I'm going to have to ask you to recall things ... no detail is going to be too small. You might find it too much."

Again, understood.

Chief came back into the living room. He had absorbed an earful from the missus, and she still hadn't seen the bruises he was sporting. He gave me the closest thing to a dirty look I had ever seen from him. It said, *If you're going to dig your way out of a hole, just don't hand me a shovel.* I gave him the unspoken promise that I'd make it up to him. Exactly how, neither of us knew.

Chief turned around and went back in the kitchen, where he and the coffee percolated. I looked at Mitzi. I thought to myself that she had aged well, that she was still hot. I had to get the thought out of my head but it wasn't easy.

12

The ashtray filled with dead soldiers. Dead soldiers smeared with half moons of blood-red lipstick.

"It's not that Martin and I kept secrets from each other. Whatever we did we did together. We shared everything except our pasts. It's always one of the things you talk about when you meet someone. 'Tell me about yourself. Where are you from? What's your story? Your family?' Martin just said, 'I'm a hockey player and that's all you need to know about me.' He wasn't much of a conversationalist, I'll grant you. He never asked me where I was from. 'What's past is past,' he'd say. 'It doesn't matter anymore.' And that's why I fell for him and I guess that's why we got hitched so quick. I had a past. I had spent a few years in Vegas. I had a few things that I regretted. Martin didn't want to know about them. He didn't care about them. It was all about going forward for him. And I thought I'd never meet a man who would look at me that way. For who I was, not what I had done.

"I never asked him about his voice. Well, I did say to him when we first met that he had a nasty cold and he said, 'Hurt myself playing hockey—stick.' And I never brought it up with him again. I just figured it was painful for him to talk about. Every word he spoke, he was reminded of it. I wish I could have heard what his voice was like before it happened. I'll bet he had a beautiful voice.

"It was all so fast, that weekend together, but I knew in the first five minutes that I'd never meet a man like him. I hear them talk about 'unconditional love' on those talk shows. That wasn't what I needed. It wasn't what he wanted. It was the one big thing: *Don't go there.* Did I think there was pain in his past? Sure, everybody has some things they want to get away from. My parents were gone from my life. He never asked me about them, never asked to meet them. I never asked to meet his."

A string of pearls fingered. A pale beige compact opened and snapped shut.

"He called the gas stations 'the family business.' I never met his parents or heard about another member of 'family,' even second- and third-hand. He grew up outside of Swift Current. In Herbert. I met an old woman, two houses down from here. She said that her son had taught him at the school out there. She's dead now. I've never been out there, just passed the exit on the highway. I'm told it's not much. I know that there are gas stations there and I know that one of them was the family business. Whenever I asked him how many stations were in the chain, when he was thinking about buying a new one, he counted them by name and Herbert was always the first.

"Mostly, though, I stayed out of his business. He hated travelling for the company. Most trips he did he'd come back the same day. Two, three, four hours the same way. Once a month he'd go up to Prince Albert. That was his longest trip and he'd have to stay the night and he just hated that. 'I hate P.A.,' he'd say, and he'd come back from there in a bad mood.

"He wasn't happy these last few weeks or so 'cause he was going up there once a week rather than once a month and he had to stay over each time. It started the week after New Year's. I remember how bad the roads were and I tried to talk him out of going, but he said that he had to. Then the one time he was up there overnight I had to call him to tell him that there had been a robbery at the station Walt works at. Walt had a gun pulled on him and he was beaten up with a black eye and they couldn't make out anything on the security camera. There was only so much money in Walt's float. Every two hundred bucks he had to deposit it in the security box and had no way of getting to it. Three men with ski masks. It was awful. Walt was shaken up. When he came back Martin felt so bad. He tried to help him in every possible way.

"I'm sorry. I don't usually smoke in the house. I gave up smoking more than ten years ago. More than that, I guess. I fainted when the officer told me about Martin, and when he helped me, y'know, to get some fresh air, I saw his partner having a cigarette. I asked him if I could have one. I sent Walt out to buy a pack. You never smoked, did you? I smoked when I met Martin all those years ago. Why start again? Maybe I just want to go back. I don't know."

The empty pack pitched. A fresh one cracked.

"The broken stick? He gave it to me after the game. He told me to keep it and said that I had to show it to him whenever I thought I should. He had promised me that we'd get out of L.A. as soon as we could. He had talked about going to Europe to play. But before the playoffs—who was it you played? Edmonton, right?—Martin had talked about staying another year in L.A. He thought he'd get traded and land with a team that wanted him. I was mad about it, mad as I ever got with him. I don't know what happened other than that goal and he never talked about it, except for what he said right after the game. 'If I ever think about breaking a promise to you again, show me this stick.' And I never had to. When we got to Germany it was just fantastic. Martin picked up the language incredibly. After four years he was just about completely fluent. He told me that he even had dreams in German. Anyway, they talked to him about staying on and coaching over there, but he said he had to come back. 'The family business.' It was the first I'd heard of it, but I didn't ask him about it. I knew he was coming back 'cause he had to, even though he wanted to stay. I didn't think I should show him the stick. He had kept his promise to me."

A lighter clicked three times before flaming up. The well of fluid almost emptied.

"He really didn't talk about his career *at all*. To anybody, really. It was so strange when this man called from Regina. A professor, he said. A historian. He was writing about hockey and wanted to talk to Martin about his career, especially about that goal against Edmonton. The man called again and again. He just wore Martin down. I remember they met in Moose Jaw. Martin would never go all the way to Regina unless he really had to, almost never, 'cause he didn't have any stations or truck stops there. He met him and came back angry. Not himself at all. I didn't ask him about it."

A quarter cup of coffee spilled on the table. A paper towel turned light brown.

"Martin had his routines. He made sure he visited his stations and truck stops, one a day. In rotation. The rest of the time he'd spend in the office that he kept downtown. He went to the board meetings of the team. He went to games but not all of them. He went to the kids' games, teams in town that Mars Motors sponsored. He liked seeing kids happy. He didn't golf much. He didn't ski, although he liked to water-ski when we'd go up to the lake.

"The nearest thing he had to a vice was the casino. The Living Sky, they call it. It looks like a big teepee with searchlights out on Highway 1. It opened a few years back. He went mostly on Tuesday nights. He took a phone call for business Tuesday nights and after he'd go to the casino and unwind. He'd take out a hundred bucks or so and play a few hands of blackjack. He had a beer or two there. You probably know from when he was playing he wasn't a drinker at all, really. It was just part of socializing. He'd buy more beers for other people than he did for himself. No, I don't know any names or anything. Mostly, I guess, he'd talk to people, strangers who didn't know him. He said it was more interesting than television. I never asked to go with him. I'm sure it would have brought back too many memories, though I didn't tell him that. I had *my own* reasons for keeping the past in the past."

A pen ran dry. Another found.

"I was with a man. Not a good man. He was physical with me. I just walked out that day and he thought I was coming back, the day I met Martin. I never heard from him again. I told Martin I didn't want any wedding announcement in the paper and Martin told me that he didn't either. This guy told me that I could be a dancer. A singer. I guess I thought I could be a star. I was young and not very smart, I guess. He had me do films and other things. He would have been mad that I left the way I did. I just had the clothes on my back. I had nothing precious. No heirlooms, oh no, nothing handed down. No warning, no call. Martin said that whatever I had he could replace. He knew I was coming from a place that I didn't want to go back to."

A sleeve tugged. A throat cleared.

"The man ... he died five years ago. I always searched for his name on the internet and in the Vegas newspapers. I saw that he'd been arrested a couple of times. And then I saw that he'd died in a car crash out on the interstate. The obituary said that his wife and son survived him."

A name on a page stroked out. A question mark scrawled.

"Martin wouldn't have 'enemies.' There were 'rivals.' 'Competitors' is a better word. The Hanley chain. They have franchises for transmissions, for brakes. Dealerships for cars, new and used, in the southwest here. You hear their commercials all the time on the radio. They own some stations too. They have their offices on Main Street, up from the doughnut shop. I know that Bill Hanley, the old man, had made offers to Martin, but what they were ... well, I don't know. Martin wasn't fussy on him. I take it that he was pretty nasty."

A clock chimed. A watch checked.

"I don't know if this is helping. Do you think it's helping? I'm sorry. I don't know what else to tell you. Of course, you can talk to Bob Roth and Harry Friesen. I'm sure that anyone at his stations or truck stops will talk to you. I don't know them real well, but most of them I've met at the company Christmas parties over the years."

A phone rang. A caller hung up.

"It happens all the time."

A curtain drawn. A snow-covered lawn stared back.

"Personal effects? What Martin had on him when he ... sorry, it's so hard, but yes, the police gave them back to me. They're in the trunk of my car. I haven't worked up the nerve to bring them in the house yet."

13

Mitzi said that there was nothing wrong with Whisper. Still, things seemed to have been eating at him over the last weeks of his life. And for a guy who lived by routine, that routine was disrupted a bit over that same stretch. It might have been the imminent deal with Garageland or the piece of business in Prince Albert or the sale of the junior team or the assault on Walt or something that Mitzi wasn't aware of, one of those secrets we keep from those closest to us, something like bad news from a trip to the doctor. I know I don't share things I want to run from or deny, and I'm sure that has more to do with a certain age you reach rather than the way you're wired.

I asked Mitzi for complete access to every piece of paperwork, every computer file, every key to every drawer of every desk. And I went through them one by one.

His phone: His cell had been returned to Mitzi that morning when we left the RCMP officers to polish their brass buttons.

His daily planner: It seemed like Mitzi would be able to recite it, but there might be some variation that could be significant.

His bank and credit card statements: Ditto.

His records for the cell, home phone, and office number: Ditto.

His personal mail: She said Whisper never got more than a postcard from anybody. I told her that I still wanted to see it.

His laptop: I hit History. Nothing special. I was a little afraid I'd come across a dead man's favourite porn sites. But no. I had to peek at Whisper's email: Mitzi gave me the username and password to his Yahoo! account. I logged in. Opened and saved entries were all business. Nothing in drafts or deleteds. I turned the page after fifteen or twenty minutes.

Mitzi dropped the shoeboxes in front of me. I spread them out on the dining-room table and recruited Chief to help me piece the puzzle together. Even if you haven't left a trace of DNA or a whiff of aftershave behind you, you're bound to have left numbers, sometimes names, sometimes patterns. Forensic stuff like this would bore the shit out of most investigators but I always liked it. Reconstructing Whisper's life was like doing Sudoku.

I checked the phone records first. I took the last three months of them, making notes as I went. I checked the additional charges and long-distance calls. The outgoing long-distance calls were listed but didn't incur charges on a flat-rate plan from Ma Bell. I saw numbers in Prince Albert. I reverse-directoried them on my BlackBerry: the Best Western. A bunch of other repeaters: Each checked out as a station or truck stop on Highway 1. Every Tuesday there was a collect call from an unlisted number and it timed out with the business call that was Whisper's appointment. The call stopped coming three weeks before his demise. I cracked my knuckles and mulled it over. A business call *collect*: asterisk.

Chief checked out Whisper's cellphone and his daybook. It turned out that he had only twenty-six numbers filed in his phone: home; Mitzi's cell; the junior team's offices; Beckwith, the minor hockey association's director; Benvenuti's, which was, Mitzi said, his favourite dinner spot on Main Street; his top lieutenant, Buster Griffiths; and finally each station and truck stop in the chain. Chief reported that there was nothing out of the ordinary or ambiguous in Whisper's daily planner, no mystery set of initials. Every appointment and doing was spelled out in considerable detail, even the most mundane of life's duties, for example:

home depot, shower curtain, lights for basement

555-2509 plumber

I checked out the personal and joint bank accounts and credit cards: a bunch of automatic withdrawals. Household stuff, including the last shower curtain and fluorescent lights Whisper would ever buy. Incidental purchases when he was making his rounds up and down the Trans-Canada. Some charges at restaurants around town, a night out with Mitzi or a business lunch. Then there were the hotel charges in Prince Albert. I didn't want to raise the possibility with Mitzi, but I wondered if it might be a romantic hideaway, as much as P.A. lent itself to romance, which wasn't much. No massive cash withdrawals. No cheques made out to CASH. Everything was traceable, a row of peanut shells tracking back to a prosperous cipher. The man, to say the least, did not live large. One entry in his chequing account that made me smile: the two-hundred-dollar cash withdrawal slash donation at the Living Sky Casino. Every Tuesday. Maybe that collect business call made him feel lucky. There weren't any cash deposits on Wednesdays, so it was a safe bet that he never broke the house.

I wasn't going to be able to get through Whisper's company's books: I accessed what he had on his laptop but couldn't make sense of it without some help. I was going to need Friesen the accountant to walk me through item by item, at least for the last couple of months. He was also going to have to give me a satellite view of everything attached to Whisper's Empire. I was going to need Friesen and maybe Roth to give me an idea of any bigger plans or developments that their late client might have had in the works.

Whisper's Collected Works and Letters littered the dining-room table and made for dull reading. Nothing looked like a red flag or even a yellow one.

14

I told Mitzi that Chief and I had to look after some business and
we ducked out. We both just needed air and airing out from her
smokes. Mitzi's rambling had my head spinning and my right
hand cramping. I also felt that I could speak freely only if I got
away to a place where she wouldn't overhear me.

The charge on my BlackBerry was down. It was registering
low battery and any minute now I was going to be SOL. I
Googled *attorney general* and *Saskatchewan*, found the information
for the Office of the Chief Coroner in Regina, and hit Call,
praying I had enough juice to last a minute or two and wasn't
put on hold or directed to an automated response. It turned
out that my charge lasted three minutes. Unfortunately, the
list of options and the "one moment please" timed out at three
minutes and one second. I had to go looking for a payphone.
Even though a trip to Swift Current is like Sherman setting the
Wayback Machine for 1955, finding a payphone there was no
easier than it is anywhere else. Chief drove the Bug downtown
and I scoped the streets for a booth. People pointed and laughed

at us. Even a couple of Mounties in a cruiser were yukking it up. We passed a Mennonite family in their nineteenth-century best, and the patriarch with his beard in finest Smith Bros. form had his earphones in and was in deep conversation with the local pastor for clarification on the avoidance of oaths. I was all for stopping and asking him if I could impose and make one call, but we were coming up on the Imperial and Chief said he had seen a payphone in there.

Just inside the door there was a payphone hanging tenuously to a chipped and long-ago painted plaster wall that had been lovingly defaced by a hundred For a Good Time Call Gladyses and a hundred more pieces of dipsomaniac artwork portraying foggily remembered genitalia. I picked up a receiver that had been the filter for ten thousand Guess What Happeneds, all lies and excuses for coming home late or not at all, and a few more thousand It's Overs. I suppose that there had even been a few long-distance calls.

Again, the list of options and the pregnant pause until an operator came on board.

"Can I help you?"

"Yes, I'm calling from Swift Current in connection to the death of a friend. We're looking to ascertain the cause of death to assure his widow that there was no foul play. The RCMP are treating it as a suicide, although there was no note and no indication of any sort of despair or depression."

"If you have legitimate concerns you should contact the coroner in your jurisdiction ..."

Just the way she said "legitimate" let me know that she presumed my concerns weren't. And I was hoping to be out of Swift Current soon enough that I'd never think of it as my jurisdiction.

"... and you said it's Swift Current. Let me look that up for you. Hold, please."

And I held. A drunk staggered through the double doors and into the hall. He presumed he'd entered the men's room. He unzipped his zipper. Thankfully, he was holding too. He walked back into the main room to continue his search for the lost lavatory without bothering to zip up.

She came back on the line. "Sir," she said, "the interim coroner in Swift Current is Albert Daulton."

"Excuse me," I sputtered. "Daulton?"

My first thought was that this was a common family name in the area and that perhaps this Daulton was a cousin or even a son of the source of a good fraction of my freshest miseries.

"Let me look. Sir, I don't see any notation that he's a doctor or is affiliated with a local hospital."

I was rattled. My proper business manner became something more in keeping with the setting, minus the profanity and slurring.

"So what, you have a coroner who is not a pathologist or even a doctor?"

"In the various regions of the province, because of the shortage of doctors, the ministry appoints lay coroners. They might be law-enforcement officials. They might be lawyers. Maybe even teachers. I don't have a listing here for Mr. Daulton's occupation but I do have his phone number."

She read it off. I went to punch the number into my phone. I was rattled enough to have forgotten that the whole reason I was on this payphone was my cell dying. I didn't have a pen so I asked her to hold on for a second. I let the receiver dangle and walked into the main room. All the denizens from the previous night were in attendance and, in fact, in exactly the same place. I asked Flora and Fauna if either had a pen. They looked right through me but Flora reached into her purse and pulled out a laundry marker. I thanked her and told her that I'd be right back. I had no reason to suspect that she'd be going anywhere and every reason to think she used the marker for eyeliner.

I picked up the receiver and the receptionist dictated the number. I didn't have any paper handy so I scrawled it on the wall. I hung up the phone, dug out change to make the call, and then prayed. It just wasn't the venue for an answered prayer.

"RCMP headquarters, Staff Sergeant Daulton's office, Constable McMaster speaking ..."

I slammed the phone down.

I started back into the main room to give Flora her pen back but stopped.

I wrote down a user review on the wall beside Daulton's number.

I called the ministry back and got the same receptionist on the line. This call represented a doubling of her usual daily workload and she had made a mental note when the payphone number showed up on the caller ID.

"Can I help you, *again?*"

"I just wanted to ask you, you said the *interim* coroner for Swift Current ..."

"Yes, there has been a changeover. Swift Current actually had one of the longest serving coroners in the province until a few weeks back. That's when Dr. Russell Hodges stepped down. He retired from his position and cut back his practice because his wife is encountering health problems. He'll be deeply missed ..."

"If Daulton is the interim, do you have a line on a successor?"

"I'm not a party to the decision and the person who would know is on vacation the rest of this week and next," she said. "I'm afraid I can't help you any more than that."

She lied. She wasn't afraid at all.

15

My gut was aching with the Celebrex kicking in. It didn't kill the pain. It just moved it from my knee to my gut. I had Chief drive over to the hospital. Whisper had landed at emergency DOA Sunday morning. That was about as unambiguous as you could get; not a terribly loose end, but still worth checking out.

It happened that Dr. Dale Goto was on call. In white-bread Swift Current, a Japanese single young professional woman seemed so exotic that many townspeople presumed there had to be a scandal in there somewhere. She looked impossibly young and, for Swift Current, impossibly stylish, even in her hospital greens. She was clearly no Sweetheart of the Rodeo. When she told a nurse to "carry on," she flattened out her A like a well-born Montrealer. She had probably leaned over textbooks day and night in the Starbucks nearest to McGill's med school. That she had to go all the way to Swift Current to get her career rolling was probably a sign that she wasn't in the top of her class. That she went all the way to Swift Current was a fair reading of her determination. She was the type who wouldn't have given me a second look when I was in my twenties. She would have thought I wasn't serious enough. She might have been right.

"Excuse me," I said and got her attention, although she stopped mid-step without turning to face me. She intended to give me seconds of her time and not a whole minute.

"Doctor, I'm Brad Shade. I'm a friend of Mitzi Mars, the widow of Martin Mars, who was brought to emergency Sunday ..."

"Yes, I remember," she said, with a get-on-with-it impatience. "He was found ... in his car."

She developed a case of acute sensitivity mid-sentence. That I was a friend mattered, even if I wasn't as close to Whisper and Mitzi as she'd presumed, and she made the leap from the clinical to the bedside manner.

"Yes, I was wondering if you recall any details from ..."

I struggled to come up with the right word.

"... his arrival."

It was recent enough that she didn't have to go to her notes.

"Lividity," she said.

I was clueless. She went on without my needing to ask.

"Livor mortis. Put simply, Mr. ..."

"Shade."

"Mr. Shade, his colouring was normal."

She turned to face me. I had been deemed worthy of a minute or two of her time, so long as she wasn't called away to attend to a frostbitten kid or a guy who'd been run over by a snowplow.

"I was told that he had died of carbon monoxide poisoning ... that he had taken his own life in a car with exhaust. And I'm saddened by that. Still, I was struck by the fact that his colouring was normal. In cases of carbon monoxide poisoning the skin virtually always turns red. Cherry red is the way they describe it. And it was absent with Mr. ..."

"Mr. Mars."

"Yes, Mr. Mars. Several hours after death in other cases the skin goes blue. That was the case, at least as I observed it in my notes. Blotchy too. Again, this would have been consistent with death by most causes but not with carbon monoxide poisoning. Very unusual. I doubt that one case in a thousand is like that, one case in ten thousand."

"So you had reason to suspect that the cause of death wasn't what they suspected."

"I'll just say that it was a *very* unusual case. His blood was an unusual colour as well. A purple tinge. I don't know what other contributing factors there might have been. Cold weather? A reaction to the prescription he was on? I don't know. That would be work for a pathologist more than someone like me here in emerg."

"Was there any follow-up?"

"I assumed there would be an autopsy. I extracted urine and twenty mils of blood. I sent the samples off for testing, which would be blood type, alcohol, poison, and so on. I made a notation with the samples that the suspected cause of death was carbon monoxide. And then when I came in for my next shift I was told that there wasn't going to be an autopsy."

"Were you surprised by that?"

She sighed. "I'd be surprised if a summer wind blew through here," she said. "I wouldn't be surprised if someone was brought in with alcohol poisoning or some type of overdose. I get that enough. I had it on Saturday night and Sunday morning—it was busy enough before they brought your friend in."

I tried to drag her out of the social morass and back on to Whisper's file. "Did the blood work come back?"

"The results have come back but I haven't had a chance to look at them. I've been run off my feet, to tell you the truth."

"I know I'm asking a lot," I said, "but is there a chance you could have a look at the blood work?"

She told me that she would make a point of squeezing it in if she had a spare moment in her chock-filled shift, which was going to end in a couple of hours.

And finally I asked her if she knew of any way that she could put me in touch with the recently retired coroner, Dr. Hodges.

"A very nice man," she said, going to her BlackBerry and scrolling through her phone book, "and it's just awful about his wife."

16

We pulled up to the gas station on the east side of town. The sign read MARS GAS, the letters set against the ages-old company logo, a crudely drawn version of the fourth big rock from the sun, canals and all. The sign wasn't lit up. On a night when the Red Planet was lit, it would have been as remote as the real thing. There wasn't a business or home within a quarter mile, only one other commercial property, what used to be a KFC that had gone out of business and been boarded up for ten years. The rest of the landscape was a wheat field that was in no danger of being consumed by Swift Current's suburban sprawl, all the mall and big boxing and franchising gravitating closer to the town's centre. When you'd pull off the Trans-Canada, a sign on the ramp pointed you north for Mars Gas and nothing else because there was, in fact, nothing else.

The streetscape wasn't scenic. The layout of the station was as diagrammed by Daulton.

I had called the Joneses and asked them to meet us. I wanted to check with the son for yet another blow-by-blow of the morning in question. I wanted the father along for the ride in case he had any input and to keep the son at ease. We sat in the car for a couple of minutes, idling, waiting for their arrival. Another RCMP cruiser went by, this time with two young Mounties in the front seat and somebody hunched over in the back. The cruiser slowed down and they gave me the Prairie *Malocchio*, but after taking a radio call they moved along.

All the coffee I had drunk was overtaking me and I had to use the john. Thankfully, I had the key that Derek Jones had given me and got out to avail myself of the facilities.

I went up to the front door. CLOSED UNTIL FURTHER NOTICE read an improvised Magic-Markered sign taped to the window. I peered through the window. I saw little green men on the desk, giveaways for kids. Cans of oil, antifreeze, and windshield-washer fluid passed for decor. And just as Daulton had laid it out, Derek Jones would have had no view of the back of the building until he walked through the back door.

I took out the key that Derek Jones had given me and unlocked the main entrance. At that point the Joneses arrived and they took it on a jog up to the door in my wake. Chief brought up the rear in a walk. I slipped my boots off at the rubber mat by the door and stepped onto the cold tile in my socks. The floor was immaculate except for one set of boot prints, Derek Jones's from his tardy sweep of the building on the fateful Sunday. No site inspection by the RCMP officers on the scene, no surprise.

"Just stand here, don't walk on the floor," I said and the three stood by.

It looked and smelled like every other service station that you'd come across. No matter how big the operation got, this was still where Whisper hunkered down to do his office work. Given the annual revenues, Whisper seemed to have been determined

to keep it looking like a humble operation. His desk was lined
with photos of Mitzi, group shots with his employees, even one
of him on the ice a few years back with a bunch of eight- or
ten-year-olds at a charity skate. Letters of thanks from charities
hung on the walls scattershot and crookedly.

Other than the wind howling outside, the younger Jones
rubbing his ungloved hands, and Chief exhaling, the only sound
in the place was the low hum of an old refrigerator in the office.
And the only thing that mitigated the smell of gas, oil, and
exhaust was the scent of coffee coming from an ancient Bunn-O-
Matic machine perched on the counter of a mini kitchen unit.
I opened the refrigerator and was careful not to leave fingerprints on the handle. Just one lonely egg-salad sandwich spoiling
in there. I shut the door and looked at the coffee machine. It
was still on. That stood to reason, I figured. Once Derek Jones
had called emergency and the Mounties arrived on the scene,
the station had been taped off, for once going by the book and
treating it like a crime scene. There was no going in to turn the
coffee machine off. I did. The coffee had evaporated and the
glass was hot enough that it might shatter if left any longer on
the burner. In a sense I might have been tampering with a crime
scene, if a crime had been committed. It just seemed like the safe
and practical thing to do.

"This is how you found everything?"

"Yeah, exactly. I didn't touch anything and this is how I
remember it."

"The alarm wasn't on?"

"No, I gave the police the number when they got here and it
turned out that Mr. Mars had spoken to them and told them he
was working late and would call them when he was through."

"The coffee machine on?"

"Yeah, I guess."

"Don't guess," Ed said, looking ready to swat the kid in the back of the head.

"I didn't turn it on," the kid said. "I'm not much of a coffee drinker."

"The floor was mopped?"

"Yeah, I guess," he said and caught himself before he saw his father's withering look. "Yes, it was mopped."

"Is that out of the ordinary?"

"I hadn't thought of it, but maybe. It was pretty sloppy out there."

"And the mop ..."

"They keep it in a closet off the men's washroom that you go into from the one side of the building."

"So you can mop your way out and leave no boot prints?"

"I guess, yeah."

"Don't guess," the father said.

"Yeah," the chastened son said.

"You haven't talked to anyone about what happened besides the Mounties, right?"

"They told me not to and I wouldn't want to. Nobody. Nobody."

When I turned off the coffee machine it made me think of the photo on the front page of the *Booster*, Whisper holding his coffee mug from the Berlin Ravens. I grabbed a pen from the counter and used it on the handle to open the single cabinet. There were a couple of glasses, left over from some promotion, each featuring the logo of the Swift Current juniors. There were two generic coffee mugs in the sink. No Ravens mug. I presumed that the photo must have been shot elsewhere, at one of the other locations. Maybe it was a file photo from last year or years before. At least that's what I thought when I went to pitch the gum I had been chewing for a couple of hours. I

pushed open the lid of the trash out by reception and it was full
to overflowing. Sitting on top of a week's worth of detritus was
the Ravens mug. It looked intact. I left it there and held on to
gum until we were off-site. It didn't add up, holding on to a mug
for more than a decade and then tossing it for no reason.

Ed Jones said no repairs would be done on the site for a while
"out of respect" and that he and his son were going to shuttle
the Taurus in the bay and the wrecks out back to the garage
downtown, where they would be serviced. Derek found the key
for the Impala and was able to start it without a boost. When it
rolled uncertainly out of the lot his father followed in the almost
as shaky Ford. They'd be back for the Summer of Love microbus
about twenty minutes later and the Taurus twenty minutes after
that.

In the meantime, I scoped out the location, the main reason
for the trip out to the station. I wanted to figure out if anyone
driving by or in and around the station might have seen what
went down. One walk around the building, though, confirmed
what Jones had told the Mounties and what they had told me:
There was no way Jones could have seen Whisper's car out back
and he wouldn't have heard it idling. He wouldn't have heard it
even if the pedal had been to the floor. And if he couldn't have
seen or heard it, no one driving by could have either.

I walked around to the back to see if someone might have
seen anything: nothing but another infinite white harvest. Not
even a gravel road in the distance to throw a crease in it. In the
summer perchance a gopher with binoculars would have seen
the scene unfold.

17

Chief and I sat in a German bakery on the main drag a few minutes before it closed, nursing coffees, hogging a table by the single electrical outlet, and waiting for my phone to charge. I was going to have to track down the historian who had pestered Whisper for an interview and ultimately coaxed it out of him. Mitzi didn't remember his name. It was the historian who was pestering, so there would have been a fusillade of incoming calls from the crackpot to the Mars's home phone, nothing that showed up in phone records. Mitzi's info, a university professor in Regina who was a hockey historian, gave me something to work with: I Google-searched *hockey, history, research, regina, saskatchewan, university*, and sundry other terms. The search yielded nothing useful. I tried to see what I could find in university calendars online. No one teaching a (Mark-Inflating) History of the Rinks course. Not a sniff. Picking out someone who would fit the profile should be like picking out Waldo from the team picture. The professor remained emeritus from the investigation.

I called my local back in the east end of Toronto, the Merry Widow. Nick answered. The proprietor was in his usual good mood.

"You know you left a tab here last time," he said.

I did and I knew he was going to mention it. I asked him if he had seen Dave Pal around. Pal didn't exactly stand out in the crowd. He was a guy of average height, average weight, a bit better than average head of a bit more than average grey hair, a bit thicker than average glasses. He was easier to hear than spot. Pal was the bar's resident hockey history maven. Fact is, he wasn't just knowledgeable but zealous about it. Who else puts on exhibitions of feats of memory by reciting the lineup of the Kenora Thistles' Cup-winning team? When I'm in the house for such momentous though unbidden demonstrations I get my nose out of the glass and heckle something like, "Hey Herodotus, exactly what did you do during the war?" Such points of real history are lost on Pal, who's the foreman on the afternoon shift at the Lever Brothers plant. He had sought out the company of other bores by taking out a membership with AHHP, the Association of Hockey Historians and Preservationists. I didn't have much time for Pal. I'd never really forgiven him for ratting out my number and email to one of his cronies, who filled my voicemail with bended-knee requests for an interview for a research paper he was putting together on Montreal's last Cup winners, otherwise known as My Shining Moment.

"Dave's at the end of the bar," Nick told me. I had factored in the two-hour time difference and knew Pal would be there. "I'll give him the phone but don't tie up the line too long. There might be people phoning in for reservations."

"Always a first time," I said.

I could never have imagined that this day would come, but I actually needed Pal. If anyone was going to know about a guy who was obsessed with hockey history, it was bound to be someone likewise disturbed.

"Hey Shadow," Pal said with unearned intimacy. "You still out West?"

He was proud to possess knowledge of my whereabouts. I got down to business but kept my fingerprints off my intentions. "Yeah," I said. "I was just wondering. I heard that there's a guy, probably a member of AHHP ..."

I said it like he always did: *ap*, rhymes with *crap*.

"... who was doing something on the L.A. and Edmonton series back in '92. Guy in Regina. A professor or something. Does that sound familiar?"

It did. "Sounds like Stu Gowan, but I don't know that he's a professor," Pal said. "That would be pushing it. He's an instructor at a community college there. I'm not sure what he's an instructor of. I never spent too much time with him. Not real popular with the other members."

Sounded like the geek who the geeks didn't like. Not especially intrigued, I plunged ahead anyway.

"So do you know anything about what he wants to do with the L.A. and Edmonton series?"

"Yeah," Pal said. "He wants to make a movie out of it. The last meeting he was shooting his mouth off about it. 'The story needs to be told,' he was saying. There's some good stuff. Y'know, John B. Harris's curtain call, Hunts's breakthrough, Mars's big goal, the broken stick and the disappearance and everything."

Paydirt.

Five minutes later, a Google search and my winning streak hit two. Like Dave Pal had said, Gowan wasn't quite the academic he made himself out to be. He was an instructor at a community college, basic bookkeeping, closer to high school than university level. Doubtless he felt compelled to have time enough to dedicate himself to hockey history so he maintained part-time status. His number was listed.

It figured it wouldn't take much to wind up the Good Professor.

"Dr. Gowan," I started, "my name is Brad Shade. I'm in Swift Current for the funeral of my old teammate Martin Mars. Martin's widow told me that he was working with you on a project about our team back in '92."

It was a dangle that caught him leaning the wrong way. He struggled to keep his skates under him. "Yes, correct," he said, affecting an ivory tower decorum that must draw laughs from the C students in the back row of his classes. "Martin and I were close. It's just another tragic point in a complex story ..."

He kept on. When it came to his sense of narrative, it was clear he was a number cruncher, not an artist.

"Professor Gowan, I'd like to help out. It's terrible that Martin won't be able to and I know he'd have liked to have seen the project through to completion."

He couldn't conceal his shock at this unexpected stroke of good fortune: I was volunteering with enthusiasm for something that Whisper had to be dragged into and seemed to regret after the fact.

"I'd be honoured," he said. "I'm sure it would have been what Martin wanted."

Bullshit.

"I'm going to be in Saskatchewan for a day or two, " I said. "Would you like to meet up?"

"I'm sure that I can clear some time," he said. Weeks, probably.

We set up a time that night when I hoped to catch up to my luggage at the Hotel Saskatchewan. Just as I was about to sign off I heard the beep of another call coming in and bade the Professor a quick adieu.

"Hello," I said. It was the last word I got in.

"You need to leave town. You and Geronimo."

A heavy breath followed and then a click. I checked caller ID. Unknown. I tried to think of a way that the bikers had tracked down my number. The easy answer: They shook it out of the motel owner. They had done a lot worse in their lives and I figured they were a legitimate risk to do a lot worse to us. They'd already kicked the shit out of us in a bar fight, so I couldn't figure out why they would want to raise the stakes and stalk us. Did they mistake us for someone else? Did they imagine we were working for someone? In the end, it didn't matter. No good reason and no bad one would make the threat feel any less real.

"Wrong number," I said to Chief. I didn't want to have to find money in the scouting budget for danger pay.

18

It seemed like Martin's demise might be good news for Old Man Hanley. If Hanley was in the bidding for the deal with Garageland Canada, he'd have one less significant rival with Whisper out of the way. If there had been any sort of professional animosity, it would go a long way to explain why No. 51's mouth watered when I rang the Pavlovian bell, the mention of Whisper's name.

It was the stroke of five. Hanley's simple storefront offices were where Mitzi had indicated, just up from the drive-through exit, where the locals drove into this cold town with a cruller in one hand, a coffee in the other, and the steering wheel between their knees. The lights were on.

We hadn't let Mitzi know about our first brush with the old bastard. I had to get a face-to-face with him, something we could keep on the down low from the widow. I stopped at Mark's Work Wearhouse to get a white shirt that might offer a patina of respectability or at least distract a receptionist from the rumpled jacket over it.

The matron who took Hanley's calls and tracked his appointments looked like his work wife, dedicated, long-suffering, unnoticed, ignored. Her hair and skin and manner were as grey as a February sunset in Swift Current. Her glasses had gone out of style five years before. She didn't know or didn't care or actually embraced the notion that they made her beady-eyed.

"I'm sorry I'm late," I said, walking up to her desk. "My BlackBerry died on me and it's gone to a better place."

"Well, I'm sorry, who is it you're looking for?" she asked.

"Mr. Hanley. I should be down there if you look," I said. "Bradley Shade from Petro Tech."

No downward glance. "I'm afraid there's nothing in his daybook," she said.

"I know that he spoke to one of our junior representatives at a trade show," I said. "Damn, I have a new girl. She assured me that this was all looked after. My secretary had to go on long-term medical leave. Carpal tunnel."

I was sure that a few more head fakes and dropped names were going to get me into the office but they weren't necessary.

The door cracked open. "Dot, get David for me," Old Man Hanley said.

"Mr. Hanley, there's ...," she said and then stalled out. She feared both bothering him if I was a nobody and offending me if I was a somebody.

Anything less than an instant "Yessir" wasn't going to sit well with him. "Dot, I said ...," he grumbled and stuck his head out the door. He saw me and then figured out where our ships had passed the previous night. We both got our snarls up.

"What the hell are you doing here?" he said. "Dot, call the RCMP. This man is trespassing."

"Whoa, tiger. I'm just here to invite you to Martin Mars's funeral. I'm the social coordinator for the Widow Mars. I just figured you'd want to be there. I feel awful about our little misunderstanding last night. I guess I was stricken with grief."

This was mostly for Dot's benefit, although provoking Hanley was as fun as getting dealt both bowers and the trump ace in a hand of euchre.

"Cut the crap, sonny. I don't know what your game is but you'd better scram before I have you removed forcibly."

"I'll leave when I'm ready. I just wanted to breathe the same air as someone as lucky as you, a guy whose chief competitor decides all of a sudden to jump out of a plane without a chute. Seemed to work out pretty well for you. Convenient."

"I have no idea what you're talking about."

He was among the most unconvincing liars I had ever met and I had the acquaintance of hundreds of coaches, general managers, agents, reporters, and players whose alarm clocks failed to ring in time to get to morning practice.

"I'm interested to know where you were Saturday night and Sunday morning."

"None of your business."

"It should be the Mounties' business, though."

"If it is I'm sure that they'll take it up with me. But they haven't and won't."

"It's a small town. There are only a few rocks I have to look under. The first one I looked under I found your idiot son."

There was no chance that he'd think I was insulting No. 59. It was pretty clear who the idiot was in the pairing.

"Dot, dial 911."

"That won't be necessary. I'll see myself out. I'll also see my way back in at some point."

I wasn't done with Hanley, just done for now. I scrammed but before I did I glanced at the mantel by Hanley's office door. An eight-by-ten glossy of two football players, Nos. 51 and 59, an imperfect match. Yeah, that swinging dick at the I and the wounded kid at the sports clinic, living proof that everything good comes into the world with a corresponding evil. With the number Chief did on 51's beak you'd have been able to tell them apart when their football sweaters were in the wash.

19

Chief was getting restless but doing his best not to show it. I told him we just had a couple of stops to make and then we could get back to Regina.

First stop: the Living Sky Casino. I buttonholed a bartender there. I had a beer and Chief a soda water that he barely touched. He'd had so much coffee we were going to have to make three pit stops on the trip back to Regina. The bartender's name was Ray and, to be blunt, his clientele was like the Merry Widow's. *Homo intoxicus* was elbow to elbow with *Homo emptipocketus*. They had been there since lunch. Ray was going to have another bad night.

I asked Ray if he knew Martin Mars. He did. Like bartenders everywhere, he had a natural rumple that bonded him with the usual supplicants. Like bartenders everywhere, he talked to strangers. Like bartenders everywhere, he seemed to talk freely but also gave the impression of knowing more than he was telling.

"Marty would order drinks and I could hardly hear him over this racket," Ray told me. He had a booming voice, all bass, no treble, but I had a hard time hearing him over the white noise from the floor. The slots seemed to pay off in sound, not cold, hard cash. Those lining the craps table yelled, begging their money to jump back in their pockets. The roulette wheel spun with the ball rolling like it was chasing Harrison Ford in *Raiders of the Lost Ark*. The only silence was found along the bar, where the wounded were self-anaesthetizing before they had to either explain or cover up their losses.

"Was he a hard drinker then?" I shouted.

"Didn't ever have more than a beer," said Ray distractedly, as he searched for his lighter in advance of his scheduled smoke break. "He bought other people drinks and sat there nursing a ginger ale listening to them."

"He didn't go to the tables?"

"He played the five-dollar blackjack table over there," he said, pointing ten o'clock from his post. A woman manned the table, high mileage, with blond hair, black-and-grey roots, and black-and-yellow bags under empty eyes. She was standing across from our dancing partners from the night before at the I and the probable source of the subsequent threatening phone calls, Butch and Sundance. I had a better look at them than I'd had during the previous evening's festivities: They were wearing vintage black leather vests, and the crest sewn on the back announced them as Loners. They wore heavy-metal T-shirts, Iron Crosses, and neither cologne nor deodorant. They were banged up, but not as bad as Chief and me. They were getting too old for this stuff, like Chief and me. Unlike Chief and me, they were in full denial of this fact.

Butch and Sundance were the only players at her table, but the dealer didn't seem to mind. She engaged them in small talk and laughed. So desperate for attention, I figured, she had long ceased to care about the source.

"You don't throw out guys wearing colours?" I asked Ray.

Ray explained to us that these days leather with their patches carried about as much weight as a Montreal Maroons sweater, Allegiances to the Long Gone. "They don't ride anymore. They were in jail for a long stretch and had their bikes taken off them by the cops and put up for auction. Poor fuckers, when they got out of jail they found that the Loners didn't exist anymore. They fell in with the Angels and these boys were on the outs. No friends left. New generation, I guess."

I knew all about obsolescence but didn't go into it. I watched the dealer wave over a girl to have her drop comp drinks for the Rebels Without a Club. "She seems to have tamed them," I said. "I can't see her and Martin Mars, though."

"Nah, Marty just talked to her. Five bucks a hand until he went bust. He bought a couple of drinks before for one or two of the guys. And then he'd wait until there was no one sitting at the table and he'd go over and play."

"Always the same?"

"What do you mean?"

"In a good mood, down mood, pleasant, businesslike, whatever."

"Look at what I look at all night," Ray said. I scanned the bar and his point was made. "He was happier than these guys. I mean, I'm taking care of them, but whenever I'd look over it seemed like he was concentrating hard. He talked to her while she was dealing. She'd space the hands out so long as it was just him and not people waiting. And if he ever won, which I think he did once or twice, he'd tip her big. Any money he brought he left here, one way or another."

"What's her name?"

"Fern."

I hit the ATM. I took out two hundred dollars and balled up the receipt so that I wouldn't accidentally look at the balance.

Fern Maclean had a smoker's sallow complexion, and the overdone eyelashes, liner, and makeup gave her raccoon eyes. Her hands were bare of any jewelled ornamentation, densely veined, and skeletally thin. She had led a hard life. In another town she might get a job in a casino but they'd hide her in the back. In Swift Current there were no lookers to bump her from her gig. Anyone with looks had a ticket out of town.

I sat at her table. Chief didn't bother to come over. I busted. I won with 17. I lost with 18. I lobbed her a softball.

"Marty Mars used to play here, didn't he?"

"I could always count on him," she said. "He was like you. He didn't have a system either, unless you count playing hunches."

She said it with an effortless stone face. She was street smart and she liked to show it. She wasn't long on emotion and didn't feel obliged to apologize for it.

"I'm a friend of Marty's. I played with him in L.A. I'm just trying to help out his missus to see what was going on with him. I guess you know he died ..."

"Suicide," she said. "I heard. That's too bad." Broken up she wasn't. I pretended she was.

"Yeah, he was troubled," I said. "He'd have to be to do something like that. I'm just wondering if you saw something, anything." I slid a fifty-dollar bill across the table. She pocketed it and thawed a little.

"Marty was a good guy. I'll miss him. I mean, his coming here helped break up my shift. And I'd tell him about my problems. I've had a few ..."

Too easy to believe.

"... and he'd listen. He didn't say much. But a change in him before he did what he did? No, I didn't see anything at all. Same Marty."

"I got to ask, was there ever anything between you two?"

"The table, the cards, and a short stack that shrivelled quickly," she said, letting me know that by her reckoning she'd given me fifty dollars' worth. "No, really, he wasn't my type." Her words were pretty chilly. She made it sound like Whisper wasn't her blood type.

20

Chief was letting the Bug warm up in the casino parking lot. We waited for the windshield to defrost. I called Harry Friesen at home. The accountant picked up on the second ring. I asked him to look for any irregularities in the books, anything that had changed over the last two or three months. He was ready to take this as a personal insult, as if nothing irregular could have slipped by him.

"Nothing improper, just any sort of change, even the slightest thing," I said and told Friesen that whatever the cost of his time Mitzi would cover it. He told me that he'd give it a look overnight. He said he owed it to his favourite client and would call me in the morning. He was onside.

Just as we were going to pull out I saw Butch and Sundance file out of the casino. Sundance was limping, only his heel touching the pavement, his ankle locked. He hadn't been limping when he bull-rushed me the night before, not when he beat a fast retreat either. I watched them shoehorn themselves into the front seat of a black Hummer. I put it at being a couple of years old, but even so it would have been beyond the means of those two if they were trying to earn an honest buck. Evidently, they weren't concerned with trying to stay inconspicuous. More likely they were advertising their bad intentions.

21

I went back by the hospital. The old bat at reception gave me a cold look. My photo was probably pinned to a bulletin board in the security department and I was atop the list of emergency-wing pests that were to be ushered back out into the cold. She paged Dr. Goto on the intercom, and after a twelve-second conversation on line one she pointed me to the hallway.

"What room ...," I started to ask.

"Just keep walking," she said, as if she would have been happier pointing me to the exit.

I walked down the hall and at the end of it Dr. Goto popped out.

"Oh, Mr. ..."

"Shade, Brad Shade. Call me Brad."

"Okay, Brad, I did get a chance to look at the results."

"And ..."

"The blood work was inconsistent with carbon monoxide."

My look was that of a D student in a remedial grade nine science class.

"Carbon monoxide binds with hemoglobin. It's exponentially more likely to bind with hemoglobin. And carbon monoxide wasn't present at all. Not even at the level that you'd see with a living patient who's an occasional smoker. There was a minute presence consistent with someone ..."

"... who had worked in a closed area around cars with fumes?"

"That and any number of conditions, I suppose."

"So he didn't die of carbon monoxide poisoning."

"That's not my determination to make."

"Okay, if it's just us talking and this is unofficial. If it was up to you."

"There's nothing approaching lethal doses of carbon monoxide present in the testing results."

"Any possible mix-up?"

"Well, a confusion in the possession, mislabelling, clerical error. Never say never, but no, I called the labs and spoke with someone there who double-checked for me."

"Okay, so your unofficial, purely hypothetical position would be that the chances of a mistake are approaching zero," I said helpfully. "He died of something else."

"If that was my determination to make, that would be the determination I would make."

"And any idea what the cause of death would have been?"

She went through her dance about her job and a pathologist or coroner being in a better position and more qualified to make the determination. I was going to interrupt her when she mentioned the coroner. He might have been in a better position, but I'd have bet his medical background was limited to rudimentary workplace first aid.

Finally she came out with it.

She told me what had shown up in Whisper's blood. Lethal.

Readily available. Impossible to trace for purchase. Rat poison. Cyanide. That was the purplish tinge.

A minute later I caught up to Chief in the parking lot. Chief had kept the Bug running the whole time. The low rumble and the exhaust billowing out of the tailpipe had my mind racing, imagining the scene behind the garage that night. Whisper strapped in the front seat with the motor running, Whisper slowly dying, Whisper already dead when the key in the ignition was turned.

22

Dr. Hodges's number and address were listed and I cold-called him in person rather than on the phone. I imagined that he screened his calls. I also imagined him busying himself about the house with chores and his wife's upkeep. The way Dr. Goto had laid it out, his wife was near bedridden with a bad back and a variety of arthritic ailments. Moreover, for reasons that she never explained to him, she hadn't left their house for almost three years even prior to the onset of her joints' violent protests. Arthritis and anxiety were one hell of a daily double.

We arrived to see a promising sign: The doctor's Volvo was parked in the driveway of a comfortable but hardly ostentatious split-level. I went up their plowed path and left Chief in the Bug, where he watched powerlessly as a bunch of kids pelted the windshield with a fusillade of snowballs.

I knocked on the door. Nothing. I waited thirty seconds and knocked again. I heard a small rumble inside, signs of life. One more knock at another half-minute interval got Dr. Hodges to the door. He had a determined and austere leanness, starting with a flat stomach and running right through to a grey moustache trimmed to pencil narrowness. He exercised self-control so that he could preach it.

"Yes, can I help you?" he said, giving me a look from head to toes and back and judging me an unfortunate case if not an unsavoury one, a drop-in patient who was coming down with something, coming down with everything.

"I hope so."

"I'm unfortunately very busy. I can't invite you in right now. Can you call back later?"

"Dr. Goto at the hospital sent me. I need your help. And I need your help quickly or an injustice might happen."

I tried to push all the right buttons in one breath. Dr. Goto represented a referral and a first pass through screening. The necessity of his help was a play for a sympathetic reaction from a man in a sympathetic business and also a stroke of his ego, the implication being that his expertise left him uniquely qualified to help. Of course it worked.

"Go on."

And I did. I explained to him that I was calling about the death of Martin Mars, which the RCMP was treating as a suicide by carbon monoxide poisoning. I explained what Dr. Goto had turned up in her slightly more than cursory lab work, wholly at odds with the Mounties' theory about the death. I explained some other curious circumstances, such as the seat belt, the cassette player, and the behaviour of the victim in the days and weeks leading up to the death. And, saving my biggest swing, I told him that his successor as coroner in the jurisdiction had decided not to order an autopsy.

"I was worried that something like this might happen," the

doctor said. He couldn't be bothered to hide his low opinion of Daulton. "I can make a phone call to my successor but I can't overrule him."

"Can you call the provincial coroner's office? Would that get him off the mark?"

"Better not to do that as the first salvo fired," the doctor said and I knew he was right. Better to be clinical with this sort of thing, better not to get emotional with a guy who seemed more of a bureaucrat than a law-enforcement officer, and better to gently offer sage counsel to a guy striving to serve the public in a role that found him completely over his head.

"Can you see if the Mounties will go back over the scene?" I asked him. "Just a nudge in that direction for Daulton. Once the toxicology report is filed. The station has been in lockdown. I have a key to it."

I didn't mention that I had been out there and worked my own casual search. I didn't mention that I had turned the coffee off. I didn't mention that I had seen the Ravens cup in the trash. If anything came back in the toxicology report they were going to be doubling back and doing a more intensive search.

"I'll do what I can," the doctor said. I sensed that he was energized by the call to action once more.

I thanked him, though maybe too quickly.

"It has been a few years since we had a homicide out here," the doctor said, a comment on the improbability of one blowing into Swift Current with me, and also a comment about his former position, which had been slightly more than honorary and nothing less than dormant.

I asked him to humour me. "Oh, and don't tell him that we talked," I said. It was an important request, though one that didn't enhance my credibility. I had to hope that he didn't take me for a crank and I couldn't be sure.

Just at that point, I heard a woman calling from what I presumed was a bedroom in the back of the house.

"I won't," he said. "Frankly, I'm not sure you're aware of this, but you didn't tell me your name."

Once I gave Dr. Hodges my phone number and email address my business in Swift Current was done, at least for that day. I had other transactions to look after in other places.

23

Chief and I checked back in with Mitzi. I told her, truthfully, that I had a couple of things to do back in Regina, foremost among them being reunited with my suitcase and my computer. I didn't tell her that I'd be relieved to look in my rear-view mirror and see a town overpopulated with supposed good guys and well-established bad guys who would mess us up and even do us physical harm.

Chief's Jeep wasn't going to be ready for at least another day, but that was something we'd have to work out later. The Bug went from being the most conspicuous car in Swift to the slowest on the Trans-Canada. The gutless shitbox didn't even meet the limit full bore. Under the speed limit was fine by me anyway. The road was messy. The traffic was heavy, a lot of transports desperately trying to make up for a day lost to Highway 1's closure the previous night.

We were a half hour on the road back to Regina when I told Chief to take the exit ramp. He rolled his eyes. We had practically a full tank of gas at this point. I had used the washroom at

Mitzi's. Chief knew I wanted to pull over for a piece of business. He probably had a sinking feeling when he saw the sign on the road: HERBERT NEXT EXIT.

We rolled past the two service stations at the end of the ramp. The larger one was a Mars Gas station. The lesser was a ramshackle independent gas seller who probably had his pumps rigged.

"Go straight," I said. "Give me five minutes."

We would have had four minutes to spare if we were just going to take in the sights in beautiful downtown Herbert, the one short block of it. The retail hub was dark: a greasy spoon, a Chinese restaurant, and a Salvation Army second-hand store. The town's memory bank was boarded up: a museum with a joyous mural that had been painted by high-schoolers on its brick side. The one light on the main drag came from the *Herbert Herald* headquarters, established in 1885, which would have been the era when Herbert was last a thriving community. I told Chief to pull over. "You can keep it running," I said, vouchsafing my intent to keep it short.

The newsroom was humming. Actually, the one lonely staffer was humming distractedly to fill in the words to a song he half-remembered. He had his back to me and was focused on the screen of a pre-millennium computer. He was engrossed in a write-up of bridge-club results. He tore a page of the *Herbert*'s current newsstand edition into tiny pieces, folded them into bite-size squares, and chewed them instead of gum. He didn't hear me come in the door.

"Excuse me," I said and the guy almost fell out of his chair, choking down his pulpy wad. "I was wondering if you could help me."

"Our offices close at five," he said, either oblivious to the fact that it was after the close of business or resigned to the reality that there was nowhere better to go. "Give us a call in the morning."

I was trying to picture the other person who would have made this an "us" operation. A two-dollar bet on the chances of this unlucky soul both writing for and delivering the *Herald* would have paid $2.80.

A second after he tried to blow me off, he determined that I wasn't there to be blown off. Scoop came up to the counter. His hair was unruly, even arbitrary, curled, matted, dirty, and colourless, like a size seven-and-a-half dustball. Everything he wore was five years old, maybe ten, and machine washable except for the boots that hiked his Dockers up to his shins. Coming out of community college, he had been told that he was going to need the real-life hands-on work experience that a small-town weekly offered. It had probably been the other person who made appearances in the newsroom, the proprietor, who had told him that. And that would have been when Scoop's Dockers weren't faded and stained and his dream of Big-City Glory didn't have holes in its knees.

"A friend of mine died Sunday ..."

He pulled a card out of his desk drawer. "Here are our rates for death notices," he said. "The people at the funeral home in Swift usually take care of that for you."

I inhaled and made a supreme effort to will up patience. I glanced around the newsroom. On its walls were cheaply mounted pages from notable events across history. The most recent one was in the year of my birth. The front page that day had been given over to a photo of the ribbon cutting for the town's centennial project, the Herbert Museum, with a mayor wearing a sash and a scissors-wielding girl in a swimsuit modest enough for Bible camp.

"I'm not here about a death notice. My friend died in Swift

Current. He grew up in Herbert. I was just wondering if you could help me track down anybody who knew him."

"I know most folks in town," he said, as if this were a bragging point.

"His name was Martin Mars," I said, and then I spilled out the thumbnail biography, ending with the fact that, as far as his widow knew, he had grown up in Herbert.

"Yup," Scoop said with the authority of the chronicler of Herbert history as it unfolded. "That would have been the original Mars Gas station that you passed coming off the highway. There's a plaque up in the diner that says the business was founded there back in the '70s. I don't know the family ..."

"Martin's parents died more than a decade ago."

"I can ask around for you."

I was sure he could fit it into his busy schedule. I was also sure that he would turn it into an item for the *Herald*'s next edition. I gave him my number and email and the details for the funeral. He said he would be in touch.

Chief didn't bother asking me how it went. He pulled away wordlessly and I didn't bother to point out the original link in the Mars chain out by the Trans-Canada.

"No more stops," I said. "I promise." And we were good.

24

The rest of the drive back to Regina wasn't triumphant, but Chief and I couldn't have been happier if we'd been in the lead convertible in the Cup parade. Chief didn't even mind when I nodded off for an hour. The most important thing to Chief was the prospect of sleeping in his own bed. It was ten o'clock when we got back to Regina. Chief would be tucked in for the night at ten fifteen. He was going to tell his missus nothing about our overnight detention. He pre-empted questions with fictions. That welt where the skull ring had landed, that was a fall on the ice in Mitzi's driveway. His exhaustion, that was a by-product of my snoring like a chainsaw. He would strip down when she was out of the room so that she wouldn't see the bruises, the biggest being where Butch had cracked the chair over his back.

I spun my own story. En route I had phoned Stu Gowan and told the Good Professor that I had a couple of loose ends to tie up, players to go talk to, coaches to meet, before we could sit down and fill in the blanks on his study of the life and times of

Martin Mars. I was buying myself time. I told Gowan that I'd meet him at quarter after ten at an internet café that was open 24 hours. I had nothing to do other than check in at the Hotel Saskatchewan and check in with Hunts to let him know that I had fulfilled our team's obligation, such as it was, to the Widow Mars. Then I'd hose off a couple of days of sweat and grit.

The internet café was down the street from the Hotel Saskatchewan. I knew what the scene would be and that he, in a slight upgrade from Scoop's packaging, would be the least funky thing in there. The staff and clientele would be pale, thin-wristed Donnie Darkos dressed in black and starved Nancy Noires whose parents were appalled by their piercings and tattoos. These would be kids the Good Professor passed in the halls of the school every day, oblivious to their snickers. Gamers would be on the computers, wielding machine guns and throwing grenades on generic war-strewn streets that were still more interesting than the ones where they lived. The music would be some gawdawful shrieking, some shaven-headed woman, I imagined.

I was able to spot the AHHP's Black Sheep from the sidewalk. He was sitting in a window seat and wore style-free cords tucked into his boots and an unpatterned and unravelling sweater that might have been bohemian on someone else but just messy on him. He waved me over to his table and we exchanged pleasantries. Even my feigned enthusiasm couldn't match his genuine excitement. He opened his laptop. He positioned it directly between us. To him it was a thin, hard plastic conduit through which my elemental experience would flow and achieve immortality on his screen and, if his fondest delusions came true, on the big screen too.

"This was always a historically important project, but I think it's even more important now given the unfortunate and premature passing of Martin Mars," he said. He prattled on, affecting a patois that would have suited the dean of classics at an Ivy League school. It was all I could do to keep a straight face.

"He was a good friend, so I'll do whatever I can to help," I said. "How much had you talked to Wh—, uh, Marty?"

"We were very early on in the project ..."

It was a fudge that crossed the line into a lie. He was representing this as an authorized work when, in fact, he solely initiated and owned it. This made me even more suspicious of everything he said.

He turned on his data recorder without asking if I minded and jumped right into questioning, as if he had a cab waiting and a meter running.

"Exactly what happened on that last goal?"

"What had Marty told you so far? Maybe I can fill in the blanks."

His disappointment crashed like a porcelain cup on a hard tile floor.

"Well, let's just talk about it through your eyes, shall we?" he said.

I barely stifled the urge to say *We shan't*. "He walked out on you, didn't he? He didn't want to talk to you in the first place, did he?"

Gowan didn't say anything. He didn't look up from the screen. He did turn off his recorder. This was something he didn't want preserved for posterity.

He was dispirited enough that I felt I had to give him a little hope. I had to promise him a quid pro quo, even if I wasn't going to tell him why I needed his quid and didn't intend to provide him with much quo.

"You recorded the conversation that you had with him, right?"

He nodded. *Yes* was stuck in his throat.

"I'll help you if you give me the sound file or the transcript or both," I said. "That's my only condition. No, check that. It's not my only condition. You have to give it to me *now*."

"I can't do that," he said. "Not right now."

"Sure you can," I said. "Your data recorder is right there. If the interview is still on it, let's put it on a memory stick. And any notes you have, you're going to send them to me by email. I'll wait with you until they're in my inbox."

He hesitated. I put some physical menace and truth behind it. It required no effort. It came from the heart.

"You're not leaving without me getting it," I said. "My friend's death is under my skin. I might do something rash. I've been having a bad day. *Days*."

I ended up buying a memory stick at the cash. Five minutes later my demands had been met. Gowan had the aspect of total defeat. A guy being stretchered off the ice might give a thumbs-up to let his teammates and the crowd know he's okay. The Maverick Historian had the last grain of self-importance kicked out of him.

"Okay, how did your talk with Mars end?" I asked. I figured that something had to have set him off.

"It was out of the blue," he said. "I don't know what happened. It seemed pretty innocuous."

Gowan opened the twenty-eight-minute sound file on his computer and fast-forwarded to the 27:30 mark. There was no hearing it above the music. I went over to one of the gamers and pulled the kid's headphones off. His machine-gun fire in a virtual war zone came to a halt.

"There's a peace treaty," I told him. "I'll be back in a minute and I'll give you an autograph."

I plugged in the headphones and turned up the volume. Gowan's voice came through.

"Tell me about your brother. Was he a player? Did he have an impact on your career?"

Radio silence followed, then a door slamming, and then a click.

"What's this about a brother?" I asked him, taking off the headphones. "Where did you get that from?"

He told me. I went back to his apartment so that he could show me and back it up.

25

Unsurprisingly, Stu Gowan was a bachelor. His one-bedroom apartment was just a couple of minutes from the coffee shop and dark when we arrived. He flipped on the light and the strewn blankets and pillows made it obvious that he slept on the couch. The bedroom he used as an office space and archive. The dust on his desk was as thick as ash at the foot of Mount St. Helens.

He went to the top drawer of a teeming metal cabinet and took a yellowing mimeographed program out of the file. He flipped through the program until he found the right page, one that had a deep crease and a stain from a coffee cup. The gloss had worn off the paper.

27
Martin Mars
Centre
5'4"
120 pounds
Birthdate: April 1, 1965

Birthplace: Biggar, SK
Hometown: Herbert, SK
Parents: Edgar and Winnie Mars
Quote: "Everything I learned about the game and everything else I
learned from my brother."

"What the hell is this?" I said.

"A program from the 1977 provincial peewee final," he said, as if I should have known. "I know it's just a mimeograph, but that's part of its charm. Four boys in the final ended up playing major junior. Remarkable, isn't it?"

"Exactly how the hell did you dig this up?"

His answer went back to his complete psychopathology. "I have the complete set dating back to 1970," he said with a sense of misplaced pride.

Why was a question that I didn't bother asking. If I had to guess, the Good Professor went to these tournaments in the hope that he would not only witness the arrival of a future pro star but also would have on hand proof of his attendance and maybe a collectible that could be auctioned online. I read about an auction of a bunch of cancelled cheques signed by Gordie Howe and bidding on a set of Bobby Hull's false teeth.

"Were you there for the tournament?"

"Yup," he said, and again he puffed his chest out, proud of what only he imagined was a coup.

"What do you know about Mars's team?"

"The Herbert Hatters ... played in a tiny old rink ... a Quonset hut ... "

He carried on with the Requisite Nostalgia Clichés as if to a score from a tinkling piano and against a backdrop of a montage of old snapshots. I thought about more immediate concerns.

I looked down the Herbert lineup and came upon the coach's name. "What about this guy, Lefty Boylen?"

"Great hockey man, career minor-hockey coach, dead, oh, I dunno, 1998, '99 ..."

I grabbed a pen off his desk. I wrote down the names of the Hatters. I didn't bother with a couple of brothers named Smith, a player named Davis, and another named Miller. The hopes of tracking them down through directory information weren't exactly remote, but I went straight to the more uncommon names: Zawatsky, Kudstra, Epping, and Tollesen. They'd be easier to find.

I bade Gowan adieu. I told him I'd be in touch. I didn't fear him running off. The Good Professor wasn't about to light out for new horizons. Not with an apartment overflowing with old programs and signed pictures and framed sweaters. Nothing could separate him from his treasure hoarded over a lifetime.

26

It was late, but I had leads and had to try a round of calls. I first tried Boylen in the provincial directory. It produced a couple of hits. Neither were related to the late coach.

I found a Zawatsky in Melville, about six hours from Herbert. When I called he had just made it home from a meeting of the town council. I told him about Mars's death and said that I was trying to break the news to Whisper's friends and family. I said I had no contact number or address for the brother.

"Honestly, we never had much to do with him," Zawatsky said. "He had that throat thing. Could hardly speak a word. Strange kid, but he could really skate. I don't remember him having a brother, but it was a long time ago. I remember his parents moved to Herbert that year or a year or two before. Otherwise, there's not much I can tell you."

The others I managed to track down, four in all, knew nothing more than that.

The only place he had a brother was in that program. I tried to calculate the odds of the quote being attributed in error:

probably no more than one in five, even for the amateur-hour volunteers who put the program together.

Mitzi said she knew only of the parents and never met them. Relatives weren't discussed. I checked Mars in the Saskatchewan directory. Lots of Marshes and Marshalls. No Marses.

I had just about resigned myself to drilling another dry hole when my cell vibrated: C & B HODGES.

"I think I have good news," Dr. Hodges said. He was a professional who favoured lowering the bar to heights he and events could comfortably clear. "I made a call to someone who shall remain nameless because he's of little importance to you. He is of much importance to the interim coroner. And a full investigation will be undertaken belatedly. One can only hope that no potential evidence has been lost or compromised."

He didn't bother noting that Dr. Goto's blood analysis was going to have them looking for a potential source of a lethal dose of a poison that might have been washed down by coffee. He also didn't bother noting that an investigation that came as a result of pressure from Daulton's boss's boss would be done to the letter.

In the background I could hear Mrs. Hodges calling for him and he said he had to go.

"Thanks for this," I said.

"Not at all, pleased to help," he said and sounded wistful. He was going to take care of the personal obligation that had thrown his public service, with this brief exception, into total eclipse. The call he made upstairs, calling in a favour, might have been the last act of his professional career. Sort of like my last game and those of many others, I thought.

27

I went down to the bar in the Hotel Saskatchewan's lobby. I needed and deserved a drink. Beers poured on my exhaustion would throw me into ten hours of rapid eye movement and a few episodes of reverie played out in my subconscious theatre. Such were my good intentions.

Tuesday night was a slow night for the bartender and the waiter. There were lots of empty rooms at the inn. Many of those occupied were reserved for members of the Anglican clergy who were gathering for a conference the next morning.

The stand-up had a small gathering. Two tanned businessmen from the Sun Belt were talking through their hats in a winnerless game of one-upmanship, every round producing a bigger boat, a pricier country club, and another thousand square feet to their McMansions' floor plans. I would have given a C-note for an auctioneer's gavel to bring the bidding to a close. I turned my back to them and focused on a threesome at the other side of the bar. At first glance I guessed that two young lions were leering at their cougar secretary, but the plot thickened on further review.

She was a Woman of a Certain Age dressed too well to be on a secretary's salary. Her face looked like it could have been carved out of Ivory soap and was framed by a couple of densely filled cubic feet of raven hair. She didn't need to enforce any deference. She was in command. And the boys weren't leering. They were sucking up and it had to be *up* because in her spiky heels she was all of six feet and more. They were the subordinates, she the Executive Dominatrix.

First take: I glanced. Second take: red light flashing. Third take: solid green. I stared. She caught me staring and didn't mind. She stole looks back, like she was emailing me confirmation of a reservation. Not that it was going anywhere. Not that I had that in mind. She liked something she saw and I liked everything in my range of view. Innocent stuff, beat the hell out of a silent bar-side vigil.

My phone hummed and shifted on the bar toward me. It was Sandy. My conscience was on line two. I let them both ring through to voicemail.

One lapdog went to the sandbox. The other asked the bartender for the cheque so that he could make a big show of springing for their drinks. I took three small sideways steps along the bar, never raising my elbows off the stained oak, and leaned forward, fetching a napkin, as if I had come all that way for nothing else. She knew better. She seemed happy about it. She was.

"Do you come here often?" I asked.

"I've come here for years."

"I always end up here too when I'm in town on business," I said and told her what that business was. My explanation wasn't self-important. It was more self-deprecating. I was the most casually dressed guy in the room, the staff included.

"You meet interesting people here," she said.

"I have in the past."

"So have I. Not as often as I'd have liked, though. I'm Donna."

She didn't come to the bar looking for me or anything like me. She came to the bar looking for a release from pressures at the office. As the roles assumed by her lapdogs suggested, it was *her* office, which turned out to be the office of the Attorney General for the Province of Saskatchewan. She was the number two there, runner-up to only the Member himself, who was usually preoccupied with debates and shouting and desk thumping and whispers behind the curtain over in the Legislature. Those who walked the red carpet on either side of the chamber knew her, but only as much as she needed them to know. They knew that, when the Member stood up and made his pronouncements in the Assembly, his words were her words, every speech and talking point. She didn't say that directly to me or, I suppose, to anyone. She had risen up through the ranks of the AG and learned how to be discreet. If you couldn't read between the lines, you didn't deserve to know.

We talked a lot. One night wasted in the I and the holding pen at RCMP headquarters, the next well spent in an oak-lined bar with a beautiful, powerful woman who lacked only one thing you'd expect of someone like her: a big rock on the third finger of her left hand. No rock there at all. The space was conspicuously and promisingly vacant.

A couple of emptied glasses later, she looked over her shoulder distractedly at the reception desk across the lobby. Late-arriving Anglicans were lined up, heads bowed as if in prayer for upgrades. She didn't turn her face back toward me. "You don't remember, do you?" she said as if she was talking to no one at all, almost out of my earshot.

I must have looked puzzled. "I have a pretty good memory," I said. My memory was cued again between "pretty" and "good" when Sandy called again and the BlackBerry shook. I powered off the phone and the pangs.

"Do you remember your first time?" she asked.

"If I told you about it I'd be more embarrassed than when I told you what I do for a living." I left it at that.

She looked down at her drink and stirred it with her finger. "I feel the same way," she said, rattling the ice cubes and more. "It was here. With you."

IT CAME FLOODING BACK and the undertow was washing me out to sea.

The Donna I met when I was eighteen was freckled. Back then she was blond. But freckles fade away and blond hair will darken and hold dye as well as any other.

Back then she didn't need to do a thing and relied on natural gifts. All these years later she took her appearance seriously, and it went a long way to make others take her seriously.

That night all those years ago I went down to the bar with a few other guys from the junior all-star team and was having a Canadian in a bottle. I learned about the better things later in life. She came in with some friends, obviously underage, the whole lot of them. They were turned away. I caught her eye and sent her a look that expressed my regrets. I told her I had a better place to go. Thought it took courage, years later relabelled it conceit. She smiled. My roomie on this trip was a big, dumb, talentless defenceman. He was a passenger who didn't belong on our team, but at that moment the more pressing issue was that he didn't belong in my hotel room. I told her to wait and ran upstairs. I took off my running shoe and my sock and put the sock over the doorknob, the universal sign of your roommate getting lucky.

It was her first time. It was my first time with her.

WEDNESDAY

We were the last in the bar. The old guy in the black vest and bow tie was wiping and rewiping the century-old woodwork that our elbows were resting on. We weren't delaying the inevitable. We were letting the pressure build.

There was nothing said when I signed the bill, when I dug out my room card, when we both stood up, when we both walked to the elevator, not even when the elevator doors shut and we started to rise up to the seventh floor. By that time she had reached up and wrapped her arms around my neck and her high heels were an inch off the floor. By that time I was imagining what I wanted to do with her first.

It was all a rush. I swung open the door and grabbed her arm just above the elbow, tight enough to bruise her. Thankfully, it was going to be cold enough to get away with long sleeves until July. She hit the king size like it was the landing pit and she had just won the Olympic high jump, back first, legs in the air, sighing ecstatically. I didn't bother turning off the light I had left on. I was glad that I did because it was going to be beautiful to watch. We had kissed enough on the elevator, in my opinion and hers. I pulled her by the ankles so that her legs were hanging over the edge of the bed and I pulled hard on her panties, hard enough that they tore away like a Velcro strip. I buried my head in her Brazilian, between her tan lines. She had managed to get away to the Caribbean for a week and her bikini waxer could have offered a two-week guarantee without a worry of customer complaint. Her sighing became hard breathing and I could feel her muscles quivering. She grabbed me by the shoulders and pulled me up. She was writhing under me trying to peel off her clothes and mine. And then all of a sudden she pushed me hard, both hands in the chest.

"I want it like this," she said.

As is my nature I was eager to please.

She stood up and grabbed me by the wrist and led me to the long vertical mirror that was near the short hall to the door. She liked to watch, she said.

She bent at the waist and pushed her ass in the air and leaned against the wall with hands on either side of the mirror. She had ink, a representation of the f-holes of a violin down in the small of her back. She looked in the mirror and into my eyes as I went deep inside her. She closed her eyes and bit her lip and her head whiplashed in a machine-gun rhythm. In the hallway I could hear young voices, stoned voices, not kids, too late for that, but a metal band that was crossing the Prairies in a van. And laughter. It didn't matter. They weren't going to keep us up.

I held her tight by her waist. I could see her rib cage swelling with each deep breath. I looked at her face. And I looked at mine. I had done mirrors before. Mirrored ceiling in Vegas even. But I had not done mirrors in a long time.

I looked at her in the mirror and listened to her voice. I hadn't recognized her at the bar, and even when she dropped the bomb I didn't know whether to believe it. I did at that moment, though, when she started making noise. In her reflection I saw her teenage face accessorized by her adult life in between. I liked what I saw in that face, but not mine looking back at me. I looked older than I expected, older than I liked. Lined face, softer body. I wasn't aging as well as she was. Leaving the light on didn't seem like such a good idea after all.

I was somewhere between H.G. Wells's *Time Machine* and "Letters to *Penthouse*."

"I thought of you all the time," she said, looking back at me in the mirror, "like this."

I made it last as long as I could. On this count awkwardness was a benefit. And when I finally crossed the goal line and caught my breath, I choked trying to find something to fill the silence. "I couldn't help myself when I saw you again," I said. It was true as far as it went. I'm trying to remember a time when I could help myself.

TWO AND A HALF DECADES: There was no catching up all of it in our pillow talk. I turned off the lights in the room, a forgiving darkness. We were illuminated only by the washroom light that I had left on. She had her back to it. She was a silhouette beside me. I could feel her hot breath on me. When she closed in I could feel her pulse.

She was strategic for a moment. She picked her words. "Funny, I've gone to that bar for years," she said. "That's where I met my ex. A Revenue Canada convention. And when the divorce was final, that's where I celebrated."

Funny, that she did. Funny, that she'd go where we met and had a night that we thought about thousands of times thousands of miles apart. Funny, that she'd go and not know she was looking for that *something*.

I wasn't going to go cosmic on her. I confessed. I had her address all those years ago. I had never dropped a letter down the Culver Mail Delivery System or in a mailbox. I had taken her phone number with me and never called. I knew how hollow *cosmic* would sound. It was physical before and physical again. We were better sweating than trying to sweat truth out of each other. We were better straining for *it* than for answers. The sheets were wet but not with tears. No tears, ever.

I had taken her address and phone number all those years ago, but now I couldn't for all my trying remember her last name. When she went to the bathroom to take her contacts out I rifled through her purse and found her business card: Donna Bodnar. It didn't sound familiar. Might have been that she stuck with her ex's name. I didn't know and didn't ask. I dropped the card in my shoe at the side of the bed.

She shut the bathroom door behind her. She had seen everything up to that point clearly enough, but with her lenses in too long she decided she could use her imagination the rest of the way.

"It's going to be a long morning," she said at 4 A.M. "But it's worth it." The present tense: the indirect promise of more. She kept it.

Between her held breaths, between her *oh yeah*s, between her glances into the mirror, years tumbled out. She had gone to law school hoping to become a court crusader and only finding out late in the day that she felt more comfortable on a squash court. She had taken a government job at a pay scale befitting her sheepskin. Two loveless marriages left her with regrets. She regretted marrying a guy who had played a bit of hockey but didn't make it to junior, a trend of watery failure that tracked through his life off the ice. Most of all, she regretted that she hadn't gone into divorce practice.

I started to tell her what I had gone on to do after that night following the tournament. She stopped me. She knew and she told me all that she knew.

She was a grown-up and I liked that. She wanted no apologies and she gave none.

"I had your address too," she said.

I HAD SLEPT MORE in the holding pen with Chief than I did in the Hotel Saskatchewan that night. I spent more time that night in front of a mirror than I had getting fitted for every suit I'd ever owned. She told me that she was going to have to get up early to go home for a change of clothes. She didn't want to use a sick day, not after being out with her lapdogs. People would talk.

I looked out the window. It was 6 A.M. so I rang room service and ordered breakfast. Twenty minutes later, when we both staggered over to the mirror again, I heard a door knock. I told the young guy pushing the cart that I needed a minute but took at least ten more. Afterwards, I went to the door in the bathrobe that hung in the closet. Only then did I realize that all our thrashing had been a no-cover, no-minimum, Amsterdam-worthy live show for passersby, a full five hours of it. When I had thrown her on the bed I had left the door open. It didn't bother me as much as her mirror fetish.

I signed for our meal. She ate her bacon with her fingers, like it was crispy strips of me. We made promises to each other. I didn't know if she intended to keep hers and I didn't know if I'd keep mine.

I watched her shower and then I watched her dress while I did the same. I had no reason to get such an early start but did so out of consideration and admiration for her. I walked her to the sidewalk and flagged her a cab. The wind hit us as if a chill of twenty-five years of distance between us was picking up where it had left off.

And then I felt a fist crack the back of my head. It was the sensation of a restraining order being violated.

"Oh for fuck sakes," she said. "I'm calling the police."

Gasoline, meet Fire. Her ex-husband was in my weight class, but a night of parking outside the Hotel Saskatchewan had taken a bit of sting out of his best shot. It had staggered me but not come close to dropping me. I turned and he wound up for a second swing. The old doorman at the Hotel Saskatchewan's main entrance stepped outside just in time to see the ex-husband dropping, his back hitting the sidewalk and crunching the salt, his head disappearing into a snowbank. His eyes were wide open and focused on the stars the other side of the clouds. His chest was heaving, though.

She summoned the cops. She told me to beat it. She didn't want me to get involved. I was going to be an innocent bystander who'd decided not to stand by any longer than necessary.

"I knew ...," she started to say but ran out of words.

I raised my right hand and gave her the stop signal. "Don't," I said. "Just call me later so I know you're okay."

"I'll be okay," she said.

I looked over at her ex. He had turned on his side but was no threat to get up. "That's the thing about divorces," I said. "They're never final."

I gave the doorman twenty and then another. He hadn't seen anything. And he had seen her before.

Sex and violence: I recommend the Hotel Saskatchewan.

2

I sat in the window of a coffee shop down the street from the hotel, nursed a decaf, and waited for my pulse to clock down. I saw a couple of college students, a smiling Girl You Bring Home to Mother in a bushy fur hat and a lanky Fair-Haired but Bed-Headed Guy, walking by the window, her huddled inside his down jacket, both of them laughing. This was their glorious present and I envied it, but my jealousy was tempered with the knowledge that one day they'd recall a time when they were undefeated and made the mistake of believing that they were undefeatable.

I thought about the past. It was never behind you. I saw the cruiser pull up and two officers asking Donna questions and her ex raising himself out of the snow, though his ass was still on the pavement. They cuffed him even though he was in no shape to resist. They offered him a ride to the police station. They insisted. She looked down the street when the cruiser pulled away. She looked but couldn't see me. It was an awful look. I felt for her in an entirely different way.

Before I could work up any sympathy for a guy whose life was going to get more miserable and more expensive, my BlackBerry pinged. It was Sandy calling from her office. In defiance of my nature I managed to feel awful.

"You sound exhausted. Are you as bad as you sound?"

I answered the query the way she offered it and reassured her that, no, I was probably not quite that bad. I told her, yeah, I was tired, rundown, and probably coming down with a bad case of something. I didn't tell her that it was a bad case of conscience. She'd always cautioned me about the dangers of self-diagnosis.

"Up all night," I said. Technically true.

I told her the plans for the day or days ahead. "I'm doing it for her," I said, *her* being Mitzi. "She's in a bad way and wants some answers. And something is wrong about the whole thing. I owe it to Whisper. I'm just trying to do the right thing."

It must have been the full catalogue of wrong things that made me less than convincing. She didn't bother with Socratic questioning or cross-examination. She went straight to thesis and verdict and expressed her displeasure.

"I had to call you," she said. "You didn't think to call me. You know that I worry about you out there. And you just send a text, not even a voicemail. A text. That's not how you treat someone you love. Respect, concern ..."

She rhymed off items for a shopping list for the next time I went to the supermarket to pick up a personality. Or maybe she was dictating a personal ad she was planning to place.

Her goodbye was not final, just rote, somehow worse than final. I tried to believe that it was just Sandy having a bad day at the office. That didn't work at all. I was guilty on all counts, a repeat offender. That I wasn't aware of any of this until she pointed it out only made it worse.

While I was on the phone with Sandy, I had a Google alert

for the Swift Current juniors. The paper in Regina had a report
that the franchise was in negotiation with three potential
buyers who intended to move the team to Grand Forks, Fort
McMurray, or Anchorage. In fact, the high roller in Anchorage
talked boldly about bringing two teams to the state, pointing out
that the regional airlines he owned could help out with travel
issues for other western league teams. "I'll offer it up at below
cost," Daddy Coldbucks said munificently. For every sale or
move of a franchise in the pros, in junior there were about ten
bad rumours. The more outrageous the backstory, the less likely
that there was fire with the smoke. Still, given the ten-to-one
ratio, I had to make it at least a three-to-one shot that *something*
might be happening. For every three noisemaking clowns like
the Anchorage blowhard, there's one guy with gelt and tight lips
who isn't available for comment until after the big deal closes.

3

I waited outside Regina's downtown library. The staff were a couple of minutes late in opening but this was inconveniencing no one else. Finally, a librarian opened the door. She had horn-rims and her hair up. I'd have put her at a well-preserved forty and she clearly worked at it, a streak of purple in her hair being just a hint of a wild side. She looked nothing like every librarian who'd scolded me over overdue books at the Boston College library. She looked like every librarian who took off her glasses and let down her hair in old-school classics on Spectravision.

She smiled when I stepped inside and stopped shivering. She smiled when I kept my voice low and asked where back issues of the Prince Albert paper were. She pointed me to shelves weighed down with a ton of newsprint in perfect daily order. I had tried to do my searching online, but the web archive material for *The Prince Albert Daily Herald* went back only seven days. I was looking for events in P.A. when Whisper's visits had become more frequent.

I carried a pile of papers to a century-old oak table. I assured the librarian that I'd keep the papers in order. I was everything she ever wanted in a man. I had respect for library protocol and the Dewey Decimal System.

The P.A. paper was easy to leaf through. Births. Deaths. Weather. Fundraisers. Wheat prices. Classifieds. Farms up for sale, which doubled back to Deaths and Wheat prices. Days passed by in the fifteen seconds it took me to flip through the pages. I was looking for a business story, a commercial deal that had sparked Whisper's interest in this singularly uninteresting place.

I stifled a yawn. I caught the librarian looking at me. I had to try to stay focused. I came up to the days before Whisper stayed overnight in P.A. for the first time.

Then I hit the jackpot.

In the pile of papers, there was just this single day that the front page of the paper had something resembling front-page news. P.A. was awakened from its slumber by an attempted murder. The photo above the fold was a decades-old portrait that looked like the one on Whisper's hockey card. At least if Whisper's hockey card picture had been taken by a mug-shot photographer.

> *A convicted murderer remains in critical condition after a stabbing at Prince Albert's federal penitentiary.*
>
> *Wolf Martens was rushed to Prince Albert's Mercy Hospital with multiple stab wounds Tuesday morning, a spokesman from the Department of Corrections said.*
>
> *Officials said that no charges have been laid and the assault in the maximum-security facility is under investigation.*
>
> *Martens was sentenced to life for the murder of his father and brother in 1974. Martens confessed ...*

The reporter reprised details of a stabbing that had left a man face down in a pool of blood in a basement apartment on the less-picturesque side of Regina. The reporter reprised the details of an even more awful crime, the stabbing of a nine-year-old and the disposal of his corpse in a dumpster, his remains never found. Wolf Martens had pleaded guilty to the murders and a variety of other counts and was sentenced in a court around the corner from the Hotel Saskatchewan. Martens's story in court, the same story in the newspapers almost thirty years ago and on the pages more recently, was fiction, as it turned out.

I flipped through the papers for the days that followed Wolf's ambulance ride to Mercy's emergency. The day after he was still in critical condition. Three days later he was listed in serious condition. And that was the last mention of Wolf Martens in the P.A. paper. Even on the slowest news day in a Town of Happenings Few and Far Between, the slow, painful recovery of a guy serving a life sentence gets bumped off the page by eighteen-wheelers rolling over, road closures, and 4-H Club meetings.

I looked up when I stacked the last paper in a neat pile. I caught the librarian looking again. This time she didn't turn away. I smiled.

I Google searched *Wolf Martens* and *murder* on my BlackBerry. I found a brief entry in Wikipedia that gave the very abridged account of his story. I searched the name in images. The mug shot came up. So did photos of Wolf, handcuffed, being led out of court. The resemblance to Whisper wasn't uncanny but their faces had the same Teutonic engineering, hair and skin the same dark Bavarian paintwork. Wolf being led away in cuffs was a smaller guy than Whisper had been, as if shrunken by a string of sleepless nightmares.

The librarian was worked up to the very edge of Come Hither.

She moved her nameplate on her desk, just in case I might have missed it: ALEXIS STEWART, PERIODICALS RESEARCH DEPT.

"Has anyone told you that you look like that hockey player who was married to that actress?"

"I used to get that all the time," I said.

WOLF MARTENS'S INCARCERATION explained the collect calls, the only way inmates can call long distance. It would also have explained Whisper's monthly trips there. Martens's stabbing would have explained the timing of Whisper's more frequent overnight stays in P.A. None of it explained why Whisper was dead, though.

I had to go to P.A. I had to talk to Wolf Martens. There are loose ends and then there are loose ends. There was no knowing the story of Whisper's death without knowing the story of his life, and the fact that Whisper had gone so far out of his way to conceal his connection to Martens made me believe that the convict could tell me a story that no one else could tell.

4 _____

I passed the doorman. "Good morning, sir, welcome to the Hotel Saskatchewan," he said, tipping his hat as if he had never seen me before, smiling because "good" didn't start to cover it.

I went to my room and called Chief. He picked up even when SHADOW showed up on his call display.

"Did you get a good night's sleep?"

"Oh yeah," I said. "Listen, do you know anybody up in P.A.?"

"I know lots of people. Why?"

I told him why. I told him about the guy who had been stabbed, the guy I thought was Whisper's brother.

"Shit, I played junior with a guy who's a guard at the pen," Chief said. "Todd Kilmer. Killer could have played some college hockey in the States but he got married young and wanted to stay close to home. He got a call from the coach of the prison workers' team. They had a job opening and, y'know, they put in a good word."

Chief filled me in. He had Kilmer's cell number. Chief told me to let him know that he gave me the number and that he had been meaning to get in touch. Chief seemed relieved that I hadn't asked him to make the call for me.

I called and left a message. I sent a text. I didn't go into any detail about Whisper, about Martens. I figured that would be enough to scare Kilmer off getting back to me. I waited. I killed time in my room, checking into our scouting database for new entries. I figured I needed to remind myself about my job before Hunts felt like he had to. Just a couple of entries. Our Quebec guy wrote long, meandering notes about players of marginal interest, as if he were trying to talk his way into liking them. Our Russian guy wrote in broken English and I didn't like his read of players' strengths and weakness in games. His say-so was the basis of our drafting a couple of guys who never bothered coming to North America.

Kilmer called me back when he was on his lunch. I filled him in. He knew all about Martens. He remembered Whisper coming in to visit him. Monthly. The paperwork had to be submitted for each visit, security clearances, background checks, even though Martens wasn't organized crime or a career criminal. The bulls had to make sure that Martens wasn't being used by hard-core cons who'd use anybody and anything in max security. Kilmer had talked hockey with Whisper.

"Yeah, Mars told me the two of them were cousins," Kilmer said. "Told me his side of the family just shortened their name."

Kilmer didn't know that Whisper was dead and he was certain that Martens didn't know. He had been part of the detail at P.A. Mercy. The nature of his job: He had to stand guard against any attempted escape by an inmate who for the foreseeable future could only leave in a body bag.

"Martens isn't out of the woods by any stretch," he said. "They had to remove his spleen. He was fifty-fifty to make it when he went in. And, yeah, Mars was there for stretches. He was pretty

shook up, for sure. He probably shouldn't have been let into the
room right after Martens was stabbed. The paperwork wasn't
done. I went off the books on that." Kilmer caught himself. He
realized that he had said too much.

"You're not going anywhere with this, right?"

I told him I wasn't and said that he'd done the right and
reasonable thing.

I asked Kilmer if Martens was lucid. He was. I asked if I could
get in to see him. Kilmer gave me the standard lines about the
protocol of applying through official channels, about the time
involved. I told him that this had to amount to special circumstances, the near-fatal wounding of one, the apparent suicide
of another. I also told him about Mitzi and how she wanted
some final answers about Whisper's death and knew nothing
about the real reason for his visits to P.A. That got him. After all,
Kilmer saw life in the pen at ground level, not as a bunch of files
and policy positions in an office in Ottawa.

"Our supervisor is assigning the detail for guarding him in the
hospital. It's all off the sked and voluntary overtime. I've done
the past couple of Fridays. I know the guy who has the assignment this afternoon. I can work a trade with him. He's junior to
me and owes me a favour. He won't ask any questions."

I wondered why he was going out of his way. I had told him
that I was working with Chief. Still, that shouldn't have been
enough for him to rework his schedule and call in favours. I
nudged him on it, not asking why he was doing it, just telling
him that I knew he was doing Martens and Mitzi a real service.
That was enough to get him off the mark.

Kilmer said that he thought Martens should have never
been in maximum security, that medium would have been fine.
He seemed to think that Martens was more mentally ill than
criminal.

"He passed up a bunch of chances to apply for parole," Kilmer said. "It's not rational."

It was a long way from the most irrational choices Wolf Martens had made.

5

I went to the outlet to rent a car. The guy at the desk remembered me. "Do you have anything high-end?" I asked.

He gave me a PT Cruiser and said that was all he had. "Some sort of convention going on," he told me. When I sat behind the wheel, I realized that the previous renter had been the size of a jockey and the seat was jammed. It wouldn't slide back an inch. I would have tried to exchange it but I saw a long lineup at the counter. Wedged in so tight that I just had to take a deep breath to hit the horn, I drove off trying to imagine Anglican ministers in executive cars.

6

At least I'd have work to do for my day job when I was in Prince Albert. I wasn't going to try to claim the trip on my expenses, because an item like that, something way off my approved budget, would stand out in the audit that Grant Tomlin planned to put our department through. I wouldn't have been trying to pull a fast one, but it just might look that way enough to give the rest of my expenses more intense scrutiny, a headache I didn't need. No, having a game to watch Wednesday night was about keeping my conscience clear and the off chance that I might see something other scouts might miss. Skipping out of any chance can become habit-forming, and next thing you know you're taking every available shortcut rather than working in the scouts' default mode, trying to squeeze in as much as humanly possible.

Medicine Hat was playing that night in P.A. P.A. had a player that I was interested in, a gawky left winger, rail thin, but a hard worker. I had seen him three times and he'd left nothing on the table. He emptied his pockets, every last bit of lint, every shift. He didn't look like a star. He was a red-headed stepchild, all

Adam's apple and acne. I hoped he was going to fall to us in
the fourth round in June. I had to see him again to make sure
that I didn't have him wrong. He was reason enough to go to
P.A. That's what I told myself driving to P.A. when I could feel
my body stiffen in the seat. Arthur felt like violin strings being
wound tight, ready to snap. I didn't want to take the pills and get
the gut pain on the drive.

My cell vibrated. I pulled it out of my jacket with my right
hand while keeping my left on the wheel. I was speeding to
Saskatoon, where I'd have lunch and then finish the drive to P.A.

It was Scoop from the *Herald*. I hadn't expected he'd get back
to me so soon.

He had asked around about the Mars family.

"From what I *gather* in my *reporting*," he said, imagining that
he was manning the desk at the Paris bureau of *The New York
Times* and not gnawing on a stack of back issues in the *Herbert
Herald*'s spartan newsroom, "the Marses were originally from
Roslynn and moved here from Regina in the '70s. That's where
they operated an Esso station, pumps and lunch counter. They
moved to Herbert when they bought an independent station
and that's the one that started the chain. The Marses were
awfully private people. Weren't much on small talk, though
you'd think that would just go with running a diner. Minded
their own business."

It was only interesting as far as it went. I congratulated him
on his spadework with half my heart and then nudged him on to
the matter of Whisper.

"Yeah, well, according to an old customer of theirs, a retired
farmer, the Marses had a boy. He said he thought they were
pretty old to have kids."

I mulled over the possibilities, attached alternative theories
to the hazy memories: The Marses had raised a nephew or

a grandson as their son, or maybe it had been a foster-child arrangement or even a legal adoption.

My hope for semi-ironclad answers was a guy manacled to his hospital bed, a guy whose keeper considered him insane.

7

In person, Kilmer looked all business, 100 percent by the book right down to the comma and semicolon, what you'd expect from a guy whose lighthearted moments on the job were as rare as harmonic convergences. He had a thick frame and thick hands like a butcher, again what you'd expect from work that had a lot in common with moving meat from slaughter to a locker. I could tell that he had played. He had scars that he didn't get on the job. If they had been injuries picked up in the workplace, he would have sought other gainful and less painful employment.

"I can give you five minutes," Kilmer said. "Have to see how he's doing. He's tired and he's drugged still ..."

I was going to need more than five minutes to get something that could put us, Mitzi, Martens, and me, in the same neighbourhood as closure and the same area code as justice.

"And the one person who came to visit him died ...," I said.

I wanted to say "his brother" but I wouldn't have taken that suspicion to the bank. It was just based on that one line in the program the Good Professor had shown me, my gut reaction when I saw the photo of Martens in the P.A. paper at the library, and a guess dressed up as intuition. I was almost ready to make the leap but didn't want to spook Kilmer.

I showed Kilmer Whisper's obits in *The Globe and Mail* and *The Southwest Booster* but wished I had a photo of him slumped over the steering wheel to show him, something to shock him and break down his stiff defences against emotional manipulation. He had been a confederate when I first spoke to him, but upon my arrival he seemed to have a host's remorse and waning enthusiasm. He could read people pretty well, and I suppose he could read my need becoming desperation. He didn't know about the threatening phone calls and I tried not to let on that this was more than a mission of mercy, but he knew *something* was up and I wasn't advertising it.

"You know his story?" he asked.

"Just what I read in the paper from the stabbing."

He pointed me into the room. The door was propped open. He could sit in the hall and see Martens and me. Even though my voice carried, I'd be out of the guard's earshot.

"He confessed to the murder of his father," Kilmer said. "He doesn't seem like a murderer, but a lot of murderers don't."

I couldn't stare down Wolf Martens's demons. I had to appeal to his inner angels, dormant, incarcerated in their own way. As far as Kilmer was concerned, I was there as the messenger, the bearer of the worst possible news, the Good Samaritan with the awful task. Of course, he didn't know that my task was a fair bit more complicated than that.

I thought I was ready for it. It was like everything else in a hospital. What you think you're ready for ends up being something that you're not ready for.

8

An IV running into a vein on the heavily taped left hand. Handcuffs unnecessarily binding the right to a hospital bed's railing.

"Who are you?"

Fluid drip-drip-dripping in the bag. A monitor blip-blip-blipping in close rhythm.

"It's about Martin? You're a friend of Martin?"

All worldly possessions sitting one atop the other on the table beside the bed. A ballpoint pen atop a red notebook and below that a Bible.

"How? How did it happen? When? Martin?"

A scaffold holding up a small television, not activated, not watched, beside the hospital bed. Daylight but no sunlight coming in half-opened blinds.

"What car? My old car? He wouldn't do it. I rebuilt that car, bought it for nothing and rebuilt it over a couple of months. I gave him that car when he was just a kid. I drove him out to Herbert after everything happened. Took the plates off it and left it in the Marses' lot. Left a note in it and told him to look after it for me. All these years he promised me that it would be there when I got out. He thought that would make me want to get out. I don't want to. Never did. Less now than ever. My brother wouldn't do it. Never. Something had to have happened. What aren't you telling me?"

The hand tethered by the tube weakly taking *The Southwest Booster* from the visitor. The visitor opening the paper to the life stories of those whose stories are at an end.

"It doesn't make sense. I guess nothing does. He wanted me to get out. He said he'd look after me. I didn't want to get out. He didn't tell anyone about it. He didn't even tell his wife about it. That's what he told me."

Eyes too weak to read more than the headline looking away from it. A failing hand putting the newspaper on top of the red notebook.

"He told me to hang up if she ever picked up the phone when I made the collect calls. I did. He didn't want her to know and I wanted to be left alone. I wouldn't have blamed Martin if he didn't want anything to do with me. He did anyway. He ended up becoming a good man, far better than me. I ruined my own wretched life. And my father's. I failed him and it ended up that I got him killed."

The call for the doctor over the intercom. His name repeated.

"He was the head of the colony in Roslynn. He was very good with anything to do with machinery. He was less good with people, I think. I got baptized. I got baptized earlier than most. Eighteen. Same thing, to prove my father's devotion more than mine, I suppose. He wanted it. And then I got sent off to school in Regina, mechanical engineering. I was going to come out to the colony after I graduated ... *graduated* ... but I knew from my first day in class that I wasn't ready. I wasn't good enough. I had gone from a one-room classroom ... I was the only kid doing high school work, the next oldest was in grade eight, even my little brother was there too ... I had gone from there to university, a big campus, classes with a hundred kids, hundreds of kids. I wasn't ready. *Jung und dumm.* I didn't tell my parents I was failing. I didn't tell my parents I dropped out. That was even before the Christmas exams. I went to work at a gas station, part-time and then full-time. Met Monica there. I worked for cash. For the Marses in Regina. They had a station there they were selling. They had just bought one out in Herbert."

A plastic cup of water half-emptied. A small bottle of orange juice full and untouched.

"I went home for Christmas. I didn't feel it in my heart anymore. If I hadn't been baptized I could have walked away. It's different when you're baptized. The worst sin there is. My mother got sick when I went back to Regina in January. I thought she got sick 'cause of me ... what I'd done. She should have gone to hospital. It would have been routine. But she wouldn't leave the colony. My father didn't want her to, either. He should have known. I never forgave him for that. He wanted to put her health in the hands of God as proof of *his* devotion. Other people on the colony would have been fine with going to the city to see a doctor. But my father wouldn't, and even though my mother knew she needed help she *obeyed* my father."

A breath drawing in not all the way to the chest. A breath leaking out like the tiniest puncture in a soft bicycle tire.

"My mother died. I came back for the funeral. I thought of what would happen to my little brother if he ever got sick. Thought about *sick*, anyway. Didn't count on *hurt*."

A hand shifting an inch inside the straightjacketing thin white sheet. The imprint on the pillow shifting with a head turning.

"He was playing hockey on the pond with other colony boys. All in hand-me-downs. Our father flooded the ice. He put up the boards. It was something that an elder had done for the boys, and when he got too old and couldn't do it anymore our father took it over. Didn't like hockey, just thought it was a way to honour the elder. The boys from the colony couldn't come to town to play in the leagues. Could only play among themselves. The one day, Martin—I mean, it's not even his name but I've had to call him that all these years—Martin got his skate in a rut and fell into the boards. Headfirst. Last thing he remembered. He broke his cheekbone around his eye, had his teeth busted up. I called to talk to him and our father. I drove right out and I took him into the city. My father didn't even want to do that ... said it would heal. They kept him in hospital overnight and did surgery on him the next day. Reconstructed him. And then a couple of days later they checked him out and I took him back to the apartment where I lived with Monica."

A head ducking from the hallway into the room. Two sets of eyes looking upward at the clock on the wall.

"Yeah, I had fallen. Completely fallen, I guess. I knew I couldn't go back to the colony.

"And our father came for Martin. He went by the hospital and they told him that I'd checked Martin out and gave him my address. And when he came he knocked on the door. Martin was on the couch, watching hockey on TV. I was letting him rest, hoping he'd sleep. We don't have TVs on the colony. Never seen a game. Didn't even listen to one on the radio. He was falling asleep. Monica was in the bedroom, having a cigarette. There were bottles around. There was other stuff, yeah. There were drugs. And I answered the door when our father knocked. Monica was expecting some guy that she sold stuff to, but it was our father and he saw everything. He understood it right when he saw it."

A head ducking back out of the room. Wheels of a gurney humming in the hallway.

"He pushed his way in, shouting. Had a temper. He said what would people on the colony think if they saw this. 'Why did God test me like Job?' He knew I was lost just having a television, and he could see the beer bottles and the vodka. And he thought I was corrupting Martin. He grabbed me. He was big like Martin. He pushed me down."

A folded hospital gown waiting for the nurse on the next shift. An empty bedpan hiding under the bed.

"No, Martin was tired and drugged. He couldn't get off the couch. He was half-asleep. But yeah, he saw it. And Monica did. All of the noise got her out of the bedroom. She was half-naked."

Chin falling slowly to chest. Head bobbing once.

"I had fallen, yeah, completely."

Eyes closing slowly and tightening. An invisible hand drawing lines on temples.

"I had met her at the truck stop. She worked there. She drank. She did drugs. Other stuff. But she was my first and only. She had me work for her."

Eyes opening and looking for a window. Eyes finding only a curtain drawn.

"Yes, I love her. Monica. Monica ... Harmon. She took me in when I was alone in the world. She saved me."

A hand reaching for the top sheet. The sheet ruffling faintly when pulled up to a shoulder.

"He shouted at me, the worst possible things. He said he didn't deserve a son like me. He shouted at her. He pushed me when I tried to get between him and Martin. He hit me. He said he would call the police and we'd all face God's wrath. He grabbed me and shook me. I didn't fight back. I'm not a fighter.

That wasn't our way, the way I was raised. That didn't change in me, I guess. But Monica grabbed a knife from the little kitchen and she ran over and stabbed him. In the neck. Just once. He fell. At my feet and I saw all this blood. His eyes were open and looking up like there was no ceiling."

A hand reaching up to a sheet to cover a bare shoulder. A handcuff rattling against a rail.

"I kneeled beside him and prayed. Martin was drugged and on the couch, too weak to get up. Monica grabbed stuff she had in the apartment and got it out. Drugs. She told me to pick up the knife and I did. And then she grabbed Martin on the couch around the neck. She choked him. He saw it. Her stabbing our father. He was frozen. He couldn't speak but she thought he was gonna tell somebody about what he saw and so she choked him. I got her off of him but she had already crushed his throat. She squeezed the voice out of him. She sank her finger deep into his neck. Into his windpipe. He gagged. He coughed. I had to peel her off him. I checked to see if he was breathing. He nodded. She took her stuff and left."

The clock stretching the minutes. The clock not quite grinding to a halt.

"I called the Marses and asked if they would take Martin in for the night. Until my father came by to pick him up. Said that my father was at another colony on business. That I had a conflict with a class I was taking—they thought I was still in school. Couldn't be left alone. They said they would do it. So I drove my Mercedes out to Herbert and dropped Martin off with them. I told them my car had problems, didn't think I could drive it back. I drove it 'round the back of the station and took the plates off it, put a note for Martin in it. The Marses got a trucker, a regular who had driven up from California, to give me a ride into Regina."

Words exchanging outside the open door. The wind faintly howling outside a window sealed fast.

"When I got back I went to a payphone. Our phone had been cut off. I called the Marses, called them collect, and told them what had happened. I asked them to look after Martin 'cause he couldn't go back to the colony. He had no family no more and just awful memories. He needed a new life. I knew the Marses liked kids and had just the one son who'd died in an accident years back. They told me they would do it and they did."

A clipboard hanging on the wall. A corkboard for cards and best wishes holding only tacks.

"When I got there my father was still on the floor in this pool of blood. Monica had come and taken all her clothes out."

The ticking of the clock outpacing the drip-drip-dripping and blip-blip-blipping. The squeak of a nurse's running shoes in the hallway.

"I went to the police and told them that I had done it. They asked what happened to my brother and I told them I killed him too and got rid of the body in a dumpster. They thought I killed him but they never did find a body. They might even still be looking for the body for all I know. There's no harm in talking to you about it, now that Martin's gone. I pleaded guilty to whatever they wanted to charge me with."

A head turning on the pillow. Eyes almost focusing on a hazy presence barely seen but heard and felt.

"No, I don't know where she is or what she's doing. I wish I did. I don't think Martin would have found out where she'd gone. He never said anything about her. I wish I knew. She took me in when I was alone in the world. She was a few years older than me but it didn't make a difference."

One in a white jacket and another in a government-issue uniform walking into the room. Both wordlessly expressing in their own professional capacities that there would be nothing else for today.

"No, I haven't applied for parole but I'm not afraid of anything out there. I'm afraid of the wrath of God. That's all that I'm afraid off. I want to be with Monica. I always did. If she's not there for me, then I don't want to go anywhere."

A head on a pillow turning again to watch a projection on the ceiling. A projection denying its lonely audience any chance to control or influence or dissolve or resist its images and shadows.

"Years later I started getting letters. It was Martin's handwriting but he signed as a cousin of mine. Put a picture of the Mercedes in there too. That's how he got ahold of me and first visited me when he was heading off to play hockey. Martin told me that he didn't remember that night. I hope he wasn't just saying that."

A voice from the door saying, "Okay, *time*." Words leaving no avenue for appeal.

"I've ruined more lives than my own. Leave before I ruin another."

A hand, not a failing one, picking up the newspaper and the red notebook under it but not the Bible. The fold in the newspaper keeping the red notebook out of sight.

9

I walked across the street to the coffee shop to grab Kilmer a large double-double and myself an extra-large black. I ran through my brief time with Wolf Martens. Shame had eaten away his soul and gnawed on the bones left over. He wanted to ponder a wasted life in seclusion. Solitary confinement suited him.

I tried to imagine the Voice of God that Wolf Martens heard. I suspected that the voice was like a basso profundo with a computer-generated echo punctuated by thunder. God's not on my speed-dial nor me on His, but when I do call Him the line is usually busy or goes straight to His voicemail. Whenever He has picked up, He has sounded sort of like James Garner.

I always think I'm prepared for what I'll see in a hospital but I never am. The cuffs on the right hand wouldn't have been tight if they had been looped around his biceps. His wrist was no thicker than a chicken wing. MONICA and a heart with black ink dripping out of it were unevenly tattooed below the knuckles of his right hand.

Martens's story seemed a quarter inch from flush. A couple of washers were left over after assembly. I didn't completely trust his version of events leading up to the father's murder, but the biggest pieces seemed to be in place. If true, he wasn't a perp so much as a collateral victim. If just mostly true, most likely the case, he was an accessory. He had kept the bloodhounds off the little brother's trail all those years at a price, one he paid when the judge piled it on in sentencing. I didn't believe that he had been the one who'd reduced his brother's voice to a whisper. That he had choked him. If Martens had done the deed, Whisper wouldn't have driven hours out of his way to pay him visits and try to talk him into applying for parole.

I tried to game out Martens's story with what came years after. It hadn't been just a crushed larynx that had rendered Whisper mute, but also a strain of post-traumatic stress disorder. An identity concealed all those years had calcified into non-being. His carving by Iron John had evoked the anger of his father and broke the seal on Whisper's emotional tinderbox. His mother's death and his father's murder, both wrapped up in perversions of devotion, had made him keep his distance from religion. And even still, no matter how haunted he was, he had held on to the values of selflessness and generosity from the colony.

I was out of the cold and in the lineup for coffee when I got around to the notebook I had lifted from Martens's room. It was a red hardcover appointment book with a binding elastic that kept the pages crease-free. He had printed his name but not an address on the front, a match for the left-handed scrawl on the note in the Mercedes owner's manual. I flipped the first leaf and came to a calendar spread across two pages. Martens had circled a few days with notations. The rest of the book dedicated a page to each day and every passing hour in the business year. He used it as a diary and a chapbook, collating his random thoughts, a few passages in broken German, a language that had been taught in the colony's one-room school and used by his father in belittling him. He also drew in it in pencil and ballpoint pen. Fields. Barns. Humble homes. The horizon. The sun. He had a comfort level with or fond recollection of inanimate things more than people. Only two people were drawn in the pages. One was Whisper, probably at age nine or ten, on skates and in a wool hat on what looked like a frozen slough. The detail made me think it had been drawn from an old photograph. The other was a young woman I didn't recognize and seemed to have been drawn from memory.

When I flipped through to the back cover a folded piece of paper fell out. It was a photostat of an entry in a program. A quote was underlined: *"Everything I learned about the game and everything else I learned from my brother."*

IO

"What's the prognosis?"

"He goes back this week," Kilmer said. "Tomorrow, maybe the day after. It's all OT, a guard here twenty-four hours. We're not budgeted to do it a week at a time. He's weak but he's out of danger."

When you're millions of dollars of beef under contract to the club and have a boil to lance, you get the undivided attention of a battery of medical experts. When you're in for murder and your vital organs have been shish-kebabed, you're on a conveyor belt set on high.

"I gotta ask," I said. "Would he get compassionate leave for a family funeral?"

"Depends how close the relative is," Kilmer said, making it sound like a long shot.

"What if it was his brother?"

"The one whose body never turned up? That he confessed to murdering?"

I nodded in the affirmative.

"And what do you have to back that up? I mean, you don't have to prove it to me but you'll have to prove it to somebody who can get approval on this."

I thought about it. I ruled out DNA testing. That would take weeks—too late. The traditional standby would be more time-effective. "If they were looking at a missing persons or search for human remains they'd have his dental records on file," I said. "He suffered a fractured cheekbone and had surgery to repair it right before he went missing. Something would show up there, maybe."

Key word: *maybe*.

Kilmer tried for a second to keep an open mind about it, no small feat for a guy who slams cell doors shut for a living. Kilmer said he didn't know, even if all this were demonstrably and convincingly true.

"Has he ever talked about what happened before?" I asked.

"Not a word. I mean, I've heard other stuff."

"Stuff" included the name tattooed on Martens's right hand. I asked Kilmer if he knew Any Stuff at All about a woman named Harmon. The guard had dropped his guard before but raised it again, clearly. He wasn't going to get into specifics. It was final, like he had turned the key in the lock.

Kilmer ducked his head back in the door to Martens's room just to make sure that he was still breathing. It wasn't visible, just audible. Kilmer didn't look at him with resentment or even bafflement. He didn't quite have all the pity beat out of him as he crossed off days to his retirement. One of the last ounces he reserved for Martens.

I gave Kilmer my business card. I thanked him and he asked if I was driving back tonight. I told him I was going to the junior game first. He said he was too and that his son was on the team. I told him that I'd watch for his kid. He told me not to bother.

"My son's the backup goaltender," he said.

II

I sat in a booth at Boston Pizza. A copy of the local rag had been left there. The sports section was given over to a preview of tonight's game. The bump in unemployment claims in town was the big news on the front page. Reading about it only brought home what I could see out the window from my seat: a bunch of shabby guys stepping reluctantly out of a mission into the cold for a day of loitering at the time when the fortunate were rolling in for shifts in the office, the store, the warehouse, the factory, and, yeah, the penitentiary.

I was going to have a four-hour drive back to Regina after the game. My third instinct was to find out exactly what happened to Martin Mars. The quest for truth was running a few lengths behind my first instincts, staying alive and staying employed. Good news on No. 1: It had been a day since I'd last had my life threatened. No news on No. 1A: That passed for good news.

I opened the red notebook again. The first entry was printed more neatly than the declaration of love tattooed on his right hand.

And all that believed were together, and had all things in common.

I flipped ahead.

The verse had a Biblical rhythm to it, but as a Sunday-school no-show I didn't recognize it. Fooling around with Google a few days later I found out it was from Acts, which I couldn't have told you is the fifth book of the New Testament. I found out later that it was a verse that was a cornerstone for the Hutterites. The founder of the Hutterites, a guy named Hutter, gathered his worshippers around a blanket and had them toss in everything they owned, their devotion being defined by their willingness to give up personal property for the communal good. The story goes that Hutter and his people were peace-loving peasants who resisted war and war taxes. Authorities meted out justice as they used to see fit in Moravia and burned him at the stake. A bunch of those who succeeded him were similarly incinerated. The Hutterites didn't wait for the Moravians to become infected with religious tolerance or run out of matches. The worshippers beat a retreat across the pond, just like the Mennonites and the Amish. It would take a lot to get me to move to rural Saskatchewan but I suppose religious persecution would do the trick.

Only when I found out about the story of Hutter's founding of the sect did the first line in Martens's own words start to make sense.

> *I have nothing to put on my blanket, no goods that are my own but this notebook and Bible.*

All that line had me thinking about was the blanket that hung on the wall in Whisper's living room. Mitzi said she couldn't understand his attachment to it. It had been a reminder of who he had been, where he had grown up, and how he had wanted to live his life.

I didn't have to dive deep into the book to figure out that the self-prosecution of Wolf Martens aspired to match the persecution of the Hutterites centuries back.

Confession

It's because of my failures in faith that I failed in school when I was sent off. It's because of my failures in faith and in school that I couldn't go back. I brought shame on our family. I am ashamed that I still hate my father. That he put being a leader in the colony ahead of caring for my mother. I do hate him for that, still. I was guilty and will be forever guilty in my heart for hating him. I did not murder him but I did get him murdered. And when I go down into my heart I am ashamed that I do not mourn him as I should. Monica was the angel who avenged when I was too weak to do it myself. She cut through the knot that tied me to my faith and the colony. And when she did that she pulled down all the bridges behind me. I cared for my brother enough that I didn't want to send him back across bridges that were no longer there ...

The first forty pages of the notebook were thick with confessions that were in a left-hander's backslant but printed neatly and legible. Though the entries were random and almost incoherent, elements of the story were consistent with his account in the hospital ward. His father had painted his ambitions on his older son when he wasn't a suitable canvas. When he was in the process of falling out of school, he began to fall in with the wrong people. Having failed and landed in the margins, he looked for approval and acceptance elsewhere, standard attraction and indoctrination for the criminal enterprise. And Monica Harmon was, from his account, even idolized, an enterprising criminal. He had landed a monster who impressed him as an angel, which is what only the most monstrous of monsters are able to pull off.

I was deep in meditation of the tumults, cosmic and domestic, when the waitress came over to my table to take my order.

While waiting for a hamburger, I sent a text to Sandy. She would have been seeing patients. *It looks like I'll be back Fri pm @ earliest.* Profuse apologies and backpedalling followed. I didn't expect her to be happy that I was another couple of days on the road. I knew she wouldn't be happy that I had to settle for a text, but I wasn't up for another sparring session and being reminded, fairly I guess, what a shit I was.

I had a call to make after I searched for a number. From the automated switchboard I selected the staff directory and waited to hear the name that had stuck in my memory. "I wonder if you could help me," I said. "I was in your archive when you opened this morning. I was looking at editions of the Prince Albert paper from a month or so back."

"I think I remember you."

I pictured her twirling her hair around her finger and biting her lip.

"I'm wondering if there's any database or listing of newspaper stories in Saskatchewan dating back to the early '70s," I said.

"That point in time is too early for any online newspaper search engine, certainly with the provincial papers," she said. "The Regina and Saskatoon papers are in the National Newspaper Directory listings. Do you know what year you're looking for?"

"Around '74. Maybe '75. I'm looking for stories about a double murder, probably stories that came out after the trial."

"That would have been a big story," she said. "I have a friend who works in the library at the paper here in town. I'll see what she can pull for you."

I tried to imagine how I could repay this smouldering volcano and all I could come up with was offering my body for human sacrifice.

Mitzi was the next order of business. I stuck to my need-to-know approach. I felt faint pressure from the right-to-know angel on my shoulder but looked the other way while I made my call.

"I'm here in P.A. looking into whatever the business deal was that Martin was planning to invest in," I said. "It doesn't appear to have been anything out of the ordinary."

I looked heavenward out of fear of incoming lightning.

"The funeral is set for Friday," she said. "Just a small service at the funeral home. Early in the morning. Just a few people will come."

"Are you okay?"

She said she was. I doubted that but let it go. We said our goodbyes.

My BlackBerry vibrated just when my plate was dropped in front of me. Harry Friesen was calling me back.

"You say there's nothing in the books any different?"

"Business was very steady. Expenses constant. No unusual one-time expenses."

"Anything?" It's through persistence that coal becomes a diamond. Not this time, apparently.

"That's been the nature of Martin's business. All locations show steady revenue. Small expenses in maintenance but really nothing significant. Some repairs were incurred with the robbery. Some vandalism, a broken window."

"Were there any changes in the payroll?"

"It's a high-turnover business," he said. "Lots of minimum-wage or slightly better positions, part-time workers, kids mostly. I really don't see any red flags there."

"Any disgruntled employees or former employees who might have gone postal?"

The accountant assured me that the employees of the Mars company were by and large thoroughly gruntled.

"I can assure you Mr. Mars made sure his long-term people were well compensated and had benefits other similar companies didn't offer," he said. "He was very fair by nature."

That would be one explanation for his hockey career being somewhat less than satisfying, if not for him then for those people who paid him to play. In the game, fair play is soft play.

Still, I gave it one last shot. "Check the rolls. Any names not on the last pay run that had been on the sheet the month previous?"

"Three that I can see that are outside the part-time minimum-wage student bunch," he said. "Stanley Smith. Herb Lacker. Vivian King."

Friesen said all three names sounded familiar to him. He also said that, based on their pay scale, he figured that Smith and Lacker were mechanics in the company's top scale, and he presumed King was the manager and bookkeeper of the auto-parts dealership and farm-machinery-repair operation. "Three semi-senior folks." I asked him to email me their addresses and personal info on file and any contacts.

When I pushed away my empty plate the waitress gave me a dirty look. Although the air in the restaurant was polluted by strains of Lady Antebellum, she thought that my voice had been a little too loud when I was making my calls and I had fouled the scenery by having written on paper placemats and napkins.

Four o'clock, business hours were winding down. I had calls to make and I could do it from the limited comfort of the PT Cruiser's front seat. I had to ring up the folks who knew the stories of the three senior employees who had been dropped from the payrolls over the two months before Whisper took his early and involuntary retirement. Stanley Smith and Herb Lacker were straightforward. Their managers said they had been model employees and good guys. As Harry Friesen had presumed, they had been mechanics for Mars Co.

"Stan turned sixty," the station manager in Estevan said. "He salted away some pretty good money over the years and he did a bit of independent work on the side. We threw a hell of a going-away party for him at the Legion. His brother has a condo in Florida. He's been down there golfing ever since."

Scratch Smith.

"Lemme tell you, we'll miss ol' Herb," the station manager in Kindersley said. "He's helping out his older brother with the

family farm. I guess the brother took ill and all the kids have run
off to college and the big city."

Scratch Lacker.

I called Mars Co.'s head office in Swift Current and tried
Vivian King from the business directory. I thought that her
phone line might not have been disconnected, but when I
punched K-I-N-G into the directory it bounced back: "No
matches were found." I pushed the zero for the receptionist and
gave her a bullshit story about King calling me up with regard to
a line of credit to finance an extension, a sunroom. "I'm afraid
I can't help you, sir," the secretary said. "I've never heard of, it's
a Ms. King, is that right? Are you sure it's Mars Gas that she
worked for?" I asked her to patch me through to her superior.
The same drill. No Vivians. No Kings.

From what Friesen told me, Vivian had drawn the third-
highest wage in the office and no one there had any idea who
she was.

I called the accountant back and he assured me that King's
placement on the head office's roll was no clerical error. I asked
him to pull up any relevant records of her employment. He put
me on hold. My luck: the Starland Vocal Band's "Afternoon
Delight." He came back on the line and put me out of my misery.
"I have her papers and there's no reason given for her termination," he said. "The space is blank. That's unusual, at least for the
way Martin kept records. And I can see from the Save function
that it was actually Martin who filed the termination and not
someone else from the office. Again, unusual. Roth was cc'd on
the file."

After I was through with Friesen I called up Roth. The
lawyer said that any firings of senior people went through his
office and he did recall the King file. "I thought the blank space
was unusual," Roth said. "This was a termination. I remember

asking Martin about it, y'know, possible issues with wrongful dismissal and the like. We would need to cite cause, I told him, but he said that court was the last place Ms. King wanted to go."

I didn't want to bounce the name off Mitzi. I didn't want to plant any seed about infidelity if there hadn't been any or even if there had, even if Whisper was paying for some on the side.

One last call. It went through to voicemail.

"Ms. King, yes, my name is Val Avery ..."

Whenever I had used aliases in my old job in investigations I had picked out names of obscure character actors. It distracted me from this line of work's wretchedness.

"I was just poring over the books here in our accounts office and it seems through an oversight ... and I apologize for this ..."

I adopted the Canadian default posture of apologizing for something without any cause.

"... but we have failed to compensate you for vacation time owing. There are just a couple of forms that I need you to sign. I can come around and give them to you, witness it, and file for prompt payment. I also wanted to clear up any questions you might have with regard to your benefits coverage going forward. I want you to be assured that it did not end with your departure from Mars Co. ..."

I went on to other small fictions that would put money in her pocket. I gave her my cell number. I opened the PDF Friesen had sent me and made a note of the address on file.

It was just under two hours before game time. I drove over to the arena early.

13 _____

"That's the kid I'm watching. I love his first step. He gets from zero to sixty in two strides, even with the puck. Never cheats. Pays the price."

I was in a corner seat and Kilmer was beside me. His thighs were so wide that he had to sit with his knees together so they didn't spill out over the side of his seat, standard stuff that applies to any pro or a lot who only got as close as he did. He had played the game and he saw what I did. Only after the first period did he tell me that it was his sixteen-year-old's first season of junior, that his son had been a sixth-round draft choice, that he was going to get more games next year. Kilmer didn't bother telling me that Junior was on the small side. The program listed him at five-eleven and the program lied. The kid sat on the bench, a baseball cap on his head, and opened and closed the gate.

I asked the guard about his own playing days. He was sheepish. He confessed to a crime of his own imagining.

"Never got a sniff with the pros," he said. "In four years of junior my team made the playoffs two times and we never won a round. In my last year, we were out of the playoffs by Groundhog Day and I knew I'd never play another game that meant anything. And I kept trying but it was gone. I tried to tell myself to sell out and play with an edge. *Be an example for the younger players who are gonna be back next year and might go somewhere.* Didn't work. I got in more fights the last five weeks in junior than I had been in the three and a half years before. I got in fights at practice. I lived wild ... off the rails completely."

A goal was scored. The cheers drowned out whatever he was reminded of.

I told him that I was the same way when my career in the league wound down. He sighed and nodded.

I left the game with a couple of minutes to go in the third period. I started up my car and waited for the seat warmer to kick in. I sent a text to Chief to let him know where I was. I passed along the relevant info, that the kid had a goal, two assists, and a couple of posts thrown in for good measure. *Back in Reg in am.*

14 _____

I put my key in the ignition. Before I pulled the car out of park and before my seat ceased to feel like a block of ice, I opened up my laptop. I presumed that part of the waitress's indignation at the Boston Pizza tracked back to the fact that I had availed myself of a plug beside the booth for recharging my MacBook. I opted for a little uneasy listening for the road trip: the Good Professor's interview with Whisper.

GP: This is hard for me to ask, but how did you hurt your throat?

WHISPER: Took a stick there. I was, I dunno, ten, twelve, thirteen. It was a long time ago. It's better now than it was. There was a whole year that I couldn't talk at all. Coulda been worse. I know I thought it was going to be the end of me.

GP: What was it like growing up in Herbert?

WHISPER: Oh, I dunno. Really, I don't remember too much of being a kid. I was like everybody else. Played hockey there. I got a late start. Once I played I played a lot, though. We played outside some. Seems like we could play outside back then a lot more than you can now. My folks were good about it. My father never played. He worked a lot and he was older, but he drove me to games. He ...

It was a story but not his, a story told as infrequently as possible rather than lived out. The Canadian Idyll was his cover story for a Canadian Gothic.

I rolled down the highway, no one behind me, crossing paths every five minutes with an eighteen-wheeler going the other way. The only radio station I could get clearly was one of those conspiracy and mystery phone-in shows. Callers fearful of terrorist attacks on the water supply and power grid asked the host if a month's worth of supplies in their underground bunkers would see them through to the other side of the end of the world.

15

My mind raced. Every time I passed a tractor-trailer I glanced in the cab and imagined the driver had smoked Monica Harmon's weed and popped her pills and snorted her lines and bought her hot wares and screwed her working girls and maybe even her. Maybe he partied with her. Maybe he mourned her. Her chosen professions and vices hardly promoted longevity.

I passed stations and checked the time, 11 P.M. I looked for the right place to pull over. I was looking for a place with a fleet of eighteen-wheelers parked in neat rows in the adjoining lot. I was thinking of the old saw about truckers knowing the best places to grab grub on the road. I doubt any of them kept a Michelin Guide in the glove compartment. The low-fuel warning beeped just when I saw the lights of the biggest truck stop between Saskatoon and Regina.

I sat in a booth in the restaurant. The sign above the preferred counter space let interlopers like me know that it was reserved for truckers on runs. Three seats in a row were occupied by a cumulative nine hundred pounds and plumber cracks that could have passed for parallel and perpendicular tectonic plates.

An old broad chewed gum and willed up the strength to take my order. Her script monogram said her name was Phyllis. I wanted a burger but I didn't need fries and knew not to ask for salad. Before I filed my requests, though, I peeled off two twenties, slid them across the table so that they'd be within her easy reach, and asked her if she could help me. A pair of double sawbucks could buy a lot of ice for her feet.

"Monica Harmon told me this was a good place. You know her?" I kept my nose in the menu.

"I haven't heard that name in years."

"When was the last time you heard it?"

"Like I said, years."

Phyllis was in no rush to fill me in. She eyeballed me. She was trying to piece it together: Who was asking? Cop? Mountie? Bad. Not a fit though. Customer? Supplier? Plausible. Green light.

"She had things going on at stops along the highway. The company had the gas. She had the grass and ass. Then she branched out into more dangerous stuff. She made a lot of money. If these boys ..."

She looked over at the express counter where the three hawgs were perched, piles of near-humanity who looked like they would have never had boyhoods.

"... had their way, they'd name this highway after her. They'd do anything for her."

What she said made me wonder about Wolf Martens's stabbing. Monica Harmon would have had friends in ye olde caboose. So would Butch and Sundance. Kilmer didn't know who wielded the blade. It wouldn't have been a biker. My Uncle Henry, Sarge's little brother, had worked for a couple of years undercover, getting inside the Para-Dice Riders when they were in a gang war with the Satan's Choice. Henry was lucky to get out alive but, even after he cut his hair, shaved his beard, and dialed back his menace, he never seemed quite right after that. What he always said was that a biker or anyone working for one had "a useless and dangerous pride in his work." A stabbing on behalf of a gang inside would have closed the deal with fifty perforations, probably more, delivered with certainty, sadism, and symbolism. The perp wouldn't have been a professional. Otherwise, Wolf Martens would have been on a slab. It could have been an inmate intimidated by Harmon's friends, some unlucky guy who drew the short straw and was told to do unto Wolf Martens lest the boys did unto him. Still, the timing seemed to make no sense. It would have been a fit if he had been stabbed his first month inside, when there might have been a misplaced fear that he'd trade info with the law in turn for years knocked off his sentence. It wasn't a fit, not decades later, not when a lot of those who had buried bodies were buried beside them. The Best Before Date on Wolf Martens's inside information had expired three decades ago.

This tough old broad took a hard look at me. She didn't know what I was thinking, but she knew I was thinking.

"She *had* things going ..."

She ratcheted up the surliness. She didn't want the detail lost.

"She doesn't anymore. Not that I know. She got out of business."

"Why?"

She held off the urge to call me Sonny. She did a quick survey of the room. She didn't turn around. She relied on the radar and heat-sensory system that had developed over the thousands of miles she had padded behind the counter and between the kitchen and the tables. "You don't have enough twenties to get that out of me. I don't know."

A dead end, at least beyond the fact that Monica Harmon wasn't an inmate's chimera. I ordered my burger, relish, and a coffee. I had topped up the tank but I still felt like I was running on empty and could have nodded off in the front seat if not for fear that I'd end up as dead as Whisper, done in by the cold. I put it in drive and started toward the ramp. I checked the rear-view and saw Phyllis standing outside the front door of l'Auberge Diesel. On her smoke break and on her cell.

I

THURSDAY

It was morning but dawn hadn't cracked. The road sign said REGINA 25 KM. My cell vibrated over in the passenger seat. I was going to let it go to voicemail but then I saw the call display: HERBERT HERALD. Scoop was up early to deliver something other than papers.

"This is Brad Shade."

"Brad, this is Kenneth Malling from the *Herbert Herald*. The reporter you spoke to ...." He was showing his full mastery of the obvious.

I wanted him to cut to the chase. This was going to show up on my phone bill at two dollars a minute. "You turn up anything more on the Marses?"

"I was able to contact a couple of guys who went to school with your friend before he went off to play junior hockey," he said.

Maybe there was a future for Scoop after all and he might be

able to write for and dine on a better quality of newspaper. Or
not.

"They said he really kept to himself. Total loner."

"Nothing about a brother?"

"No."

"Church?"

"Marses didn't go."

I took a flyer. "Did anyone mention Monica Harmon?" I
asked him. "Evidently, Martin Mars had a brother and Miss
Harmon was his girlfriend."

It took him a breath, a hem and a haw for it to kick in. "There's
someone here who worked as a mechanic for a couple of years for
the Marses quite some time ago, retired now," Scoop said. "He
said the Marses decided to move out to Herbert because there
was some real trouble with drugs and hookers at their place just
outside of Regina. And he mentioned the Harmon woman by
name. He said she was 'a bad apple' and that she went away to
prison on drug charges and other things a few years later."

I thought Scoop was going to waste my time. I had misjudged
him.

"Yeah, I talked to a lawyer in town ..."

Okay, knock me over with a feather. I figured there wasn't
even a justice of the peace.

"... He's retired now but his brother is a big criminal lawyer in
Regina. He said she pleaded down from some heavier sentences."

"And now?"

"She was released a few years back. She hasn't reoffended, I
guess. That's what the lawyer here says. He said he doesn't know
where she is. He also said, though, that she would ... let me check
my notes ... 'probably be well-advised to keep a low profile.'"

"Kid, you did a great job. I appreciate it."

"Let me know if there's anything else I can do for you."

I hit End and then the BlackBerry hummed again. I didn't turn my head to look at the call display. I just figured it was Scoop with a trivial footnote that he had forgotten to pass along. It wasn't.

"Shadow, I hope I'm not getting you up. I figured you'd be sleeping in after your long trip and I'd leave a message. I'm going to be in transit all day back from Europe."

It was Duke Avildsen. I didn't mind two bucks a minute with him. Duke was in his seventies and claimed with justified pride that he had been collecting cheques from the league for more than half a century. He had been a player and then a coach, although just for a while. He had been a scout with a bunch of organizations including L.A., where he'd somehow survived five different owners and eight GMs. If they dropped a nuclear bomb on an arena, the only thing left standing would be Duke Avildsen. A hundred square miles would be DayGlo with radiation, but Duke would have a lineup in his hand and he'd be circling numbers, writing notes in the margins. He always said that his goal in life was to make a case to draft a guy in the seventh round and then introduce him at the Hall of Fame induction. He had already done it once. "Just gotta do it again to show it wasn't a fluke," he said.

Duke had just checked his bags at the Helsinki airport. I had given him the plum assignment of taking in the Five Nations tournament in Tampere. I owed him at least one. Duke's grandson was playing for the American team at the tournament. The Littlest Duke was six foot four and as Canadian as maple syrup, but he had been born when Duke Jr. was playing for Oklahoma City. The older Avildsens came to the conclusion that exploiting an opportunity to play in the U.S. program in Ann Arbor was a good way to go. Duke is a proud family guy but he'll always be a scout first. When I asked him how his grandson

was playing he gave me a one-word scouting report: "Horseshit."
He also offered that he thought Duke III, at least on the ice,
took after his mother.

"I'm still out West."

"What the hell. Flights cancelled or something?"

"Guy I used to play with in L.A., Martin Mars, died. Cashed
himself out. I'm trying to help with the arrangements," I said,
looking at a faint constellation of lights on the horizon.

"Looking out for your old teammate," said Duke, whose
teammates, most of them anyway, were either involuntarily out
of the game or mortally out of commission. "That's lost these
days. So many guys switching teams, getting traded, chasing
bigger contracts. Ships passing in the night, you know. All about
a buck. Back in my day you played years together, even decades.
There were good teammates and bad ones, sure, but the best
ones were like brothers. That's how it was in Montreal. Do you
remember Doucette?"

"Little before my time but I know the name," I said. So did
any half-assed student of the game. You have to be up on your
Hall of Famers.

"I don't know if you know the story, but his game went south
maybe in his second or third season with us," Duke said. "We all
knew something was wrong. He wasn't hurt or drinking. So we
kept an ear to the ground, everybody in the room. We realized
that his wife was fooling around on him. What's more, we found
out that his wife was fooling around on him with a boxer. Do
you remember Angelo Angelini?"

"No, Duke, I'm too young and boxing's not my game."

"This pug, a heavyweight who knocked out Top Ten
contenders with a big left hook and knocked out broads with his
looks. 'Teen Angel,' they called him. 'Matinee Idol.' Guy would
sing the anthem before the fight. So anyway, we went and found

out where this Gino lived. It was only a couple of blocks from the Deuce and his missus. And so there was five of us that laid in wait for him. And we kicked the shit out of him. You know Cal Decker ..."

A great player and an awful drunk who wasted more talent than anybody back in the day and maybe ever. Yeah, I told Duke, I knew of him.

"Well, Cal Decker was a stand-up guy. He smoked this pug. The guy was on the ground, blood pouring out of him at about three or four different points, like marinara sauce spilling out of a five-gallon pot. Cal told him, 'If anything ever happens between you and Doucette's wife, the first thing I'm gonna do is go to the mother of your boys and you'll be sparring with a divorce lawyer and for sure that's out of your weight class.' And Cal said, 'The second thing I'm gonna do is come after you myself and finish what I started.' Shit, we mostly just watched Cal and peeled him off the dago at the end or he might of killed him. Cal said, 'This guy probably never won a real fight in his life.' Cal was never a fighter, at least didn't go looking for it. If it came down to it, though, for a teammate, especially a good guy like Deuce, Cal would have killed anything but his thirst."

Duke signed off right after that. I thought of that old war story, one of several hundred in the series, as I started to pass the big-box retail stores in Regina's farthest-flung suburbs. Yeah, I could see Cal Decker going to bat for a young teammate, especially when the kid had a ton of talent. But that wasn't what was in play this time. I was wading in long after hanging them up, twenty years after the fact, going the extra mile for a guy who sat in the next stall, a guy who had been my teammate for one season, a guy I wouldn't have claimed to know at all. Whisper could have used me or anyone else in the room to stand up for him when Iron John Harris was throwing him under the bus. I didn't because I didn't want to risk my own job. Going back to Swift Current, I was doing what I thought was the right thing for Whisper, but it was all twenty years too late to matter and for him to ever know. I had my reasons, I guess.

2

I met up with Chief for coffee in Regina. I felt awful. My body still ached from all the hours I had spent behind the wheel, my back was seizing up, and Arthur was letting me know he wasn't happy either about the hours of confinement. The welt on the back of my head throbbed. Things weren't going to get much better after I returned the PT Cruiser. We'd be taking the Bug loaner back out to Swift Current. Walt had called Chief to let him know his Jeep was ready.

I brought the Big Man up to speed. He took his eyes off the road and almost put us in the ditch when I told him about Martens Sr.'s murder, Whisper's foggy eye-witnessing the crime, and the Divine Miss Harmon's attempt to quiet or kill him by strangulation.

"Thing like that would mess with a guy his whole life. You still don't think it was suicide, do you?"

"I don't. He kept his demons locked away for years. It looked like that, anyway. It wasn't that he was haunted. He was chased."

It seemed like deaths were out there in every direction and

none was your run-of-the-mill departure from the mortal coil. I couldn't imagine that, near the end of this tragic arc, there'd be something so plain as a broken guy just cashing in his chips.

My BlackBerry pinged. The call display announced prompt delivery: REG PUB LIB.

I checked the time. It was 8 A.M. She said that she had something to show me. I told her that I had to drive out for the funeral and asked if there was any way that I could come in early. She told me to come to the employees' entrance in the back of the building.

I had one call to make in advance. Thankfully, in another time zone to the east, the business day had already begun for government offices.

3

"Martens, *e-n-s*, just the way it sounds, he's an inmate at the penitentiary in Prince Albert," I said. I gave the woman on the other end of the line Martens's relevant numbers that had been provided for me by Kilmer in P.A., namely date of birth and inmate number.

"This is a family member who has died?"

"Yes, a brother," I said. "A younger brother. The only surviving member of the immediate family."

My backup for that would half-fill an administrative eye-dropper. I figured I might as well pretend to be holding a hose.

"And you are ..."

It was a drill that the woman from Correctional Service of Canada had been through a thousand times.

"My name is Brad Shade. I'm a family friend acting on behalf of the widow of the deceased. I have known the deceased for more than twenty years. We worked together."

I gave it a properly grave reading. That the widow of the

deceased did not know of the existence of her husband's brother was a detail that wasn't going to speed things along. Neither was the fact that I was taking a small liberty with my claim of long-standing friendship, seeing as I had shared a hotel room with him two or three nights a week one winter and hadn't spoken to him in more than twenty years. And of course I didn't volunteer that the say-so of Wolf Martens was the only spongy corroboration of the brotherly bond. I didn't even like to admit it to myself.

"Temporary leaves are difficult but we can expedite them. Can you have the death certificate faxed to us?" she asked.

I told her that I could and took down the number that I'd pass along to Bob Roth, who had all the paperwork.

She asked if I could prove the relationship of the deceased to the inmate. I told her it would be tough when it was in fact impossible.

She One Moment Pleased me and I held in a musicless void. I sat there wondering why at least a few bucks from the thousands I sent to Ottawa every year couldn't be dedicated to some Muzak to be piped in for callers while on hold. Beats Starland Vocal Band, I guess.

After a couple of minutes and four bucks in roaming charges, the woman from CSC came back on the line.

"Thank you for holding. Yes, according to our records, there is a TL form filed for the funeral ... tomorrow in Swift Current. Transportation and security for a funeral. The filing was made and approved yesterday."

I'd had a good feeling about Kilmer but even so had under-rated him, I thought. I hadn't given him a sob story or a hard sell, but he'd have to be a stand-up guy to file the paperwork for Wolf Martens's leave. And after I thanked the woman on the line, I realized that someone with authority could probably move the request for a leave faster than the guy on the street.

4

Alexis Stewart of the Periodicals Research Department had the bound hard copies of the papers out. Six months of papers were in each volume, wrapped with heavy broadsheet-size covers. She strained to carry a year and a half of all the Saskatchewan news fit to print over to a long oak table near her desk and I saw the muscles in her upper arm pop. She had flagged coverage of the murder and the brief court case with yellow sticky notes. She kept her voice to a hush, although I hadn't passed anyone on my way in and no one else was in the line of sight. I wondered if it was just a matter of adaptation to her environment.

"I don't remember the case. Too young. Before I was born. I mentioned it to the supervisor and she said it was all over the news. I was able to get the dates from the Canadian News Index."

The index used to compile a year's worth of the big stories from papers across the country before the internet made it redundant. She gave me the full history of the reference series. She was just happy to talk to someone. She made eye contact.

"There might be some that I missed. I'll keep on it if you want ..."

Oh yeah, I wanted her on it.

"... but I thought you'd want to see something as soon as I came up with it."

The last chapter played out on the front page of *The Leader-Post*. The courtroom was "packed" for the sentencing and Wolf Martens "remained impassive" while Hizzoner told him that he was going away for life. The story noted that violent crime was almost unheard of in the Hutterite community and that these murders were believed to be unprecedented. The story noted that only one elder represented the Hutterite colony in the courtroom. There was no comment from the Hutterite elder. There also wasn't a line about the elder declining comment. It's funny. Anywhere else the case would have been sensationalized. The paper would deliver readers not just the truth but a soap opera. Not in Regina, though. Not in the '70s. Those reporting the story seemed embarrassed by it and dug only an inch deep for fear of causing their readers to push the paper away, a judgment that nothing good would come from playing out the tragedy in greater detail and that what was past was best left in the past.

The day after the sentencing, *The Leader-Post* ran this story that spilled over from the front page to a full halfway through the front section:

> Wolf Martens was eighteen and recently baptized when he left the colony to take an electrical engineering course. Though his and other Hutterite colonies keep what they believe is a safe distance from the world beyond their fences, they are by no means as isolated as the Amish. It's common for young men to go to towns and cities for extended periods for schooling so that they can return with skills that will benefit their colonies. The society is traditional,

but there are engagements with the outside world. Wolf Martens's went terribly wrong.

Not long after Martens left the colony for Regina last year he struggled with his schooling. "He was a below-average student," an instructor at the community college said. "It was clear that he lacked the background in math and sciences to make a real go of it. I think he understood his predicament better than any of us did. And I know he was distraught."

Said one classmate: "Martens didn't connect with me or anyone else in the course even when we tried to reach out to him. We knew he was failing. It's a tough course but it's easier when you have friends you can work with."

The breaking point, it seems, was the death of his mother, Helga Martens. No death notice appeared in the local paper and members of the colony declined to comment, but one local health official, speaking on background, said that Martens had a bleeding ulcer that could have been treated with the proper medical attention. "When they finally called for an ambulance she had already lost a lot of blood," the official said. "She had been complaining of intense pain for several weeks but refused to go to the city for treatment or even have a doctor come out to the colony."

According to police documents, weeks after Helga Martens's death an elder had driven her younger son, Hugo, into the city and left him to stay with his older brother, Wolf, overnight. Hugo, then age nine, needed surgery and wouldn't be fit to travel for 24 to 48 hours following the procedure. Members of the colony have said that the Martens were concerned with Hugo's staying overnight away from the colony for the first time. Wolf Martens assured them that he would take care of his little brother and drive him out to the colony when he was fully recovered.

Though members of the colony have declined to talk to the media about Wolf Martens, it appears that he never returned after *his mother's death. If he had any contact with his father it would have been by phone or letter.*

According to one police official with knowledge of the investigation, Wolf Martens became so distraught after his mother's death that he decided to disavow the Hutterites. He also dropped out of school and started drinking. "He took a series of minimum-wage jobs but never stayed more than a couple of weeks at any of them," the police official said. "He became involved in illicit and illegal activity."

For a few days after his surgery, it seems that Hugo Martens stayed with his brother and they remained out of touch with their father. At present the whereabouts of Hugo Martens's body remains unknown.

Technically true. The RCMP wasn't reopening the cold case, but I was trying to find out what happened to Hugo Martens. At least what happened to him besides becoming Martin Mars.

I was reluctant to take up any more of the librarian's time. Then again, that she had already volunteered so much of it made me think that she wouldn't be completely opposed to volunteering just a few minutes more.

"Is there any way that you can search the online newspaper database for any reference to Monica Harmon and a term like *drug* or *court* or *sentence* for me? I promise I won't ask for anything more. I'd appreciate it."

She had no idea why I was asking for all this. Though she was locked away in a library, walls of books and a big oak door separating her from the real world outside, she seemed to sense that these weren't casual searches I was asking for and not morbid curiosities either. She checked the spelling with me and keyed it into the database.

Twenty-five hits in *The Regina Leader-Post*. About the same in *The Saskatoon Star-Phoenix*. Even a few in the national fishwraps.

I stood behind her as she scrolled down the screen and I scrolled down her. "I hope you weren't insulted when I said you looked like that hockey player," she said without looking over her shoulder and realizing that if I hadn't been I was now.

5

I called Sarge with a name and a date of birth. Or at least day and month of birth. I told him that I wasn't sure of the year and that it fell into a range. It complicated what was a hassle to start with. He heaved a sigh. He said he'd have them run for me but let me know without saying so directly that what was a favour I shouldn't have asked for had turned into a big favour even he shouldn't ask for. He told me that he'd picked up a hat trick in the police versus fire department old-old-timers game. He said that he took two minors as well. "Horseshit calls," he said. "When are you coming home, anyway?"

"Soon," I said with confidence that wasn't well-founded.

"I'll put in a call to a buddy of mine down at Metro headquarters and I'll call you back if anything turns up," he said, and he would do just that.

6

"It can't just be that he feels guilty. He should have been able to get past that. It has to be something more."

I had Sandy on the line while Chief drove. I had to raise my voice to make myself heard above the old Bug's strained whine. He kept his eyes on the road and expression unchanged while I gave her the rundown. Yes, it was a neat bit of distraction and manipulation, but though she knew it she didn't care. She approached someone in need of her help unconditionally. Hearing about other people's problems distracted her from problems of her own, those being me. Examination rather than self-examination, it wasn't just her job or her calling. It was some personal need. She had empathy enough for the two of us. That being a good thing. She reminded me that some people want to do the right thing, but no matter how many times she did I willed myself to forget or deny the fact.

I wasn't worried about roaming charges on this call. I spilled out the whole bottle. I was telling her about my visit to Wolf Martens and the events that had landed him a small room in the

Hotel Nowhere and a shiv into his organ collection. As always, she found my amateur psychoanalyzing amusing.

She gave me half marks. That's half more than usual, but she's a tough marker.

"It's more than guilt," she said. "It's shame. You feel guilt when you've done something wrong. And guilt's not a bad thing by any stretch. At least you can tell the difference between right and wrong with guilt. But shame is what you feel when you believe there's something wrong with you. There's not a lot that I can tell you ..."

The irony kicked in later. She was talking about Whisper's brother but she could have been talking about me. Not that she knew. Not that she didn't.

Sandy launched into her usual advisory whenever I solicited her help. Usually I went to her when I had an enigmatic or troubled kid or a deeply troubled parent whose issues might be a portent of bad things to come for a son who might represent an eight-figure investment for our team. She doesn't like it much when I ask her for help on this stuff but she inevitably caves, as she did this time. No guarantees, no warrantees, and, if someone asks, you weren't talking to me. Opinions rendered are for entertainment purposes only and do not represent clinical diagnosis as accepted by the Canadian Psychiatric Association. Void Where Prohibited.

"... but I suppose it's almost like a perfect storm of shame. His failure in school especially when his community had invested hope in him, his failures as a son and a brother, his failure in his faith after being baptized ..."

"Yeah, it came up in the newspaper stories," I said. "It's one thing if you leave the colony before you're baptized, but it's another if you leave after."

That had stuck with me after reading one of the newspaper

stories the librarian had dug up. In the absence of comment from any Hutterite elder, a professor of comparative religions told a reporter that Wolf Martens's baptism "required obedience to God's call" and "commitment to live the course of his life in our community."

"I read somewhere that shame is a sickness of the soul," Sandy said. "Whatever else he might have been suffering from, almost certainly depression, alienation, and inferiority, maybe paranoia, maybe compulsions, would have been magnified by the shame he felt. It's not just that shame can cause retreat and surrender," she said. "Another common response is violence and self-destructive acts. Could he have done it? It would be consistent with some reactions to shame. Could he have not done it and confessed to it? It would be consistent with some reactions to shame."

I didn't feel inclined to explore my own ambivalence, the jangle of nerves and pain in my gut when I allowed myself to drift back to the night at the Hotel Saskatchewan. The *nights*. If you drilled down deep you wouldn't hit shame, and whatever you did hit I wouldn't ever want to know. You can know too much, even about yourself.

I told her my take about Wolf Martens and matters of the spirit and faith, every last high-minded detail, but then I realized it was a dropped call. I didn't know how long I had been talking to myself. It felt like five days.

7

We turned off Highway 1 and rolled into beautiful downtown Swift Current. I kept an eye out for Butch and Sundance's Hummer but saw only an RCMP cruiser set up for a speed trap. I held my breath. The cop with the radar gun gave us a dirty look but didn't wave us over.

I called Kilmer. I wanted to make sure that he had the details right for the funeral. My call went through to his voicemail. I figured he was on his shift. I left a message, asking him to try to call me later on, letting him know that I'd heard about the approval of Martens's temporary leave.

My BlackBerry vibrated and I hit the button. I guessed it was Kilmer calling me back.

"That's a really bad move coming back here ..."

I pulled the phone away from my ear. CALLER UNKNOWN. Again.

"You should go get Geronimo's car there and give it a test drive for four hours or so. Or you'll go home in bags."

Click.

I didn't say anything to Chief again. I turned my head and looked out the passenger window. I tried to figure out how we had been spotted. I tried to figure out how I should take the threat. Someone who had gone to the trouble of tracking down my number and keeping a claustrophobia-inducing close watch on us had to be taken seriously. And when someone had gone to the trouble of poisoning a harmless guy like Whisper and trying, fairly successfully, to cover it up, I had to take everything seriously.

Chief looked over at me and I forced a smile.

"Another robo-call," I told Chief. "I won a cruise vacation."

"Maybe you should take it," he said.

"Yeah, maybe I should. It's for two. You want to go?"

8

I was in the lineup at Wendy's and Chief was in the head, busting the seal. I was tapped on the shoulder. It was Old Man Hanley.

My reflex reaction: It was no coincidence that our paths crossed. He could have spied the Bug from his office window, I thought. He could have been the source of the anonymous threats, though he wouldn't dirty his own hands with any follow-up, I thought. "If you're here to threaten me or chase me out of town, get on your horse," I said.

It was all I could do to resist the urge to spice up the rhetoric, but I'd probably have violated a local bylaw that would see me thrown into stocks in the town square and forced to wear the Scarlet F.

Old Man Hanley put up his hand in the universal sign of cease and desist. The folds in his forehead relaxed but didn't quite disappear. The blood vessels in his nose and across his cheeks burned a little less threateningly.

"I appreciate what you're trying to do for my son," Old Man

Hanley said. He was a man uncomfortable with the phrase *thank you.* He rarely had the occasion to use it.

I looked out the window. No. 59 was outside. Perched on crutches. I nodded. "No problem" was all I said, not fully erasing my sneer. I didn't need to go into my reasons. I wasn't about to tell him that he could never know his son's pain the way that I could. From what No. 59 had told me, his injury might have been worse than the one that wrecked my career. Nerve damage, that's just about as bad as it gets. I'm a cold-hearted bastard about a lot of things, but I can't be about an innocent kid in for a lifetime of pain.

Chief came back from the head, took one look at Hanley, and engaged his death stare, hotter than the heat lamps warming the burgers. I told Chief everything was cool. If we could ever figure out how to harvest Chief's surging testosterone, we'd be able to shut down nuclear plants across the country.

Hanley turned to the Big Man. "I was thanking your friend," he said.

Chief was suspicious of any peace offering. I was too. On the ice, when it's time to go, everything is honest and inevitable. "We're cool, everything's okay," is the prelude to three-quarters of the scraps I've ever been a party to off the ice.

Hanley jumped back in where he had left off with me. "You're right," he said. "He is a good kid. It's almost like he sees things more clearly since he got hurt."

I could have told him that getting hurt has a way of pulling back the gauze, lifting the fog, and throwing everything into sharper focus.

Old Man Hanley kept talking. "He told me that he didn't realize what the game was until he had to watch it on crutches. 'It's not that special. I don't want it anymore. There are other things.' That's what he said to me."

"That's pretty smart," I said.

"I want you to come back to my office," Hanley said again. He nodded his head. His office was a one-minute walk away.

"Okay, I'll just let Mitzi Mars know where we're going," I said. I keyed in her number and rang through to voicemail. I sent her a text as well. That would have been enough to scare Hanley off trying anything funny or unfunny.

Hanley led the way and we went in single file across the snow-covered street. I followed. Chief was behind me. No. 59 brought up the rear, negotiating the snow and ice on his crutches. It was like a Swift Current variation on the cover of *Abbey Road*.

We took our places in Hanley's office. "I understand that you have been taking an interest in Martin Mars's death," he began.

"How would you know that? Your friend Daulton tell you that?"

He ignored me.

"And I understand that you have, what, an interest in me as ..."

"As a suspect," I said. Some of the lustre had gone off our new-found friendship.

"You're making the presumption that there was a crime committed and I have no idea what you're basing this on. But just so you don't waste any of your time or mine, I can tell you that Martin Mars's death would be adverse to my interests."

"What is it that they say about business? If you can't beat them, kill them."

"I wasn't out to outdo Martin Mars. There was no 'beat' in this at all. And Bob Roth can vouch for that if you don't believe me."

"How do you figure?"

"Roth put together our partnership on the Garageland deal. To whatever extent we were fighting for our pieces of the market, Garageland was an opportunity for us only if Mars and

I did it together. Neither one of us could do it on our own. The Garageland chain was beyond our scale. We're not big businesses. We're very successful small businesses, but we both knew our limits."

"Why didn't Roth tell us this? Why didn't you tell us?"

"One, he couldn't have known that you would have been interested. Two, there was a matter of confidentiality involved. He would have breached it if he told you, and whether Martin Mars is alive or not, we still have an agreement."

I must have looked unsatisfied. I was.

"Here's the paperwork," Hanley said, pulling a folder from an old-school filing cabinet and pushing it across his desk. The contract was thick, initialled throughout, signed, witnessed, and apparently legit. When I called Bob Roth after I left the office he vouched for it. In fact, the lawyer said that the last points of the contract were being hammered out late in the previous week, with a race to have business finished by the end of the business day Friday.

Still, I had to see if Hanley could account for where he was later that Saturday night and Sunday A.M. When I asked, No. 59 piped up and said that he and his father were at a game at the arena, that they had taken three employees and sat in the company's box. Hanley piped up to say that they had retired to the Legion for drinks after the game and No. 59 had acted as a designated driver, dropping off the lawyers and his father's employees before going home to watch a late rebroadcast of *Hockey Night in Canada*.

"Mars's death complicates everything going forward," Hanley said. Things were looking slightly less complicated for me with Hanley out of the mix. One name stroked off the list, two when I factored in No. 51, the thuggish, able-bodied son, acting as his father's factotum.

"So if you had no reason to want Martin Mars erased from the picture, who would?"

Hanley had his own theory, one that had more than once crossed my mind.

"I'd look at the team," Hanley said. "I don't know what kind of game Beckwith is playing. I know a lot of us who've invested in the team over the years are worried about how fast he's moving on this. We've put money in and it could turn out to be a bad investment if the bidding isn't straight."

Hanley's instinct, as always, followed a buck, and he said that he had heard that Beckwith's business was struggling these days. "There are more housing stops than starts around here these days," Hanley said. "A lot of people are struggling, but could someone use a one-time injection of capital? Beckwith sure as hell could."

9

When Chief and I walked out of Hanley's offices, my BlackBerry pinged. The caller ID gave me UNKNOWN. When I answered I kept it low-key and waited for the other party to speak first. This wasn't the same Unknown as the threats, though. This Unknown made herself known to me, volunteered it. Five minutes later I was knocking on Unknown's door and trying to remember that line of bullshit about vacation pay and benefits I had strung on a voicemail the day before. It was something I could dispense with as soon as the door cracked open and I recognized the face looking out at me from behind the chain.

10

"Well, this is awkward. What should I call you?" I asked her. "Fern? Viv?"

"What do you want?"

"Well, I guess you've figured out that I'm not Val Avery and that there's no outstanding vacation pay and your next trip to the dentist will have to be out of your own pocket, unless the casino workers have their own plan."

Telling me to go fuck myself would have taken too much effort and given away that any of this mattered. She blew smoke in my face like she was spraying me with nicotine-based Mace. My eyes watered and I waved my hand.

"Any particular reason that you have two names? One at the Living Sky, another one on the Mars payroll. You do get around."

"A girl is allowed more than one name," she said.

I didn't have to roll my eyes to get a further explanation. I just did so for my own amusement.

"I have an ex-husband," she said. "I actually have two, but the one ex-husband is my special problem. He's out East, thankfully, and if I never see him again it will be too soon. My account is under my name, the one I used when I was still married. But at work and out in public I'm using my middle name and my maiden name. I don't even feel comfortable doing that. But you can't be too careful, especially with dangerous people."

"And your ex out East ..."

"A court has ruled that he's dangerous. I'll just leave it at that."

Any claim to victimhood was nullified by fraud.

"You have my condolences but now, about the way my friend tipped the dealer, your no-show job with Mars Gas."

"Oh, I *showed*. I showed to answer the door and unchain it and welcome him into this house. Not daily, but weekly. He strung me along. He said he was going to leave his wife for me. He said she was frigid. I guess I'm a career sucker for lines of bullshit. It never happened and was never going to happen. He put me on the payroll and told me that I should quit working at the casino, but I told him that I had to get out of the house to do something or I'd lose my mind."

Ah, an admitted grifter with the Old Protestant Work Ethic. Very admirable.

I hated to admit it, but the kept-woman story stood up on a first pass. Back in my awful interlude between my playing days and my scouting job, my days working for the investigations outfit, I had turned over stones of many rocky marriages and found women like Maclean/King, those who lived in a damp, dark, immoral murk. More than once I came across a guy having an affair who would go see the woman on a regular basis in a public place. It was usually in a workplace, either hers or theirs. It would be brazen enough to be exciting and would be a neat bit of subterfuge, leaving people to think that they would hide it better if any fire were there.

I told Maclean/King that what Whisper had done outside

the lines of his marriage didn't matter to me and I wasn't about to loop Mitzi in. I was trying to give a freshly minted widow closure, not compound her grief.

"Tell me about your ex," I asked.

"There's not a lot to tell," she said. They always say that when there is.

"Try me. Or at least humour me. You know, sexual jealousy as a ..." I didn't bother to complete the unthinkable thought. She had neither looks that killed nor looks to kill for. Whisper got better cooking at home.

"Like I said, he's out East. He's in Windsor. He worked in a casino there. So did I. That's where I met him and that's where I left him. Now he works in a bar. He's worked in so many there I don't know which one he's working at now."

"Any reason to think that he'd be out here or that he might get jealous of you dealing cards to another guy at a home game?"

She didn't bother to answer, too awful and too typical to consider. I moved on. "Where were you Saturday night?"

"Where I am every Saturday night, dealing at the five-dollar table at the casino in front of a cast of thousands, star of my own reality show under the security camera."

"Do you know who would want Martin Mars dead?"

"Can't imagine why. I told him that it was over and I didn't want his money anymore. I didn't care. I just wanted to get on with things and that's all I want now."

There's nothing so noble as the willingness to turn down cash. Nothing so implausible either. I could imagine reasons why someone might want Whisper dead, but I couldn't imagine why Maclean/King would. She was in a textbook position to extort him. Killing him wasn't going to get her "job" back. It was the one way to guarantee she couldn't. In fact, Whisper might have had reason to see her dead, for fear that she'd rat him out to

Mitzi once he turned off the tap and money stopped flowing into her account. I couldn't put extortion past her, and her place on the payroll looked like his way to pay her less painfully on the installment plan.

On my second pass, though, when I was back in the car and Chief was driving away, I gamed out the whole picture and the situation looked less clear. I thought of the other trysts I had investigated, and this one wasn't a match on a few major counts. He might have been guileless, but meeting his mistress on a regular basis in a casino? You couldn't get worse cover. Where people go to get a load on, to get into trouble, to get a momentary thrill.

I just didn't buy Whisper and this woman, not when he had Mitzi at home.

II

My cell vibrated: M & M MARS. The widow had an update for me. I tried to wipe the images of Whisper and the other woman or any other woman out of my mind. I was semi-successful.

"Beckwith called me again and said he was calling an emergency meeting of the board at the arena," she told me. "He says that he has a hard offer on the team and that there's a deadline of ... uh, I don't know. I couldn't take it all in. Anyway, he said that if I didn't have someone there, Martin's interest would just fall with the majority. It was a default something or other."

I asked her if she was able to get Roth or Friesen to attend. She said that she couldn't get through to either and that the meeting was within the hour. "I'd go but I just don't understand all that stuff," she said.

Although our scouting department's budget spreadsheet looks like hieroglyphics to me, I figured I could tell if Beckwith was trying to pull a fast one just by sense of smell. He was a paid-up member of the Association of Small-Town Charlatans but he was used to running his games with rubes and hayseeds as marks.

When we pulled into the parking lot, it was easy to tell that a meeting of the board was going on: no pickups, just imported sedans. Beckwith had a Saab 9-3 sedan with BILDIT vanity plates. Chief and I made a dash from the car to the arena. The front door was locked and I pounded on it until a janitor came over and inched it open. I didn't knock him over when I pushed the door open, but I could have. When we barged into the meeting, Beckwith had the floor and was about to push the last button. Every head that lined the conference table snapped toward us except Beckwith's. We were in his direct line of sight.

"I have two sealed offers," he said. "The first is from the interest in Alaska. The second is from another group."

I didn't like the ambiguity but no one questioned it.

"Who's the other group?" I shouted from the back of the room.

Beckwith ignored me or at least tried to. He reached for the one envelope.

"Who's the other group?" I brought it up to angry shout.

"A party that doesn't want to be named," he said. "I can assure you that the party has been talking to us since we first started looking into selling the franchise."

"Your assurances are bullshit, Beckwith," I said. "If you steam-roll this sale through, who's going to look after you? What's in it for you, a nice signed cheque from 'the party in Alaska' or from the Player to Be Named Later?"

"The latter has asked to be left anonymous in the process but has been in active talks with us," he said, still trying to clown me with a show of officiousness. On a point of procedure, though, he had me snookered. He asked for a show of hands of unsealing the bids. I dissented. I was alone because Chief didn't have a vote.

"The Alaska bid," he said and tore the envelope open. "A one-time payment of four and a half million dollars."

That set off a buzz in the room and every board member turned to one another and expressed surprise and relief that the woes were winding down, as well as fast-acting nostalgia for a team that would be gone at the end of the season. It was a distraction that Beckwith fully utilized. He put on a show of disorganization. I walked from the back of the room and around to the front, where I saw him reaching into his briefcase. He had his hand on a stack of identical envelopes, all sealed, all unmarked. He fanned them like a crooked dealer would a deck, stopping at the one third from the top. That was the envelope he pulled out.

"The second bid," he said and he tore the envelope open.

"What the hell was that? What the hell did you just do?"

Any attention I might have attracted Beckwith rediverted.

"The second bid is five million dollars," he said with theatrical flourish. "And the bid includes a provision for local hockey in Swift Current. The team will stay in town."

That last bit sounded just like a sentimental manipulation, a made-to-measure deal closer.

"Time out!" I shouted.

"You get one time out in hockey but none here," Beckwith said.

"Okay, acting as proxy for Mitzi and the late Martin Mars, I move that we have a brief recess in advance of a vote of the board," I said.

"You have the identification and paperwork to say that you're acting as the Mars proxy?" the vice-principal asked.

"It's in the car in the lot," I said. "You want me to get it for you?"

"That won't be necessary," Beckwith said unexpectedly. He didn't have a gavel but his words fell and didn't need further percussion. "The board will be in recess for five minutes. After the recess the board will vote."

A few board members ducked out for a smoke, while others busied themselves over at the side table, where a hastily prepped cold buffet was laid out. Chief grabbed two ham sandwiches. I went over to Beckwith and tried to keep my voice down, mostly because I didn't want any threat overheard. I planned to start with a threat of a legal paper-chase action and then an illegal purely physical one.

"What the hell are you trying to pull?"

"Hold on, I have a call coming in," he said, putting his hand up, dismissing me as if I were the help offering him cream for his coffee. "Yes, I would say that it looks good. It's safe. Yes, what time is your flight ..."

"Beckwith, what the hell do you think you're doing?"

"Yes, it is him," Beckwith said. "You want to speak to him? Okay, Mr. Shade, here."

Beckwith handed me the phone.

"Hello?" I said.

"I thought I recognized that voice. Same temper, dude, take it easy on yourself. You can't go 'round the world in a bad mood all your life."

"Who is this?" I shouldn't have had to ask. If I had been thinking clearly, I would have had it at "dude."

"Shadow, it's me, Stoner."

His was officially the last voice that I expected to hear on the other end of the line. To me he was always that greasy little eighteen-year-old rink rat, the kid we dragged out of the steam bath in the Mercedes. He wasn't, though. Every few months a story would pop up in the business section, a new venture, a new partnership, a new endorsement deal. His agent and business manager had managed to make him forty million on the ice and about five times as much off it. When he was an All-Star he jumped into charity work for colitis, and he had his agent and business manager park the sum of his savings in Big Pharma stock, saying it was just a matter of principle. Next thing you know, old Jed's nearly a billionaire.

I was the rule, a guy who walked out of the game with less than he had expected as his career wound down. I was an extreme example of the rule but by no means unique, a guy who walked away with nothing to show for what passed for my prime. Stoner was the exception. Just the way the stars lined up.

"What the hell?"

"Dude, Whisper called me up and asked if I could help out with the team," he said. "You're out there for the funeral? Are you in on this deal too?"

"No, I'm not in on the deal," I said. "I was in Regina scouting when I heard that Whisper died."

"Yeah, I'm going to be flying up for the funeral," he said. "I told Whisper that I was willing to beat any bid that he got for the team and I'd keep it in Swift Current. He said that having me involved would help them sell kids from B.C. and Alberta on the idea that going to Speedy Creek would be good for their development. The way that I figured it, we could tell them I was going to be on the ice with them in training camp and a few times during the year. I could set them up with jobs at my hockey schools during the summer. Top kids I could even bring down to L.A. to work out with my trainer. It would all be cool."

"You stayed in touch with Whisper?"

"Dude, if he hadn't rolled down the window I would have been a traffic fatality. 'Course I stayed in touch with him. Funny, I actually bumped into him at one of his stations. I was driving out to one of those sports banquets a few years back. We talked maybe once every month or two the last five years, I guess. He talked about you a lot."

"So you went in on this deal because of Whisper."

"Yeah and 'cause it'll be good for my brand, y'know."

He said it like he was parroting his agent and business manager when they spoke of his "transformation from hockey player to brand."

"And what about Beckwith? How does he figure in this?"

Beckwith didn't turn his head. He pretended not to hear his name dropped.

"Beckwith, oh yeah, his company is going to do the construction. Part of me coming in is a private-public thing and I'm bringing in some money to grease a development around the arena. We got a company that's designed that sort of thing around the world. Beckwith called me with the news about Whisper. That was awful. Anyway, he asked me if Whisper wasn't around if I was still good with the deal and I was like, dude, for sure, stoked."

Years in L.A. had sun-bleached his argot and cadence.

"Beckwith was worried that you'd drop out."

"Oh, for sure. I mean he hadn't been involved at all with me and Whisper at that point. But we came to an arrangement. I said, go to the market and see what anyone is willing to pay. I'll beat it by half a mil and keep the team in Swift. He said that was what he was all about, keeping the team. I told the guy that if I landed the team, he could keep his job as veep and I could go out and get a really good coach and GM. I told him, look, dude, I'm gonna sign a bunch of blank offer sheets and you just fill in a bunch of amounts going up a half mil at a time. I wanted to make sure that the people there weren't getting a haircut to sell the team to me."

Blank offers: If Stoner's business manager found out he'd need smelling salts.

Fanning the deck of envelopes, Beckwith was looking for the one that was five hundred thousand over the bid from

Klondike Ike. You only have to be so slick to run an inside game in a small burg. But the fact was, Beckwith had been moving in concert with Whisper and not working against him. He had been worried that Whisper's death might have killed Stoner's interest and crashed the deal, and that would have been adverse to his financial interests. And with no team, he'd have had no choice box at games, no seat reserved at the head of the table for board meetings, and no title. Beckwith had reason to think that he needed Whisper alive for net worth and self-worth.

The conversation with Stoner wound down. We made promises to stay in touch, ones that at least he meant to keep. Before he signed off he threw something out there. To him it fell like a feather but it landed on me like a live grenade.

"Listen, buddy, I've got to run but I might want to talk to you about something I got going on with a minor-pro team I got a piece of," Stoner said. "Probably need a coach and general manager. Might suit you. Lucky thing I talked to you. Wasn't 'til I saw you on the TV at the draft last spring that I knew what you were doing these days. You gotta learn to network."

I've always been a Hell Is Other People guy, but he had me weighing the inconvenience and pain of staying in touch against things I might have been missing.

I handed the phone back to Beckwith. A couple of minutes later, a show of hands. The Swift Current juniors had a new owner, a famous name. When he signed their cheques they wouldn't know whether to cash or frame them.

The applause was still in full swing when my BlackBerry vibrated again. I pressed it to my ear and covered the other to shut out the background noise.

"A really bad idea staying 'round," the voice said in a monotone that was more threatening than a shout. "Get your buddy's car and get the hell out of here. You have one last chance to leave or you'll be as dead as your friend. Could happen sooner than you think."

The click cut me off before I could say a word.

Chief was watching the board members exchange handshakes and hugs. I heard what I thought was a two-by-four snapping and then realized that the Big Man had one fist in the other and was cracking his knuckles. It wasn't a nervous habit. Chief had none. I didn't think anything more of it because I was too preoccupied with the latest threatening call, another unneeded supplement for creeping paranoia. He hadn't noticed me taking the call and he didn't notice me checking the source. CALLER UNKNOWN again. I looked around the room. "Sooner than you think" had me wondering if it was already too late.

12

Chief and I didn't stick around for the rest of the board meeting. Beckwith and the others were going to stay another hour to celebrate and sort out details like where and when the announcement would be made and who'd get to shake Stoner's hand first. Later on, I found out that Beckwith had moved that a crest with MM in black would be sewn on to the sleeve of the Swift Current sweaters for the next game.

Chief and I walked out into the parking lot and were ready to make a dash out to our patiently waiting Bug. We didn't make a backward or sideways glance when we went through the front doors. If we had we would have seen who was waiting for us out there: Butch and Sundance.

"Hey, Butcher, they're still breathing," Sundance said, limping forward. It was the same limp I had spotted at the casino.

"Breathing for now, little buddy," Butch said.

"Shit, Butch, if you had been able to talk you would have been at the top of the card back in your day," I said. "Oh well, that's show business."

Sundance had no idea what I was talking about. He compensated the way that dumb thugs always do, with profanity and inarticulate threats. I struck a nerve with Butch, though. He was a biker dishonourably discharged, a two-bit criminal, an ex-con but at heart a showman. Once you've stood under the bright lights and all that. Butch was pissed.

It wouldn't have been too hard to spot Chief and me coming into town. Our yellow Bug was like a Kick-Me Sign slapped on our backs. How they tracked us down was no puzzle, but *why* stumped me. Chief and I had barely made it away with our lives that night at the Imperial, so you could toss out revenge as a motive. There was no score to settle. They shut us out. Likewise, the Loners had beat it before the Mounties arrived, so they faced no charges. We couldn't do them any damage.

"We had to take it easy on you two last time," Sundance said. "We were afraid that if we hit you too hard we might end up hurtin' one of the kids. But now ..."

Sundance's words stopped rolling and his eyes started, some sort of weird delirium.

Butch picked up the slack. "The shit-kickin' we laid on you and you came back," he said. "You dumb mutherfuckers. They're gonna have to ship you out of here now."

And it was on. I wasn't optimistic. The bikers spread out, either side of us, and so Chief and I had to turn our backs on each other to face our dancing partners. Again Chief drew Butch and I had Sundance.

Butch and Chief were first out of the chute and I could hear shots traded and grunts. Chief was more beat-up than he let on to me, and I wouldn't have been surprised if he was going into this bout with a cracked rib or two or a little shoulder separation. Butch uttered a couple of unfortunate racist epithets, probably a requirement of his membership in the Aryan Brotherhood. It was a misjudgment. It flipped Chief's switch and he waded in on Butch, grabbing his leather vest in his left hand and jackhammering the biker with the other. Chief's reach was the difference maker. So long as he kept that arm straight, Butch couldn't get inside to wrestle him. After eating a dozen shots that would leave his face a swollen mess, Butch made a belated move, trying to break the straight arm by bringing down his elbow. Mistake. That only brought Chief within his wheelhouse and he needed only one punch to reduce Butch's nose to a single serving of calcium-fortified cereal dust. Chief doesn't have much of a ground game and stayed on his feet, kicking Butch right in the chops. His jawbone snapped. I felt sorry for Butch. When he woke up he was going to be on a diet of milkshakes for two months and the Dairy Queen was closed for the winter.

It was an inspiring performance, I have to admit, the stuff that lifts the spirits of the team on the ice. It wasn't inspiring enough for me to go head on with Sundance, though. I was still feeling the effects of our scrum Monday night and determined that it was better to go at this technically and clinically. I kept dancing on the outside while Sundance limped forward with the balletic grace of a B-movie zombie. I was going to pick my spot and I did. I kicked the legs out from under him, a leg sweep that you'll see in any respectable dojo. He landed on his back and snow cushioned his head from a hard bounce off the asphalt. He got back up and kept coming forward, this time with a knife that he had pulled from his vest pocket.

He took a swipe at my midsection. It was poorly timed, all windup and no payoff, like going for a highlight-reel slapshot when just a wrist shot would do. I couldn't count on his bad judgment and my good luck to last, and the longer the fight lasted the worse it was for the home team. I'd only had an eyeful of him a couple of times but I'd logged my scouting report. He had one weakness. The next swing he took, another miss, I took my chances and ran him, stomping on his boot, the bridge of his foot. The steel toe offered some protection but any shot there would serve its purpose. He staggered backward and fell to the ground, about ten feet from where his knife came to rest.

"My fuckin' gout," he whimpered.

Not so helpfully I picked up the knife before he could stagger up. He froze as I pulled it closer to his grill. "Lie down, face down," I said. Sundance should have been thankful that none of the boys in the cellblock or at the headquarters could see him now. I put my foot across his neck and gently pumped, like I was squeezing apple juice out of his Adam's apple.

"Fuck off," he said with a strangulated and sadly half-hearted rasp.

"You sound all choked up," I said, putting my heel down in search of his C4 vertebrae. If I sneezed he was going to spend the rest of his life on a ventilator.

By this time, Butch had sat up but he was willing to be counted out of the ring.

"I believe in kismet and karma but I can't imagine that this was a coincidence or something just destined to be," I said. "What the fuck is this about?"

Nothing. He tried to grab my ankle. I pushed my heel down like I was slamming on the brakes and it had about the same effect. He came to a dead stop. His hands dropped and his eyes rolled back.

"You doing this for someone?"

He turned his head and nodded. I pressed down.

"Who?"

"F-ffff" was all he could manage again.

"I'm going to give you a chance to walk away and pretend this never happened," I lied. "Who put you up to it?"

"She did," he said.

"Who's she?"

"Mother," he said.

"Your mother?"

"No, Mother, this woman we know," he said. "We're partners. She gets the weed and we know boys with a lab. It's business." Yeah, Butch and Sundance must have taken turns with the Chamber of Commerce Men of the Month Award.

"Try again," I said. This time I pushed down hard enough to make his eyes pop out of their sockets.

He panted when I eased up. "She had us get the boys at the I to rough up the kid at the gas station," he said. "She wanted them to give him a message ... that he had to settle up what he owed her and come 'round in person to do it. It's the only time she had us rough up anybody."

I couldn't see Walt being a dope smoker. I didn't give it deeper thought until later.

"And what's that got to do with us?" I said.

"When we told her that you said you were here for Mars's funeral and you talked to her at the casino, she told us to look after you."

He told me her name but said that he wasn't sure of the address. "Is it Sixteenth or Seventeenth?" he said, calling out to his fellow fallen soldier. "Sixteenth" was the muffled reply from his supine confederate. I could see how it could get confusing with the town's numbered street grid. "I dunno what the number is," he said. "I just recognize the house, that's all. I only been there a couple of times, 'cause most of the time I deal with her on the phone."

"Which one?"

"I dunno the number," he said. "There's a lawn jockey on the lawn."

Noted. Had that down.

"What about Martin Mars? You sure as hell didn't like it when I mentioned his name at the Imperial the other night."

Sundance said nothing but he was spared further violence and humiliation. I heard a car making the turn into the parking lot. I tossed the knife into a snowbank and it disappeared without a trace. I looked over at Chief. He had gone to the Bug and pulled the plastic flower out of the vase and then walked over to the motionless pile of meat in Butch's leathers. He tossed the flower on his victim's chest and then realized I was watching him.

"Got to give him respect," he said.

The RCMP cruisers unnecessarily pulled up.

13

Albert Daulton tapped a pen on the top of his desk and did his best to look nonchalant.

"You're not being charged," he began.

"So you brought us in here to present us with the keys to the city?" I said.

"Don't be smart with me, sonny," he said.

I feigned full contrition. Chief gave me That Look. "Sorry," I said. "It's just been a bad night."

"So I understand," he said. "That's the way the arena's janitor described it when he dialed 911. He said that pair started everything and you were just trying to protect yourselves."

It was a good thing I hadn't knocked the janitor to the floor when we barged in to get to the board meeting.

"So if we're not being charged, what do you need us for?"

"First, statements for charges against the Loners."

"Not going there," I said. "Not worth it. It was just a friendly exhibition of strength and sportsmanship."

Daulton had to anticipate that we might be reluctant to put our names to anything that would jam up gang members.

"I understand. The methamphetamines and weapons in their vehicle should suffice. Nevertheless, I'm going to request that you leave town as soon as you can and for as long as you can," he said.

"Sure," I said. All this lying was making it easier each time.

"Look, I know Martin Mars was a friend of yours of some sort ..."

"Teammate ..."

"Okay, teammate," he said, not amused by my continued impertinence. "But your friend died ... at his own hand. These are the types of things that we don't look at too hard for fear of opening wounds. We let the dead rest. We let life go on."

"It's swell to be philosophical about it, but the fact is, my *teammate* didn't die at his own hand. He didn't die from carbon monoxide poisoning ..."

"How do you know that?"

I told him precisely how I knew that. I told him about Dr. Goto and the absence of cherry-red lividity and hemoglobin that wasn't binding and blood that had turned purple. The interim coroner seemed suitably convinced when I told him that I had convinced his predecessor to make a phone call up to the chief coroner for the province.

Daulton didn't say, "But I can explain." He just went right to it.

"It was a mistake I made because I allowed personal feelings to crawl into it," he said. "It's not the first time I have. But I have only a couple of months until I retire, so I guess it will be the last time."

"You hated Mars that much that you didn't care how he died,"

I said. Ninety-nine percent of accusations from my side of the table to the other would have led to a world of trouble, but he was repentant enough to admit a mistake, just not the one I expected.

"No, I allowed personal feelings into it because Martin Mars was a friend of mine," Daulton said. He leaned back in his chair as I leaned forward, and Chief squinted as if his eyes couldn't believe what his ears had just heard. "Martin quietly did a lot of good work in the community. He had a big role in a program for troubled youth, kids who committed minor offences. He gave them jobs. Even took them into his home."

"Like his boarder now?" I guessed.

"Pretty typical of the boys he took in, yes," Daulton said. "We had picked him up for underage drinking a couple of times when he started working at the filling station. He lost his job and was living on the street when he was found in possession of metham-phetamine. When his case was going to court, Martin stepped forward and told the Crown he'd give him a second chance and vouch for him. The case was dropped. He did a lot of that sort of thing."

"There's a lot that you don't know about him ... he's not who he claimed to be all those years," I said, thinking I was one step ahead of him. I wasn't.

Daulton bit his lip and looked away. He wasn't used to being on the other side of the justice being done. A career criminal wouldn't blink. Daulton tripped the wire. He did everything but break out in hives. He'd hoped this tear-soluble 10 percent confessional would have sufficed. He soon realized that we knew too much for him to get off that easy.

"I had known him for years, even before he played in the league. I knew about his story, about his family."

"You know that those weren't his parents?"

"I knew the Marses, his 'parents.' I knew the old couple first and always thought it was strange that they were presenting him as a son when he clearly wasn't. I was just a constable then, first year or so on the force. I was out in Herbert a lot. People were suspicious and I was too, but I let it rest. No harm in it. People around here will talk about something and then they let it drop and carry on like they never thought or talked about it in the first place. And it was years after the Martens murder. I never put it together."

Daulton leaned forward. He lowered his voice even though no one was within earshot. "When Martin was twenty he came to me and told me that he had trouble," he said. "He told me exactly what had happened . Everything he saw."

"Why did he come to you then?"

"He had a contract offer to play hockey in the States but was going to need a visa to work there, and the American authorities would be conducting a background check, a pretty intense one. I told him that it would be better if I just wasn't involved at all, but he said that he had no one else he could ask. I spoke with an executive with the club."

"That would have been Hal Sutherin, our general manager in L.A.," I said. It wasn't until after Chief and I left Daulton's office that it would hit home: that Hal's brother, Bud, was the one tugging on John Harris's arm when Iron went off on Whisper, that Bud probably knew Whisper's backstory but didn't loop in Iron, that the Sutherins managed somehow to keep it to themselves, that it might be the single well-kept secret in a game lousy with gossip. One-third of that secret died with Hal Sutherin when he was felled with a heart attack on the seventeenth hole at Riviera, ruining a round when he was on pace to shooting his age. Another third died when his older brother, Bud, fell down the sinkhole of dementia about a decade back.

"Yes," Daulton said. "I spoke to Sutherin. He told me he

thought he had heard it all a year or two before, when a player found out in the visa application that the woman he thought was his sister was in fact his mother. And I spoke with the visa authorities. There was a significant hole where his birth records should have been. I told them just the thumbnail details, that Martin Mars's biological parents were both dead, and that he had endured a terrible emotional trauma. I didn't lie but I left a fair bit out. *Finessed* it, if you want. It complicated things but we were able to get the paperwork done. It was something that wouldn't have been cross-referenced with a years-old missing person case. I had to bend the rules but it was impossible not to be sympathetic. It was our secret."

Daulton was claiming that he was all heart when he pushed through Immigration's background check, but he was also covering his own ass for not following up on his original suspicions about the Mars family. It's one thing for a case to go cold, another to throw it in the freezer the way he had. Once he finessed the visa application, Daulton was bound in the secret more than anyone, more even than Whisper. All Whisper had to lose was his privacy. Daulton would have lost his reputation and his job just for starters. He might have even been charged and prosecuted.

"It wasn't just a secret with the two of you," I said. "There's his brother. You had to know he'd been in contact with his brother ..."

"For a lot of years, yes, I did."

"You think he knew about ..."

"About my role in all this?" Daulton said. "I want to say no, he didn't, but I could only go on what Martin told me. I've been afraid of it getting out."

"What's the old saying, it's easy for three to keep a secret if two are dead," I said. "I guess you'd be rattled by anyone kicking up too much dust around Mars's death, anyone like me."

He didn't like the dash of pepper I wanted to add to the fresh servings of his candour. "Draw your own conclusions," he said, trying to resurrect the wall. It wasn't quite as thick as onion skin.

"They're drawn," I said. For a couple of breaths we had run out of things to say. Daulton was preoccupied with the implications of somebody outside this messy loop knowing his role in concealing Whisper's secret, somebody being Chief and me, someone being anyone we had told or planned to. While this was sinking in I spied a number written down on a notepad near his phone. It was upside down but I didn't have any trouble recognizing it. It was mine. No name. Not part of a form. Just my number. Could have pulled it from our interrogation Monday night. Could have pulled it right off the BlackBerry's screen when it was confiscated by the Mounties who dragged us in. That my number was somewhere in the building wasn't surprising. That it was so handy for Daulton was telling. Another conclusion drawn: Daulton didn't charge Chief and me because he didn't want us lingering around headquarters or in town kicking up the aforementioned dust. It hadn't been Butch and Sundance or any other outlaw trying to get in my head with the threatening calls. No, the calls originated from an ID-protected cell in this shabby office in the local seat of Truth, Justice, and the Canadian Way.

I reached across the desk and picked up the paper. He didn't move. I waved it. He would be wasting his time at a poker table at the Living Sky. I presumed the last Anonymous Trip Advisory had been made and I moved on.

"It will be easy for you to figure out what Wolf knows. I was up in P.A. yesterday. I phoned in a request for the release and they told me that it had already been filed. The supervisor of the guards had done it."

That's the problem with getting an inch ahead of yourself. It always takes you a foot off course.

"No, I doubt a guard filing a request like that would have been appropriate," Daulton said, his official superciliousness resurfacing. "I filed the request immediately when I got word of Martin's death. I put the nature of his relationship to Martin down as 'cousin, sole surviving' and all the rest. I presumed it wouldn't be filed by anyone else. I know that Martin's wife had no knowledge of the brother. And it would be processed expeditiously if the request came from my office. The instructions are for the guard to deliver Wolf Martens to our headquarters and we're to supervise his leave in tandem."

It was a lot to take in and I needed a minute. Precisely why he wanted Wolf Martens to be at the service for Whisper I didn't know, but I could guess. A promise made. A pre-emptive tightening of the circle. Guilt. Daulton was about to fill the silence with his rationalizations of his past actions and inactions but I jumped in.

"You knew an innocent man was sitting in prison all these years," I said.

"I realize the justice system failed in this case. Unfortunately, you have someone who is either unstable or insane, but he has given his confession, repeated the details over and over, and been found to be competent by experts. Martin coming forward wouldn't have changed much."

"And so you know that the real perp walks, right?"

"I know the 'perp' based on what Martin told me. She did time for drug and firearms possession. Her sentence was pleaded down to a pittance. Another failure of the justice system. She's on our radar. We keep tabs. She's still in town. People like her do what they do. They know we know what they do. And they know the limits of what we can do about it. It's an elegant dance."

"Glad you can see the elegance in it."

"Martin told me their paths crossed sometimes. He never went into it, but he was such a pure spirit ..."

Nice word for a naïf.

"... he thought he could coax her to clear his brother."

Even Whisper couldn't have been that clueless, to think that Harmon would talk her way into a life sentence.

"He said, 'I'm going to get her and she's going to go away,'" Daulton said. "Look, I'm sure she's involved in the same things she's done before ..."

She worked in the navel in the town's seedy underbelly but somehow lint wouldn't gather around her.

"But there's nothing you've been able to take her down on, right?" I said. "Even though these fat ex-con bikers and kids are working for her."

"We can't close the circle, not yet, much as I'd like to. Martin said that he was close."

Close.

"You have an address for her?"

"I couldn't give it to you if I did."

And he didn't.

14

Chief and I went for coffee and meditated wordlessly, like a pair of yogis on a mountaintop. Whisper had told Daulton that he had Monica Harmon. It could have been an empty boast. Then again, it would have been one hell of a coincidence to make an empty boast about bringing down a criminal one day and be found very dead the next. Especially when the criminal you're talking about got away with murder once. Especially when you're found in the front seat of your treasured connection to your only sibling. Especially when you've been laid out to look like you checked out with self-inflicted carbon monoxide poisoning and the sum total of CO in your system equals about the same amount as you'd get on a draw of a cheap cigar.

I didn't know for a fact that Whisper had Monica Harmon cold. I was just going to presume that he did, rattle her cage, and see what fell out.

Sarge called.

"You owe me," he said.

"I owe you for everything, starting with a spectacular gene pool."

"You know, these friends of mine have more important things to do than spend hours chasing down ..."

"Sarge, this call is costing me two dollars a minute," I said, knowing that this price point would speed things along and spare me a speech.

"Just tell me one thing," he said. "How did you have the date but not a year?"

I looked at Wolf Martens's red notebook on the dash and flipped it open to the first pages. "A calendar, a day circled, and initials in it," I said. "A little guesswork, a little luck."

I left out a little larceny.

He gave me a rundown on Monica Harmon's colourful career; her many convictions; her time off the street, which seemed far too brief; the name of her parole officer; her address. He read off the area code and the first three digits for her phone number and waited for me to take them down. I took a not-so-wild stab at the last four digits.

"Yeah, that's right," he said.

Sarge was going to ask me how I knew but I reminded him that the call was costing me. Sarge is more sensitive to the value of a dollar than most, never mind two dollars. He left the *good* off *bye*.

15

I could see the footprints I had left in the snow three hours before. I knocked on the door. A couple of seconds later the peephole went into full eclipse and a deadbolt was unbolted, but the door remained chained.

She looked surprised to see me again so soon. She looked surprised to see me at all after she had made the call to Butch and Sundance. She did her best to mask her surprise. Her snarl looked like it had been sculpted in nicotine-laced wax. She again greeted me with a puff of smoke in my face.

"What the fuck do you want now?"

"We're on Name Number Three, right? No, I'm guessing you keep a couple of others alive too."

"What are you talking about? Get the fuck out of here."

She tried to slam the door shut. I leaned into it with my right hand. If I wanted to I could have ripped the chain right out of the frame and invited myself in. I fought the urge. That would give her a reason to call 911. Reason prevailed, even though my testosterone was close to cresting.

"Hey Monica, by the way, heard anything from your friend Phyllis lately? Get a call from her telling you about a dashing guy asking questions about you?"

With the mention of her square name, the name she was known by along Highway 1 and among officials with Corrections Canada, the single drop of blood ran out of her face. A twitch was a giveaway that I had pieced together who had tipped her about someone poking around a truck stop asking questions about her. Old Phyllis had given her the make and licence plate number but the PT Cruiser was a rental, no use to Harmon. I was a match for the physical description the waitress had given her, though. It wouldn't have been much of a guess on Harmon's part, not after I had quizzed her in the casino.

"I know your story, as much as Wolf Martens and the RCMP know, and I know a bit more than that, namely that my old buddy had you on his payroll until just three weeks ago," I said.

"Like I said, he was devoted to me."

"I don't know why he did it, though 'devoted' isn't on my short list of reasons why he'd want to bankroll you."

She slammed the door in my face.

16

I had Chief drive to the German bakery in downtown Swift Current. The eat-in section wasn't intimate, just tight, four small tables with two rickety chairs per crowded just inside the door. The entrance of every customer was announced by a gust of wind that blew napkins off the tables and the opening two bars from "Das Lied der Deutschen." The anthem took me back to my days playing in the German league near the end and a Bavarian babe who was on the verge of becoming my second wife, at least until she realized that I was still in the game only because I was trying to play my way out of bankruptcy. Any warm and tingly feeling the music might have induced was overridden by the wind, which had me shivering and sitting on my hands.

I told Chief I had to clear my head. Really, I was just stalling. I wasn't eager to see Mitzi again. I wasn't sure what I should tell her. I weighed telling her everything I had found out. I weighed telling her nothing.

"I didn't know this guy well enough to know what he would have wanted," I said. I looked out the window onto the street.

The street lights were on even though it was mid-afternoon. It was overcast enough to be night.

Chief made the leap, assuming that I was talking to him and not myself. "If you want to know what he would have wanted, you gotta look at what he was doing," he said. "You gotta look at what he was trying to do."

Chief didn't give it a high mystical reading. It wasn't Sweat-Lodge Wisdom he was offering up. He was matter-of-fact about it.

I turned away from the window, reached for a pen in my pocket, and started to doodle, all straight lines, all right angles.

"You know those weren't robo-calls and wrong numbers I was getting," I said.

"Yeah, I know," Chief said. "I know they weren't booty calls either."

17

"And he never applied for parole. It seems like he wants to stay in prison the rest of his life."

Chief and I sat behind BLTs we hadn't touched during a recitation of miseries. Mitzi insisted on making us something before she would sit down to hear what I turned up in Prince Albert. I had just given her a very selectively abridged version.

I left out the part about Whisper's windpipe being crushed by Monica Harmon. Whisper had avoided revealing or explaining all that could be avoided. He couldn't have written a fiction of his entire life. His voice, though, was the one thing that had needed to be explained and he had come up with a lie of convenience. I didn't want Mitzi to know that Whisper had ever lied to her.

I also left out the fact that he had placed Monica Harmon on the Mars payroll. And the fact that he spoke to Harmon on a regular basis at the Living Sky Casino. I knew that there had been nothing going on between them, but Mitzi was just too fragile. It was already all too much.

Mitzi bowed her head and sobbed softly, almost a whimper.

Her adult life was now in a whole new perspective. Maybe she had always sensed Whisper's shame. It's the leading cause of all mutations of avoidance.

I glanced at my BLT but let it sit. I'd have come off callous if I took a bite of it. Chief's stomach growled. It was unaware of the etiquette of mourning. He fought off the urge.

To Mitzi's credit, she raised her head after five minutes. To her greater credit, she moved off What Was and moved on to What Might Be.

"Is there anything we can do for Martin's brother? Any way to get him out?"

"I don't know. He's like a lot of guys in prison. He's mentally unstable. He needs help. Probably too late now."

I respected her even more. It seemed like she wanted to step into her husband's breach and try to save his brother, a complete stranger to her. That he was a convicted murderer didn't weigh on her thoughts. She couldn't think ill of her late husband's brother.

She excused herself to get more Kleenex in the kitchen. I stole a bite of the BLT, chewed hard and fast, and swallowed so that I wouldn't have a mouthful when she came back into the living room.

"I don't know if I can stay on in Swift Current," she said.

Seconded.

"It was a lonely place even when Martin was here," she continued.

I picked up the considerable slack in the conversation. I told her that I trusted Roth and Friesen to look after the business end. Even on less than ideal terms, she would get out with more money than she'd ever have a chance to spend. I told her that she could settle in a place where the weather and neighbours weren't as cold and harsh. That could have been any place at all if you took the two counts in concert. I rhymed off likely destinations: Victoria, the Gulf Coast, San Diego, maybe Mexico or the Caribbean. I left Vegas off the list—no sense leaving one bad memory for another. I told her that I'd help her as much as I could. For a minute, an awful, tasteless, glorious, opportunistic minute, while I rhymed off all these attractive choices, I painted a picture for her and, I'll admit, for myself. I thought a guy could do worse in life than end up as her winger. She was well preserved, as I noted before, and she had the wherewithal to stay stunning. What kind of guy could lust after a grieving widow? She was in the room with one. I kept thinking *too soon* but it was an effort.

She started sobbing again. I had spoken in my usual conversational voice, but if I had cranked the volume up to one hundred decibels she wouldn't have heard me. If I had put on a slide show of the choicest gated communities she couldn't have seen it from the front row. At that moment I regretted turning up anything at all about the life and death of her husband. At that moment I thought my life and hers would be easier if it had just been left a suicide.

"We still don't know ..."

That was as far as she could go and this was one blank that I wouldn't fill in for her. *We still don't know who killed Hugo Martens, Martin Mars, and Whisper?* I owed it to her to try to find out. I owed it to him.

Mitzi composed herself.

"You haven't touched your sandwich," she said. "Go ahead."

I had a second bite and even though it had been sitting there for half an hour it was delicious. The lettuce was crispy enough to have been plucked from an iceberg. The bacon crunched as if it were working from muscle memory.

"This is so good," I said, desperate to pull off the impossible, namely pushing conversation onto the mundane.

Mitzi stifled tears. Small talk was hard but still easier than the rest. "It's the one advantage of living out here," she said. "The meat from the local farms just tastes so much better than what you buy in the stores. Everyone in town has a farm that they go to for their meat ..."

She paused. I could tell from her expression that her mind was performing some introductory human calculus.

"From everything that you've told me about Martin's growing up, it makes sense now that he had me buy our meat from a Hutterite colony about ten minutes out of town. He never drove out there. He always had me do it. He said that he got lost on those back roads."

It hung out there in the silence. There had been a couple of compelling reasons for Whisper's not wanting to drive out there. That he might be recognized. That it would bring back unwelcome memories.

I lost my appetite.

Mitzi tried to distract herself with The Today and The Tomorrow. "I'm going to stay on," she said, raising her head, looking out the living-room window at a snowdrift. "I'm going to ask Bob and Harry to sit in Martin's spot on the team's board for now. Maybe I'll be able to do it in time."

"I think just Wh— Martin's memory might be enough to keep Van Stone involved with the team."

"And I'm going to tell Walt that I want him to stay on. It will be good for him and good for me, I think."

I saw no need to point out that he had a sweet deal that he couldn't come close to matching in Swift Current.

Only a couple of breaths later Walt came in the side door. We dropped the subject of Walt's Room at the Inn. Mitzi asked me my plans and I told her that I was going to book my flight, that I had to reconnect with my employer and the women in my life, those being Sandy and my daughter. She asked me if I'd stay for dinner. I checked my watch. I couldn't see heading back on an empty stomach. I didn't like the idea of stopping at another roadside place in a couple of hours. I told her that I'd be happy to stay for dinner but that I was going to have to be a bad guest and hit the road after dessert and coffee.

She said she understood. She started to rummage through the refrigerator and freezer, trying to figure what she could whip up.

"I just don't know what to do," she said. "You liked the pork chops the other day, didn't you, Brad?"

"Yeah, I did."

18

Shortly thereafter the phone rang. Mitzi took the call in the kitchen. Roth was calling to say that he had a few matters to discuss with Mitzi, some papers to sign. Mitzi said that she wanted his advice about a couple of things as well. She invited Roth over for dinner. "Nothing formal or fancy," she said. "Just some pork chops."

I cringed. The lawyer explained to her that the main course wasn't on his diet plan. I watched her drink it in with bafflement, punctuated with a shocked "Really?" Roth asked Mitzi if she was alone and she told him that Chief and I had been on-site and Walt had just arrived. He asked her to put me on the line.

"Is she still under sedation? Is she okay?"

Mitzi was within earshot, so I picked my words. "Yes on both counts, though a little shaky on the latter," I said.

"Well, I'm just worried about her."

"I'm sure it's appreciated."

"Do you think coming over after dinner is appropriate?"

Again, I looked over at Mitzi. She asked Chief if he wanted
more coffee and put another pot on. "I think it would probably
be for the better if we were all here in support," I said. At that
point it hit home that I had assumed the role of captain on the
support team of a woman I hadn't seen in almost twenty years,
someone I barely knew.

"I'll be over shortly," Roth said. I liked the fact that he was
willing to come over to the house for the good of his client's
widow and endure the fresh perfume of pork chops.

I lowered my voice while Mitzi ran the water. "Good," I said.
"But I think you should keep the paperwork to a minimum.
She's still ..."

"Fragile," he said, sparing me having to risk Mitzi overhearing.
"Yes, I'll be over shortly."

It wasn't going to be a wholesale line change, just a little relief,
but for that I was grateful. With the coffee dripping, Mitzi
began to root through the freezer to round up pork chops and
was disappointed to find that she had only enough for dinner for
three, which is to say only enough to feed Chief.

"Brad, I'll call the colony farm and ask them to put something
together we can have for dinner, but I don't think I'm up for the
drive out there," she said. "Walt can go with you."

"Sure," I said. Another mitzvah to add to my swelling number
of good deeds.

If Chief and I tried to run this errand alone, we would end
up hopelessly lost and be discovered on the side of the road the
following spring. Even if we had a GPS it would have been useless
to sort through the approximations that passed for addresses out
on the gravel rural-route side roads. Walt wouldn't offer much
in the way of conversation but he'd know which snowbank was
the left turn and which fallen road sign was the right.

Roth was knocking on the door twenty minutes later and

we headed out. First we cut across town and turned in the Bug loaner at the repair shop in exchange for Chief's Jeep.

Chief looked relieved to be behind the wheel of his usual ride and pushed the driver's seat all the way back. I offered Walt the passenger seat and stretched out in the back.

In between Walt's unembroidered instructions for right turns and left turns and go straights, I tried to make small talk with the kid. Again, it was nothing that reached the level of the Algonquin Round Table.

I asked him how he was holding up.

"Okay," he said, when he clearly wasn't.

I asked him how things were going over at the station on the west side of town, which had reopened in full.

"Okay," he said. "We pretty much had to get going. A truck was scheduled to fill up the underground tanks. We had some repairs lined up. We showed respect by keeping the station on the east side closed. I don't know when that's gonna be opened or if it's gonna be opened at all. I don't know the manager out there. I'm just glad I don't have to work there. I don't think I could stand it."

"You're good with cars?" I asked.

"Learnin'. Just the basics, though. I want to get so that I can buy 'em and fix 'em and sell 'em. Y'know, it's a good sideline."

"You bought any?"

"I bought the old Impala that was out behind the east station, right beside Mr. Mars's Mercedes. I don't think that I can ever work on that one."

"Hey Chief, can you turn the radio down?" I said. "I feel a migraine coming on." It was true but it wasn't going to be me who was knocked dizzy and reeling. The Big Man pushed the button and I reached into my coat to pull out my BlackBerry. I checked the battery and it had more than half a charge, good for a few more hours. I had an email alert. It was from Ryan

MacDonald, a scout with Boston, a complete knucklehead and ass-kisser, and, I'd safely have bet, a guy who'd be the first whizzed with budget slashing in a lockout. Despite my boundless sympathy for my fellow man, I ignored the email. I found the voice recorder icon and held the smartphone up behind the headrest that Walt was leaning on. I leaned forward so that both ends of the conversation would be clear for playback.

"I guess I could see that. What do you think of that, Chief? What he says, what was it again, Walt?"

"That I don't think I could go work on that Impala," he said.

"Which Impala?" I asked.

"The one that was parked beside Mr. Mars's Benz. That would be too hard to do."

Chief nodded his head. "I guess," the Big Man said.

I kept it in the small talk vein. "Funny, when you said that you bought something to fix up that was out at the station on the east side, I thought it might have been the van."

"That Volks' hippie wagon that was parked in the back, naw. That's a customer's. I don't know who would want to spend a hundred bucks on that old thing."

"What do you think of that van, Chief? The one we saw in those police photos of the scene behind the station."

"Couldn't tell much about it," he said, turning his head to look at me in the rear-view mirror and try to figure out where I was going.

"Take the left here," Walt said. "The road is gonna get bumpy."

It did. Our asses were put into the meat tenderizer on a low setting and change was shaken out of Walt's pockets onto the floor of the car. It was only the start of the shaking.

"Walt, how is it that you know that the Impala was parked beside Mr. Mars's Mercedes? And that it was behind the station? Or that the van back there was an old Volks?"

"I went out Monday to see if there was anything I could do."

"His car was moved Sunday morning, after the police photographer was done with it. While you were on your shift across town."

"I heard someone mention them then, I guess."

"So you thought you saw them but you had that wrong. You only heard about them from ..."

"I guess I heard it from someone, I can't remember."

"That's really curious, Walt. What do you think, Chief?"

"'Curious' is a good word," he said.

I didn't give Walt a chance to get in. "That's the sign there for the turn for the colony farm, right?" I said, without waiting for Walt's confirmation. "So you know where the Mercedes was parked and more importantly what it was parked beside, even though you couldn't see the scene from the road and even though everything was cleared away right after."

I took a little licence with "right after," not that he'd know.

"Yeah, I guess," the kid said. He looked like he had seen a ghost. I would have bet he had.

"You got all that, Chief?"

"Yeah, Shadow, I heard all of it."

"Good, I have it all here too," I said.

I hit Stop. I held my breath. I just hoped the recorder had picked up everything he had said. And it had, crystal clear, not too loud but loud enough to rock Walt's world and start lifting the fog that had settled around events that Sunday morning.

"Walt, there's only one way you could have known all that," I carried on. "You would have had to have been behind the station after closing Saturday night and before Derek Jones made the call to the police. And when you get to the RCMP station, which is where we are going from here, you're not going to have a chance to talk to anybody to set up an alibi or put together

some bullshit story about how you know so much about the
scene behind the station."

Walt stared blankly ahead. Somehow he thought if he didn't
turn his head the walls around him couldn't come crashing down.

"And Walt, I should tell you that I have worked as a licensed
investigator. I have testified in legal proceedings. That was my
job. That was what I was trained for. And Chief here, well, his
father was a war hero. He's a respected figure."

I saw no need to tell him that we, the licensed investigator
and the respected figure, had spent the night in a holding pen
at the RCMP office where we would be taking him once we
managed to turn around and head back to town.

"Walt, the way I see it, you can probably do yourself some
favours if you co-operate. I don't know why you wanted my old
friend dead. I really don't."

"No," Walt said. "He was real good to me." He closed his eyes
and his immediate future came into sharper view.

To say he was an unsophisticated kid would be an under-
statement wholly out of keeping with my character. I could have
convinced him to trade away his worldly possessions for a bag
of magic beans. If he had incriminated himself to someone in
law enforcement, a lawyer would have had a shot at bobbing
and weaving at trial. He hadn't done that. He'd only put himself
on the scene in a statement to two Not Quite Ordinary Joes,
ones without particular standing no matter how I sold it to
him. Would it stand up in court? Anyone versed in such things
would laugh at you. Thankfully, he wasn't versed in such things.
Thankfully, he had a conscience that was eating him alive.
Thankfully, remorse occupied the void where reason would have
inhabited a professional criminal or an amateur more talented
than himself.

19

Window wipers swinging in a low rhythm.

"I grew up on a Mennonite farm, went to school here in town. I knew that I didn't want to grow up in the traditions."

Tires rolling over the gravel. A massive chest rising and falling behind the steering wheel.

"I went to school here. High school. I got bullied some by the townies. Maybe I was big enough to look after myself but I couldn't or didn't or whatever. I just didn't know where to start. I gave up on school and dropped out. I still came to town like I was still going."

A dome light shining in the back seat. Two bars on a BlackBerry promising a charge for as long as it would take.

"In school, no, I didn't do drugs. Not even weed and it was everywhere. When I dropped out, though, yeah, I drank and smoked weed. One day I just didn't go back to the farm. I stayed away. And the more I stayed away, the worse it got. I did meth. I did a lot of things. I got into her for money."

A head dipping. A head bobbing with every bump in the road.

"Her, yeah. I owed her money. She said I could pay it over time and could work it off."

A pickup truck gunning it. A gust of wind veering the car off its straight line.

"I wanted to work. Not for her. I wanted to do real work. I saw a sign for help wanted at the gas station by the school. I went in and applied for it. I met Mr. Mars later on. He said he tried to meet everybody he hired. He asked me about my family. I didn't want to talk but he kept talking to me. He said that where I was living wasn't healthy. He offered to take me in and I said that would be good. And yeah, I told him about her. She stopped bothering me for a while after that."

A head turning to look out the window at the endless white blanket. Fence posts inching through the surface yards apart, if at all.

"My eyes were bad. Real bad. He said he'd look after it and he got me the surgery and after a few days I could see things clearly, clearer than I could before even wearing the glasses."

Sleet slashing across the window. A crosswind buffeting the car.

"I could have stayed there. I wanted to. I don't know what would have happened."

Tires skidding where gravel gives way to a paved road. Big hands turning a steering wheel into the skid to right the line.

"They came for me. The football players. Hanley's son and the rest. They got me when I went on a bathroom break. And they told me to go see her. They told me that I had to settle up with her. I didn't know what it was about. I went without Mr. Mars knowing. And she told me that he was out to get her. She asked me everything that I knew about him. What he was gonna do. And I told her everything. I told her, I dunno, just whatever it was I knew, and the thing that she kept asking me about was the Mercedes and how he was going to take it to Las Vegas for a rally. And I told her that he was teaching me about how to tune up an engine and how to do the timing and everything. How he liked to do it late at night. To go to one of his stations and work on it."

Night falling barely in the afternoon. A light grey giving way to a dark one.

"And she said it was him or me. Or him and me. She meant it. She said she would do it or get it done. I believed her. I don't know if you know the people she knows, but I was scared when she got the football players after me. She said they were Boy Scouts compared to what would happen next."

An old car with an old man behind the wheel crawling along the road. Other cars lining up in a procession with no chance to pass.

"She told me that her friends the Loners would give me stuff to put in his coffee, the powder. She said they kept it beside the baking powder in their cupboard—whatever it was they cut the coke or drugs with. She knew that he drank a lot of coffee, especially when he was trying to stay awake for work. She told me it would make him sick. I figured if it was in the cut stuff that's all it would do. And she told me I was supposed to call her when I'd done it. She told me that I'd better do it real soon. So I did. I went with Mr. Mars out to the station Saturday night. Mrs. Mars took her sleeping pill. She didn't know that I had gone out with him.

"Mr. Mars took the cover off the Mercedes in the garage at the house and drove it out. I followed in the Escalade. He left the Mercedes in the bay at the station so one of the guys could look at the AC the next day. I dropped the powder in his coffee and he passed out. She told me it would make him sick. That's all that I thought it would do. Then the motorcycle guys came out.

They dragged him into the front seat of the car and strapped him in and pushed the car around the back of the station. I panicked. I said there were gonna be questions. And one of them said, 'There are never questions around here. Everyone just looks the other way and you should too.'"

The first traffic light on the way into town turning red. Cars lining up, idling, exhaust drifting up and then blowing clear.

"And that was it. When it was over I drove the Escalade back to the house. And the next thing was I heard the phone ringing upstairs Sunday morning. I thought it was just gonna make him sick, that's all, really."

A thumb hitting an End button. The last power bar on the screen turning to a yellow caution rectangle.

20

"I have to tell them."

"I know."

I dialed 911 to get to the Mounties. NO RADIO SERVICE. I was going to have to run him in. The kid was no flight risk. He'd freeze to death out here if he made a break for it. He was going to come away peacefully. He wasn't going to overpower me.

I filled in the blanks for him. There was really only one blank. "We're going to drive over to the RCMP building. If you turn yourself in it will be the best thing that you can do. And if you give up Harmon and the Loners, the court, the jury, the Crown, they're going to understand that you were at risk of getting hurt or killed yourself if you didn't follow through. And if you can make the case that you didn't know it was a lethal dose that you spiked his coffee with, you're looking at a reduced charge."

I didn't think Walt was sharp enough at the best of times to put together the fact that ratting out a well-connected drug dealer and two gang members, one already acquitted of double murder, might be hazardous to his health. I underestimated him, I guess.

"I have to go back and get my insulin and my stuff."

"I can do that."

Chief shot me a look. "Shadow, we should go straight to the RCMP," he said. "The kid can tell us what he needs and we'll pick it up after."

"He'll need his insulin and whatever," I said. I wanted to ask Walt when the last time was that he'd checked his blood sugar but he was off in space somewhere. "We might not be able to get it to him for a while after he turns himself in."

"Shadow, we've just had too much trouble in this town," the Big Man said. "We have a kid who killed somebody and we're driving him around. The Mounties are gonna drop the hammer on us."

"Easy, Chief, next thing you're going to tell me that they're trying us together," I said.

Chief sighed and looked skyward as if his sunroof were open.

I turned to Walt. "Not a word to Mitzi, okay?"

He nodded. He was ruined with guilt. He was no threat to anyone.

I didn't want him confessing to Mitzi. I didn't want him around when I broke the news to her. Those options were too complicated. The Big Airing Out was something I was planning for after Walt was safely checked in with the Mounties. It had to be that way. That was My Exit Strategy.

On the drive I started to think of other complications, though. I could see myself on the hook here if anything went down less than smoothly. If any of this landed in court I might be called out to Saskatchewan again. If it came down that way I could count on the most inconvenient time. It wouldn't be the off-season. It was bound to be a time that conflicted with

my work. Maybe it would even be at the time of the draft. And
then it was going to be my ass that would be in the crosshairs of
Harmon, the Loners, and their scumbag confederates.

Fifteen minutes later Chief pulled his Jeep into the driveway.
I looked at Walt. His head was down. "Don't say anything and
I'll distract her," I said. "We'll be in and out. I'm going to tell her
that we have to go out and pick up a couple of other things for
dinner."

He nodded. Vacant stare, the puddle on the floor mat out of
focus, the prospect of the rest of his life in high def.

Walt and I got out of Chief's Jeep. The Big Man stayed behind
the wheel and nodded off.

We could hear Mitzi busying herself in the kitchen and
smell the onions Roth was chopping when we came in the back
door. It wasn't locked. I stood on the landing, just inside, while
the kid went to the basement. Mitzi came to the top of the
stairs.

"Brad, I'm glad you're back. It looks awful out there. Did you
get the pork chops?"

"No, there was a bad accident at the top of the road to the
colony," I said. "We turned around and came back. I'll go to the
supermarket. Walt'll come with me. He has to go to the drugstore. He's out of his prescription." It was the best excuse I could
come up with.

I looked downstairs. I saw Walt go first to his bedroom to
gather a few things and then walk into the bathroom. He went
into the cabinet. He pulled out his diabetes works, his toothbrush, his razor. He shut the door to do his business. Bodily
functions don't take any of these occasions into account.

"It's rotten out," Mitzi said. "We could just call the drugstore
and get them to deliver."

"No, that's okay. I have to get a charger for my cellphone too."

It was an easy line. It was true. Playing the recording for Daulton
and company was the first thing I was going to do once they had
the kid in custody.

Seconds passed. The wind howled. Mitzi was out of sight. I
could hear her in the kitchen, the clatter of getting plates out of
the cupboard and knives and forks out of a drawer. I got lost in
thought. *Do I tell her to set one less place for dinner? Before we eat off those
plates, I'll be telling her how her husband was killed. I'll have to fill in all those
things that he left blank.*

"How is Walt? I'm so worried about him," she said.

Mitzi had come to the top of the stairs to the basement. I
hadn't noticed.

I had no snappy comeback. I had known that I was going to
be asked a lot of questions over the next couple of hours, most
of them with a Mountie firing them at me with professional
skepticism and taking notes. I hadn't counted on anyone voicing
concerns about the emotional well-being of a kid who turned
out to be a murderer. Especially when the voice was that of the
victim's widow.

I heard a thud in the bathroom. I thought the kid was hugging
the bowl, tossing his cookies. That would have been par for the
course. Even I had lost my appetite.

Mitzi didn't wait for me to answer. "It's been so hard for him,"
she said. "I have to let him know that I'm fine with him here, no
matter what happens."

I heard another thud in the bathroom. I listened harder but
Mitzi kept talking.

"I know he's a damaged kid. He's got no one there for him.
The only decent thing would be to care for him. It would be
good for both of us, I guess."

No sounds from the bathroom.

"Walt," I said. "Let's go."

No answer.

I looked downstairs. At the bottom of the bathroom door a dark puddle.

I took the stairs two at a time. The puddle was gathering.

I threw my shoulder and hip into the bathroom door. The lock didn't budge. Not the first time, not the third. Finally, the screws in the hinges gave. I was standing in the puddle.

I kicked the door. My boot left a tread mark beside the knob.

The door crashed down. It landed on the kid's legs. They were splayed. He was flat out and felt nothing. An X-Acto knife was on the floor beside him, where it had fallen out of his hand. So was a note. The last pints of his blood were leaving the vessel. His eyes were open but saw nothing. His stare was empty, unfocused, fixed upward at the bathroom's low panel ceiling, as if angels were dancing there.

"Call an ambulance," I yelled upstairs to Mitzi. I picked up the note before it floated out on the rising tide of the red sea. I jammed it in my pocket of my jacket, leaving a stain that I'd only notice a couple of weeks later.

The ambulance could have been idling in the driveway and it wouldn't have mattered. There was no hope of the ambulance coming soon enough. Two minutes before would have been two minutes too late. I tried to tie tourniquets around his arms above the slashed wrists. They covered me in blood but that was about all they did. I pulled myself away and saw Mitzi standing there with her mobile phone in her hand. Her look was as frozen and faraway as the kid's. She seemed to be looking for the same dancing angels and coming up just as empty.

The ambulance made it in five minutes and the boys in the crew would have done a service if they had attended to Mitzi rather than what was left of the kid downstairs. When they piled downstairs I was standing in the bathroom doorway. I didn't try to explain anything. I didn't know where to start. Whisper's death. This kid's role in it. How I had pieced it together. How I had let the kid talk me into making a pit stop on the way to the Mounties' headquarters. How I had screwed it up completely.

21

I thought Mitzi had been a mess when I arrived three days earlier. That was nothing compared to the smoking crater of a woman left asking *why* as a pool of blood blackened at the bottom of her stairs.

I had all the whys but one. I knew why Whisper had kept his life's story and his brother a secret, even from the woman closest to him. I knew why the kid had killed Whisper, and that doubled back to why the kid had taken his own life. I even knew why Whisper's brother had owned up to a crime not his own and sought refuge in a place where others are desperate to escape. I had all the whys except the last one, why I should tell her.

I don't pride myself on having a conscience. Hard to do when you misplace it a lot of the time. Or misplace *them*. I've always felt like I had more than one conscience. Two obvious ones: one on the ice and later in business, the other with family and friends. There's another, I hate to say, with the women in my life, and that's just the awful runoff of so much gone bad, of what someone else would call damage. I guess there's a fourth, one common to all but cold-blooded bastards who would lean down to a dying man either to save him or at least have him leave a little less alone. The list is probably longer than that. If you were objective you'd say it's conscience of situation. If you were judgmental or cynical, it would be conscience of convenience. I don't buy that. I've never found conscience convenient.

I wasn't going to tell her. Not a thing more than she already knew. Life's a lot simpler on a need-to-know basis. There's no holding your cards too tight. Tell only those who need to know and only when they need to know it. Nothing more. It's all about outcomes. Yeah, maybe someone could make the case that Mitzi had the right to know about Whisper's death, murder as it turned out, but it wouldn't have made anything better.

22

Mitzi drifted off. She was still sitting on the living-room couch, slouched over on her right side. The sedative had taken hold. I pulled off her slippers and raised her legs so she was stretched out. She didn't make a sound when she slept. I had to look hard to see her breasts heave to make sure she hadn't OD'd or given up all hope.

While I was sitting shiva I thought about Swift Current. About how those who had at least suspected or even known the coach was a pedophile and decided not to get involved. About those who denied the town's and the team's role in the bus crash that killed the four kids or owed their families a debt beyond hanging their pictures in black frames in the lobby. And about those who should have known that the surviving players needed professional help after the crash, rather than letting the coach run the show so that his secrets didn't get out. So many stood by in silence, waiting for a Good Samaritan or crusader to step up and none did. They looked on, a mute choir.

Yeah, dressed up as a piece of heaven, Swift was the most awful patch of turf I had ever crossed.

But it changed for me in the living room. In the living room of my late teammate. In a living room just up a set of stairs from a three-piece bathroom flooded with still-wet blood that Chief and I were going to have to clean up. In a living room across from a sleeping widow who knew nothing of her husband's life before she met him or anything other than the work schedule of the boy who killed him and took his own life.

I wanted to think that silence was something unique to Swift, this dire and frozen place, and to those who lived there. But I had been around too long. Now I was one of them.

I suppose I always have been a keeper of secrets. It was everyday stuff in hockey, as a player, as a scout. I had a couple of terrible things done to me as a young guy in initiations in Junior A, and I did the same terrible things to the guys who came in a year after me at each stop. I still don't talk about them. Nobody does.

Yeah, each time our coach knew we were having our annual players-only party. Yeah, he knew that we were all underage and were going to get drunker than sailors on leave. And yeah, he told us that there wasn't going to be "any funny stuff" and if he got wind of it whoever was involved was off the team. "I don't want that call from someone's parents," he said. He wasn't enforcing team discipline. He was cinching the silence. The best of the veteran players always took charge of the initiation. No one would stand for the captain or the best player getting suspended or kicked off the team for hazing. There was a brutal logic to it, but we were too far down the rabbit hole of shame and guilt to be conscious of it. College initiations, peelers pulling the train or whatever, were nothing compared to what went on in junior. The rookie dinners in the league, those were nothing at all, just some pranks and coin pulled out of your wallet, which was fatter than it had ever been before.

It was too easy to make the transition, joining Swift Current's collective hush, the town's wordless chorus. I had done it all before.

Would things be better if she knew everything that Whisper had kept from her? Not that I could see. If she knew that Whisper hadn't taken his life? He had gone down a road that wound up costing him his life, different it's true, but a grey area, metaphysically open-ended. Wouldn't have changed things if she knew, a crime that now could not be prosecuted. If the boy she thought of as her son had snuffed her loving husband, the boy's protector? No, the idea that she had harboured the one who'd kill Whisper would only compound her grief.

Chief left the decision up to me, even though my last decision wasted a perfectly savable life. I didn't blame him for not pushing me to either tell all or say nothing. After all, I had dragged him into all of this.

I wouldn't tell her.

23

And that was it. When it was over I drove the Escalade back to the house. And the next thing I heard was the phone ringing upstairs Sunday morning.

One of the young officers had a BlackBerry charger. It was the source of the juice that let Daulton, Chief, and me hear the voice of a kid whose lifeless body was still warm. I hit the red End button.

"I don't know that it's enough," Daulton said.

"Not enough?" I said. "Even with the note?"

Daulton picked up the note. It was printed in caps, not written in script, and it was done in a hand that had rarely had occasion to put anything down on a page.

> *I DIDN'T WANT TO KILL MR. MARS. HARMON MADE ME DO IT. I DON'T DESERVE TO LIVE. I'M SORRY FOR EVERYTHING.*

Daulton dropped the pretense that was issued with his

uniform. "Oh, it's enough for me to believe it," he said. "And it's enough to follow up, a lead for sure."

"Yeah, that's a real lead, especially with the fact that a guy died from drinking cyanide when his car was rigged up to look like it was suicide by carbon monoxide poisoning."

"What I mean is that it's not enough for charges against Harmon or the bikers, not by itself. And not enough to get a conviction, not by itself."

"That's a pretty high bar to clear. It's not a high jump. It's a pole vault."

"It's something that we can start with."

Throw fucking caution to the wind, I wanted to say, but for once I decided to play nice. "So they're going to walk free until ..."

"Those two gentlemen in leather have been charged with several offences ..."

"OK, so *she's* going to walk free until ..."

"We'll bring her in for questioning."

"If she doesn't head off for parts unknown or go underground or hop on the back of a Harley," I said, content with a short list of snags. "Then your questions can't be asked and you have dead bodies and a dead end."

"I understand where you're coming from."

"Probably not. Doesn't seem like it, anyway."

"We need something more than this to bring her in on. Something other than this."

Daulton finished taking my statement while Chief gave his in another room. He was through first.

"Funny, that you came back to the Marses' house before you were going to take him to the drugstore on an errand," he said.

I scrambled. "He needed his insulin. He looked pretty sick. I thought he was going to drop right there."

It was a satisfactory answer. Daulton did his best to look unsatisfied.

I didn't see any benefit in disguising my impatience and Daulton was of the same mindset. I had my job to get on with and he was a clock-punched card closer to his retirement.

"If you had reported all this right away, it would have turned out much better," he said. "But you're so smart. You decided to do things your way. You're the son of a police officer ..."

"A *staff sergeant*," I said.

"You think that justice usually gets done. You think you can get it done by yourself."

"Done, yeah, but I don't know who I'd count on to do it around here ..."

Normally I would have let it go right there but I didn't like Daulton pinning this dead end on me. The assistant coach at B.C. had tagged it just right all those years back. "Shade, you've got an electric mouth," he'd said. Daulton had flipped the switch and powered it up.

"I know about you and I only just met you. You're a vet. You've been here, what ..."

"Almost thirty years," he said. He thought he was shutting me down, but no, I handed him a shovel and out of reflex he started to dig himself into a hole.

"Almost thirty years," I said. "So you would have gone out to the road when that bus flipped over and those players were killed."

"It was an awful thing."

"I'll bet it was. So was the fact that no one was found responsible or the fact that the families of the dead never saw a nickel of compensation. It was an awful thing but it shouldn't have been so awful for you. You're a professional, right? Deal with this stuff every day, right? I think the real awful part was that you knew that bus was unsafe. Shouldn't have been on the road, right?"

Not a blink. Not a twitch. Twenty-seven years of practice and he had it down.

"It must have been hard writing up that report," I said. "It must have been even harder when a couple of those kids' families were suing the team and they didn't have evidence like that in their files. It must have been really hard. That and the coach. Everybody in the league seemed to know what was going 'cept the people in this town, who should have been the first to know ... and you, who should have been the first in town to know, you with your keen insight into the criminal mind."

They brought Chief into Daulton's office just as I was in full vent. The Big Man gave me That Look.

"I'll tell you what I think of justice," I said as I stood up and leaned over Daulton's desk. "I think it gets done. Sometimes it gets done right away but sometimes it can drag on. Sometimes it's straightforward and by the book. Sometimes it's a little crooked and, well, whatever it takes."

I said a few more things, not including "Goodbye." I hit him where he lived. He had booked others for assaulting an officer when they had inflicted minor wounds compared to the waxing I gave him.

I had to get on with the Whatever It Takes. I just had to figure out Whatever That Was.

24

It couldn't have just been that Whisper had cut her off the payroll. That wouldn't have been enough. She had to believe that Whisper was going to take her down, and she had to know exactly how he had her.

Whatever it was that Whisper had, Daulton didn't know and hadn't put it together. It wasn't her identity. It wasn't her whereabouts. Daulton knew that. Her parole officer knew that too. And it couldn't have just been that she was moving weed. She was smart enough to cover her tracks. She knew how to roll around in the mud and not get caught with dirt under her fingernails.

She thought she was smart. She had a criminal's ego. And she thought that Whisper and everyone else wasn't up to her speed at all. If Whisper had her, dead to rights it had to be because she'd sold him short and overestimated herself.

The door to RCMP headquarters closed behind me and I braced myself against the cold when my BlackBerry vibrated. It was a call from Donna. I didn't take it. A minute later a voice-mail alert flashed on the screen. I gave it a listen.

"Hey, it's Donna. Just want to tell you that you're clear on that mess with my ex. I'm not pressing anything. It's just not worth it. He'd lose his job at Revenue Canada and that would be a whole other mess—our kid with school expenses and him being indigent. It wouldn't make sense for me. So he's going to keep his job holding other people's feet to the fire and appear to be the fine upstanding citizen I know that he's not ..."

She went on for thirty more seconds or so. At one moment it was practicality, the next indignation, and after that what I was cynical enough to expect in a disaster scenario like this, even with a highly intelligent woman, sentimentality.

I only half-listened at that point, though. It was after she mentioned her husband's job that I realized how Whisper had Monica Harmon. If I hadn't listened to that call, it wouldn't have come together so neatly. I was going to his wake the next day. I had a few calls to make first.

I decided it would be better to go back to Regina for the night. It was the only safe thing. If she knew or even suspected that I had the cards to play, Black Aces and Eights, a Dead Man's Hand, and that I intended to run the game that Whisper had planned, she knew enough bad people to leave me as thoroughly dead as my old teammate.

25

Bob Roth wasn't exactly clear why I had asked him, but once he determined that he wasn't breaking the law he went through with it anyway.

"Yes, Ms. Harmon. Yes, I'm sorry for calling late. I'm the executor of Mr. Mars's will. It's my duty to tell you that his last will and testament will be read in my offices tomorrow after the funeral and it is incumbent on me to inform all principals named ..."

And Roth went on. I sat beside him in his office and nodded. He looked skeptical.

A few minutes later the Big Man was behind the wheel, rolling back to Regina.

I

FRIDAY

Do Not Disturb hanging from the doorknob. Snow falling and wind blowing outside the window.

"I thought about you all the time I was driving all over. It's funny. That bump there, I fell on the ice. Lucky I wasn't knocked out."

A naked body resting up against another naked body. A shoulder feeling faint puffs of breath.

"Maybe it won't make everything right. Everything is so broken. But it's going to make at least one thing right. Thanks. No, really, I have to thank you. You did a good thing. It helped a lot. It helped me do the right thing for a guy I used to play with. At the start I didn't want to be involved, and then at some point along the way I felt like I had to do the respectable thing. God knows I've done lots of things that weren't respectable at all."

A laugh holding back. A hand gently pushing.

"No, not this."

Fingers running through hair. A bathroom light shining through a small open gap.

"How well do you know people? I like to think that I read people better than most. And I do it for a living. It's not the game. It's people I read. I don't get many wrong, but I couldn't have been more wrong with Whisper. That's what we called him. Martin Mars. Wasn't even his real name. I know now how I got it all wrong, why I did. I mistook the player for the guy under the sweater, the guy on the ice for the one in real life. Does that make sense? I think that most of the time what you are is what comes out on the ice. But not for Whisper. The exception, I guess."

An elbow bending with a hand propping up a head. Eyes finding the shape of a silhouette.

"I thought he'd be a guy pushed around in life. He was pushed around when I knew him. On the ice and off. He was a guy who walked away rather than sticking around and pushing back. He just didn't have it in him when I knew him back then, well, except that one time, that one time when he pushed back. He had an awful deal in life, turned it right around, and still had it in his mind to push back on that one thing ..."

A phone ringing once. A hand lifting and dropping the receiver before a second ring.

"Yeah, that's right. I never thought of it that way. A slow burn. Every game your name is crossed out on the roster and you have to sit in the press box. Every time you see your name and it's not your name. Every day you know your brother is putting an X through a square on a calendar. A slow burn, yeah, I guess I've never thought of it that way because I'm just not made that way. Do you want breakfast? It will take them a half hour to bring it up here."

A hand lifting the receiver. A finger punching five.

"One Canadian breakfast, one continental. Coffee and OJs. Grape jam or jelly if you have it. You can just knock and leave it outside the room if we don't answer."

A thick hand reaching behind a thin neck. Thick fingers grabbing purple-tinted hair ringed with sweat.

"What time do you have to be at the library?"

A soft hand squeezing a hard bicep. A knee forgetting to ache.

"Yeah."

A man dressed in white and black pushing a cart to the door of the room. A knock on the door going unanswered.

2

Ms. Alexis Stewart reported for duty at her desk in the Periodicals Research Department with cheeks flushed by a guy she had seen for the first time on *Entertainment Tonight* and in the March 27, 1992, issue of *People* magazine. Her memories of the night wouldn't be spoiled by the knowledge that the man she had shared a sheet with only hours before watched paramedics pull another kind of sheet over a hard-luck kid whose death would go unnoticed in the newspapers piling on her desk. It wasn't that she was cold-hearted, just that she had no idea.

3

Chief was standing in the lobby. He was on the phone with his missus and laughing about something one of the Little Chiefs had said. It was the type of call I was never on either end of. And never will be. Yeah, I had calls from Sandy, but they weren't the same. Yeah, I had calls, other calls. Something was missing. Nothing shared the same way. Yeah, I'd spent another night with my testosterone revving. That was what I had instead. Mr. Independent. I had to settle for Ms. Co-Dependent for a Night I and II.

Chief caught a look at me just as he was about to sign off. He thought I was pissed at waiting for him to get off the phone. I was just pissed about what he had, what Whisper had for all those years, what I had missed out on.

The service was scheduled for two o'clock. I told Chief that this would be a quick turnaround. That we'd be there an hour, ninety minutes at most. I don't know why he believed me at that point. Maybe he didn't.

An hour later we were passing those hydro-pole crucifixes.
I leaned into the back seat and pulled out my laptop.
"You don't mind, do you, Chief?" I said.
"Go ahead."
"Just want to look at a few reports."
I looked at reports I had on windows that I'd opened before
I left the Hotel Saskatchewan. I skimmed them. I plugged in my
earbuds and opened a sound file. That was the real reason that
I'd booted up my laptop.

> GOWAN: *On that overtime goal it was Ted Edgar who had the
> shot on net, wasn't it?*

> WHISPER: *No, actually it was Brad Shade. It was right during
> a line change.*

The big historian, he didn't even check the box score to get
the first assist on the goal.

> GOWAN: *Shade was your linemate that night?*

> WHISPER: *Yeah, he was stuck with me. Six shifts. He was my
> roomie too.*

> GOWAN: *How would you describe him as a player?*

> WHISPER: *As a player? I dunno, I always thought Shadow
> could have been a pretty good guy if he hadn't got hurt. It's how it
> goes. You gotta be good and then you gotta be lucky. Soon as you
> get hurt once, your chances of getting hurt again go way up. I was
> lucky. 'Cept for my throat I never got hurt.*

The cover story had become so much a part of him that he wove it into an answer to a question a long way from his own story. He said it like he believed it. Maybe he did.

He went on.

> WHISPER: *The one thing I'd say about Shadow was that he was the best teammate I ever played with. Not the best player by a long stretch ...*

The truth, but it still wounded.

> *... but Brad helped me, not just 'cause he was my roommate. The one thing that always bothered me about leaving the team is that I never thanked him. Maybe if I had, maybe he would have tried to talk me into sticking it out. He couldn't have done it. I never tried to get ahold of him all those years later either. I felt bad about it. I owed him something just for getting that far in L.A. It was tough, but Brad was the one guy in the room who really had the time of day for me. And a good teammate isn't the guy who's good with the stars, y'know. It's the guy who's there for the little guys, like me. He was like a brother to me.*

I felt guilty and, I admit, that's a long way from my natural condition. I felt as though I had hardly known Whisper at all. And if he felt that I was there for him, it was only because no one else was. That's how it is with a Black Ace. The other guys on the team would rather do a group hug with a quorum of lepers than be a Black Ace's best friend.

Whisper was practically asking Gowan to keep chasing that theme. I would have bet with a little prod Whisper would have talked about the hotbox Mercedes contest. The Good

Professor's lack of interviewing skills were a by-product of his dearth of social élan. He didn't think about stories. He thought about things and numbers. He wasn't even listening when Whisper was opening up. The paper shuffling stopped.

I nodded off with the buds still in my ears. The curtain dropped. When I came to we were just passing Herbert.

"I really appreciate this, Chief," I said. "I can't guarantee you that you'll have a job when we come out of this, mostly because I can't guarantee that I'm going to have a job when we come out of this. But I'll tell you, so long as I have a job and a say in who stays on the staff, you'll be there."

He nodded without turning his head. I could have said a lot more but there didn't seem to be any point. There's only so much physical and mental torment a guy can take, but he can take a lot more of that than empty promises, however heartfelt.

"I don't like funerals but the fireworks are after the service."

"I like fireworks," Chief said. Yeah, hundreds of times in his life, in his best days on a nightly basis, he had thrown lit matches into the gunpowder factory.

4

Chief and I had made good time down Highway 1. We ended up being the first in the room at the funeral home.

Mitzi came in after us. She looked fragile and weak. The black made her look even paler than she was. She came into the room with Roth on one side of her and Friesen on the other. They were positioned to catch her like a second baseman and first baseman congregating under a cloud-scratching pop fly.

"Thanks for coming," she said to me. Her voice was faint and her words were slurred by trauma, sedatives, and a couple of hours of restless sleep.

Hanley was next into the room. No. 59 was in tow and he took a seat, careful to lay down his crutches where they wouldn't trip mourners. They did the ritual handshakes. I asked No. 59 how his knee was and if he had called the ortho. He said that his father was going to foot the bill for him to fly first class to Toronto for surgery. He said that he hoped the surgery would be good enough to fly back economy. I had a life lesson for him. I told him to seize every chance to fly first class.

Ed and Derek Jones were the second family act to put in an appearance. Ed knew Roth and Friesen only passingly but shook their hands and told them to call him if there was anything he could do. The younger Jones looked like he wished he could be anywhere else, the list being topped by a poolside chaise lounge on a cruise ship with the British Virgins awaiting—the port of call, not the passengers.

Beckwith came in, and right behind him, Van Stone. Stoner looked buoyant but not improperly so. That had always been his nature, and I suppose if it had been him in the casket he'd have had the same dopey grin. "Dude, I hate all this but it's good to see you, too long, too long," Stoner said and he kept right on going, filling me in on the sale of the junior team and his plans to make it the best junior franchise in the country. Beckwith was only half-listening but still fully grimacing, knowing that the new hands-on owner wouldn't like anyone else's fingers on his prize, including and especially everyone sitting on the board.

Stu Gowan made an appearance, one that I hadn't expected but should have seen coming. At least he showed enough taste not to bring a folder of hockey cards to be signed by any former players in attendance. He had probably already added Whisper's obit to a folder in an overflowing filing cabinet.

Kilmer came in with Wolf. Wolf was wearing a suit the guard had pulled from his son's closet. He made his way over to Mitzi and shook her hand without introducing himself. At that point Kilmer, Chief, and I were the only ones in the room who knew his connection. Mitzi didn't put it together. He recognized her from photos that he had filed in his red book. I'd give it back to him at the end of the service.

Kilmer and Wolf sat in the second row of seats, directly behind Mitzi, the lawyer, and the accountant.

Daulton showed up in uniform. He was standing at the door

when Kilmer turned and nodded. Daulton walked over and sat next to Wolf. Kilmer whispered in Wolf's ear. "Thanks," Wolf said to the Mountie and nothing more. I figured that Kilmer told him not to do anything that might make a scene.

A couple of station managers and a couple of out-of-town suppliers showed up. A funeral-home staffer pointed them in the direction of Mitzi, who should have been easy to pick out by the sobbing behind the veil.

Roth checked his watch. He had thought about asking a clergyman to speak to the assembled but assumed any candidates would blow him off because Whisper had never darkened their doors nor, more to the point, dropped bills in the passed hats. The lawyer reached into his vest pocket, uncrumpled his handwritten speech, and gave it one last review.

Monica Harmon walked into the room at that point and stood in the back. I saw her first and she gave me a snarky overconfident smile. Heads turned toward her in sequence. Inspector Daulton's. The station managers'. Not Wolf's, though.

Harmon gave No. 59 a smile. Mistaken identity. He had no idea who she was.

A complete stranger walked in. He was dressed more for a desk job than for a funeral service. I didn't recognize him but I had a pretty good idea who he was and why he was there. Harmon eyeballed him once and looked straight ahead.

5

Even though the service was forgivingly brief, my mind drifted off. I suppose everyone is the same way at a funeral. Unless the deceased is your flesh and blood or your best friend, you think about your life, here and now or elsewhere and the past, not the extinguished life and exhausted time of the poor stiff at the front of the room.

There in the funeral home in Swift I thought of my days in college. I thought of a philosophy course I'd taken and a professor standing at the front of the class talking about justice, the theory of justice. I'd had an urge to raise my hand and get a word in but I didn't. I had just heard about a kid on a team we had played against a few weeks earlier. I had heard that the kid had played his last game. He was a freshman like me. He had been a defenceman. The puck had been dumped into his end of the ice and he had skated back to pick it up. A big winger had skated in after him. It had been up to that point a routine play, something you'd see a hundred times in any game. The kid had picked up the puck and the big winger lined him up. The kid could have got his stick up or the butt end of it into the gut of the incoming winger. He didn't. He played it clean. He went into the boards and broke his neck. They carried him off the ice and while this philosophy class was going on he was breathing through a tube.

I couldn't start to count how many cops my father has introduced me to. I know a hundred by name. I had a pretty good sense of what law enforcement was: something that was *only* associated with justice and never as closely as you'd like. Justice is a nice thing to kick around in a theoretical sense.

I wanted to put up my hand in that class and say that justice isn't something that *is* but something that *gets done* and too often doesn't get done. And that morality is whatever it is that you're willing to do or not do to have things done or not done to you.

I snapped out of my daydream and my thoughts went to the unlucky stiff at the front of the room. I thought of what a shitty hand life had dealt him in so many ways and how much good he had made of it. He had wanted justice to get done and he had erased a few lines and written some in along the way. He had lived by a moral code higher than mine, but he was also, down deep, a player, and for him justice and morality had been something other than theories.

6
_____

Chief and I drove over to Roth's offices after the service. I saw his car in the lot. He had left Harry Friesen to see Mitzi home and keep her company. Just after we arrived, Monica Harmon pulled into the lot and followed us into the building.

"Such a nice service," she said. "I'm sure it will be such a nice will."

I wordlessly feigned disgust and failure. I knocked on the door and the lawyer cracked it open.

"Have you started the reading yet?"

"Come in," Roth said.

Chief and I walked in and before Roth could shut the door Harmon squeezed past him. "I'm here for the will too," she said.

He put up no opposition.

"Which room is it?" I asked, though I didn't need to.

"The conference room in the back," he said. "Take a seat in there. I'll be there in a minute. I just need to collect some papers."

Harmon brushed past us and opened the door to the conference room.

Daulton was sitting at the long oak table, his uniform looking
out of place in the oak-lined space.

"Do come in, Ms. Harmon."

She looked puzzled. She looked less so when she glanced
over her right shoulder and saw the man who had been the last
to walk into the funeral home and the first to leave. She was
familiar with him. She had been seeing him on a regular basis
for a long time, a nuisance, a pen pusher, a dull man who was
almost too easy to stay two or three steps ahead of. Check that,
entirely too easy.

"Just a few things to go over, Ms. Harmon," he said. "Or
should I call you Ms. King?"

"Or Fern?" I said.

"Yes, is it Maclean?" he said. "Very good then."

I was sure we could have dug up another alias or two. The
Mounties would do just that later on.

Roth arrived with a few folders in hand and laid them out
for the man who had welcomed Monica Harmon and was more
familiar with her than the rest of us, although maybe not as
much as Whisper had been.

"Just one moment, please," he said and he asked the lawyer a
few questions in a hushed voice. He asked for a pad of paper and
pulled a pen issued by the government agency.

Harmon crossed her arms in front of her and made a show of
what she portrayed as momentary annoyance. It would turn out
to be a lot more than momentary and a lot more than annoyance. Even a hiccup can become chronic.

"It's awful about Mr. Mars, isn't it, Ms. Harmon?" Daulton
said. It wasn't his win but he was already taking a victory lap.

"Yes," the man said from behind the papers. "It has come to our attention that you have maintained a position and drawn an income that you have not reported to me as required as a condition of your parole. That's a violation of your parole, although minor compared to maintaining another identity, opening bank accounts in those names ..."

"Drawing health benefits from a company drug plan, Vivian?" I said. "For shame. I wonder whether there might not be something a little stronger than a parole violation. It's not like you broke curfew or anything. I mean, it might be something along the lines of defrauding the health insurance outfit that covered you as a Mars 'employee.' And it might be that there are tax code implications."

"So it would seem," Roth said. "It would seem that there are multiple social insurance numbers registered here."

Daulton had managed to get the number for one Fern Maclean and the account number where the casino direct-deposited her salary. When Daulton and his boys advised the casino's manager of the presence of a convict in the midst of the operation, he opted to co-operate and open his books. It had all been passed on to my good friend in the Attorney General's office who, through a third party who owed her a favour for a case that disappeared at her request, found a way to direct relevant facts to someone of influence at Revenue Canada.

"You thought you were scamming Mars, getting on his payroll. He sold you on the idea, right? Better than a one-time payout. More reliable. Cleaner. A squeeze every two weeks. *How sweet is that?* Did he want you to talk to his brother, convince him to apply for parole? Is that how you thought you had him dangling? You thought he was a mark but he was setting you up."

She said nothing. She stood still. The situation was registering, and until all the pieces fell into place, as they inevitably would, it took everything out of her just to draw a breath.

"He threatened you, didn't he? Said he was going to expose you if you didn't help him with his brother. And then you realized that he could pull the pin on that grenade after his brother was released. He was going to get his revenge one way or another, sooner or later. Unless you moved in first."

As reconstructions go, it might not have been dead-on but it didn't have to be. Maybe they couldn't hang her on murder, I thought, although I'd have banked on Butch and Sundance selling her out without blinking. In the meantime, they could slam her with frauds, evasions, and everything else, and that was a start.

"There's going to be a lot that they can shake loose," I said. "I suspect that this is only the start of it. We might even be able to coax Hanley's son and his friends to discuss your role in the robbery and assault at the gas station. There are some very big things that you might walk on, though I believe in a just universe. It's just the snowball effect, all these little things that are ..."

"Fireworks," Chief interjected.

"Fuck off," she said.

Roth and the parole officer looked a little scandalized by my lapse into trash talk and hers into profanity, but Daulton smiled.

It wasn't finished here. In a few days' time, when they were able to move ahead on the prosecution, building a case with Walt's suicide note, with testimony from the co-operating Loners, with physical evidence that included a half-empty box of rat poison found in Harmon's trash that matched residue found on the Ravens mug at the station, someone was going to have to tell Mitzi. Roth was up to speed and could have done it. Daulton likewise. It could have been anyone in the lawyer's office. Anyone but Chief and me. It wasn't finished in Swift Current, but we were.

Seemingly, Whisper, the most guileless guy I had ever met, had set up a career criminal. She had destroyed what was left of his family and he had preyed on her greed for delicious if posthumous payback.

7

Chief and I left Roth's office. While we let the car warm up we saw Daulton and the parole officer leave with Monica Harmon cuffed in the back seat of the cruiser.

Chief looked at me and said not a word. He gave me a nuanced expression that clearly begged an instruction to hit Highway 1.

"Just one last thing," I said. "One last stop."

8

An unmarked car with back-seat doors that opened only from the outside was parked in the driveway, blocking in Harry Friesen's Civic. Chief pulled up in a no-parking zone across the street. I doubted we'd get ticketed, although we were getting too used to miscarriages of justice in these environs.

I knocked but didn't bother waiting for an answer. When I walked in with Chief in tow Mitzi was on the couch across from Friesen, which I expected, and from Wolf and Kilmer, which I didn't. We had walked in a few minutes after the conversation in the living room had condensed to a hushed dialogue between Mitzi and the brother-in-law who she'd only heard of the day before and was meeting for the first time.

It seemed like they couldn't look each other in the eye. And the rest of us in the room couldn't work up the nerve to look at them.

"It's what Martin would have wanted," she said.

"I know," he said.

Five seconds of silence. Ten. I cut in. I had to, no matter how awkward it was going to be.

"Mitzi, again, I'm so sorry for your loss and I wish we could stay on ..."

I caught a look at Chief, whose expression said Be Really Careful What You Wish For.

"... but we have to get back to Regina and I have a flight to catch. I promise to stay in touch and if there's anything I can do for you, just let me know."

"Brad, I appreciate everything you've done. Everything that Martin said about you over the years, it's all true."

Friesen chimed in and so did Wolf. It wasn't a house party, but the scene had less of the pall that had hung over the household after Whisper's death and then Walt's.

"I'll walk out with you," Kilmer said. "I could use a cigarette."

Kilmer walked out behind us but he didn't reach into his jacket. He just wanted to fill us in out of earshot of the principals.

"He told me after the service that he wanted to meet her to give her his condolences and to tell her all that his brother had meant to him. And she told him what you had told her, about him being an innocent man. She told him that if he was really sorry that his brother had died he should do what Mars wanted—apply for parole. Just out of respect for him. She said that whatever it was going to cost, she'd look after it. If he needed help on the outside, she said that she'd do whatever she could. He even talked about working on cars again. He looked at the pictures on the mantel and couldn't keep it together when he saw a picture of his brother beside the Mercedes. I think that did it."

9

I was able to catch the last flight out of Regina to Toronto. For once I slept on the flight, the fastest three hours of my life.

I got the Rusty Beemer out of the parking lot. Almost three hundred bucks. I wasn't dead broke but I was dead-to-the-world exhausted. Thought I'd be gone for ten days and I'd ended up on something like the Bataan Death March.

Five minutes from throwing it in park I sat at a stop light, doing my best not to nod off, when my BlackBerry pinged. It was a message from Intel-Sec. I deleted it without opening it. The BlackBerry pinged again. A message from Hunts. I put off opening the email until the morning but it ended up being what I'd assumed, a warning that our side of the operation was going to be up for line-by-line review at our organizational meetings at season's end. With Grant Tomlin stroking out line by line, each one intended to loudly announce to our owner Tomlin's indispensability.

I had been so long on the road that I walked around my

apartment as if it was a museum display of my former life. Mail piled up in my slot, the building's dead letter office. Another way to annoy the super. I opened a letter from the boarding school and knew it was the schedule for tuition and expenses. For once I wasn't too worried. I did a quick bit of math, but before I could get to the subtraction my attention was diverted by whatever it was that I had left in the bowl in the sink. The remains had fossilized. The price of running late to the airport. The price of staying up late the night before my flight out West.

It was going to be a few days before I'd feel like I was all the way back. Then again, I only had a few days before I'd be heading out on the road again. Road Warriors, that's what scouts call themselves. That's how we think of ourselves. It's either a joke or a lie. We're on the road, sure, but we're not warriors. We're no more warriors than the World War II veterans pushed in their wheelchairs in a Remembrance Day parade. We *were* warriors, past tense. And when we were warriors no longer we piled out on the road, reminding ourselves of our places in the old wars. And when we see others in the trenches, we think we know what makes them tick, we think we know how they got there. Maybe that's the lesser takeaway from my unenjoyable stay in Swift Current. We don't really know the other guys in the room as well as we like to think we do. Not even close.

Every other time I've headed out on the road for a long stretch, every time I've spent hours and even days talking to no one other than the receptionist at the front desk of the hotel or the waitress in the restaurant or the security guard at the arena, I've felt that I had to get reacquainted with my life. That I'd forgotten a little bit of it. I looked at the picture of Sarge and me at the Quebec peewee tournament. He had his arm around me and we both looked proud. I thought of all the hours he spent with me at the arena and everywhere else. I looked at the picture of my daughter on the mantel. She was staring out at me with her mask half pulled off, perched on top of her head, and I thought of all the games she played that I missed because I was watching some useless game somewhere else. I thought of the sacrifice, hers, involuntary.

Whisper's father never had a moment like that. Whisper might have had a chance to but he didn't either.

10

"I think we need to step back," Sandy said.

She said "back" but it was *way* back. I wasn't surprised. Things just weren't that good. Maybe things had never been as good as I had thought. For sure I hadn't thought that much about what it looked like through her eyes.

She said, politely and not in as many words, that I loved my job more than I loved her. It wasn't true. I could see how she would have got that wrong. She loved her job. She loved it so much that it wasn't a job but rather work or even a service or calling. I hated my job in a lot of ways but I needed it more than I needed her. Not that no one lives on love alone, but it's an exclusive club. I wished I had a chance to give it another try.

Whisper and Mitzi had something that I'd never had with anybody. They had something that I had wanted when we went on our honeymoon and came back to Hollywood and heard cheers and signed autographs at the arena and in restaurants and even the supermarket. Whisper and Mitzi had something that I don't think I wanted with Sandy or, if I did, that I didn't want enough.

"Stay in touch," she said.

I waited for her to say that I was a good man and she didn't. She had me right.

That night I was going to have a dream. It was going to last no more than a couple of terrible breaths. A woman was chasing me out of the black gloom and I didn't want to look back, but I did and I couldn't see her.

I had one thing I had to do before I could properly set the stage for that sweat-drenched dream.

II

"You're sure?"

"I'm sure."

Nick poured me another double. He gave me a look as if he were sizing up a stranger for trouble. At some level I was looking for trouble, at another I was becoming a stranger.

"I know I look like hell. I feel like hell. I just want to drink myself to sleep."

"Not here, though," he said, sliding the rock glass across the bar. He was impatient to get to an all-night poker game in the dimly lit basement of a restaurant in Greektown.

I was watching the last few minutes of a late game. Montreal was in L.A. Two of the teams I had played for back in the day. I saw a Montreal guy wearing my old number. Somehow it hadn't been retired. Somehow he was making ten times the salary I'd made in my best year. Somehow I couldn't imagine him ever sitting on this bar stool, but then again somehow I had never imagined myself doing that either.

The camera flashed to Grant Tomlin up in the team box. He

was sitting beside the owner and giving him a running commentary. Tomlin had done the same thing on broadcasts for years but
now was doing it for an audience of one, the guy who signs his
and my paycheques. All his melodrama had been entertaining
enough on the air but it was completely counterproductive as
a management style. And by counterproductive I mean a real
threat to my paycheque, not his. He was good at telling you what
happened six seconds ago but was just guessing about what was
going to happen six months or six years from now. He said what
he thought the owner wanted to hear to land his job, and he
wanted Hunts and me and Chief and anyone else to follow his
lead. He could kiss my ass before that would ever happen.

I looked down the bar to take attendance at last call. I was as
alone as a Black Ace in the press box. The only other patron was
one of the Merry Widow's Irregulars, an old guy whose name
I didn't know. He looked weary enough to lie down in a booth
and use his coat as a pillow. He was drinking himself to a slow
death only because he lacked the ambition and commitment to
do it quickly. I would have bet his cousin in Swift Current drank
at the Imperial.

Nick tried to head off trouble, that being my thirst for another.
He caught me up on the news, that being that he was thinking
about giving cards a rest. "The other night at our game on the
Danforth a game got out of control, two guys who own restaurants," he said. "Hold'em. Basement of the Sparta. It went past
cheques and cash and everything. One guy put his restaurant
up and the other guy matched. Y'know Square Burger down
the street? Guy lost it when he got rivered. Ace. How do you go
home and tell your wife that? Thank fuckin' God I didn't have
the cards and this joint wouldn't be enough of a stake to cover
their bet. Time to get out. A guy loses a restaurant on a card, it's
enough for a guy to pull a gun. Not worth it anymore."

He was talking to himself. He went on and I didn't hear a word. He'd still go to the game.

The BlackBerry rang. I looked at the call display. A number beginning with 312, the Saskatchewan area code. The caller ID: ATT GEN. The call rang six times through to voicemail. I waited. No message was left. I checked the call history: six calls from 312 ATT GEN that night. If it had been business, messages would have been left. None were. There would be more the next day, the day after that, and the rest of the week. I'd wait it out until they came less often and not at all and she'd be safely shackled in memory again. She'd hit redial with the faint hope that the thirtieth or thirty-first time might be different. I doubted that it would be, even a hundred and thirty-first, but I couldn't say for sure. I haven't seen the survey. You keep drilling down and you might hit a heart.

I opened a fold in my wallet, just to make sure it was still there, fifth time, sixth time that night, as if it was going to burn its way through the leather and the back pocket of my jeans. One day it would be gone, all gone, like everything else I ever squeezed out of the game, but for now it eased my worries about my job security beyond the summer and let me delete unopened emails from Intel-Sec at least until the fall, when Grant Tomlin might walk through our offices wielding a scythe. It was a cheque in the amount of a hundred thousand dollars from the estate of Martin Mars, issued by the lawyer, as laid out in Whisper's last will and testament. Either he had miscalculated the interest on the five-hundred-dollar bet I had let him walk on or he had put more value in our friendship than I ever could have imagined, especially when I had sat there silently while Iron John trashed him. Maybe he had put it together that I had defended him and ratted out Iron to the reporter. Maybe he had hoped that I'd be there, that I'd go to a cold, hard place to find the cold, hard truth and set things right again. Maybe he counted on my conscience kicking in after being so little used back in my playing days. I lingered on the possibilities from the time that I raised the glass off the bar until the burn hit the back of my throat with awful certainty.